"It's too late to help Jeremy," Andrea told Doug with finality. "He's already a hard-core druggie."

"It's never too late!" Doug exploded, springing up from the sofa to start pacing around the room. "If there was such a thing as too late, *I* wouldn't be here right now."

"What do you mean?"

"I was just as bad as Jeremy, if not worse. By the time I was twelve, I'd done it all. On my twentieth birthday I threw a party and landed in the hospital, where I hallucinated for six days."

"Oh my God," she said weakly, the color draining from her face.

So now I've blown my chances with you, Doug thought bitterly as he continued to pace, *but at least you finally know me for what I am.*

Dear Reader,

In June, everyone seems to think of weddings. So Harlequin has chosen this very special month to launch a unique cross-line series we're sure you'll enjoy. In *Wedding Invitation*, a Superromance by Marisa Carroll, you'll meet the people who've created Weddings, Inc., a wedding planning service in the town of Eternity, Massachusetts. There's a long-established tradition that any marriage solemnized in the Powell chapel is guaranteed to be happy, so couples come from miles around to exchange vows in Eternity... In this first book, Eternity's own Brent Powell is marrying Jacqui Bertrand—except that the bride is no longer speaking to the groom, his mother is less than thrilled with her future daughter-in-law and Jacqui's kids are in no mood to accept a new stepfather! Be sure to watch for the next book in Weddings, Inc.—*Expectations*, by Shannon Waverly, a July Harlequin Romance.

Peg Sutherland has concocted a wonderful adventure for you, in Bali, where Daron Rourke has a secret life—under a *Pirate Moon*. But Grant Hilliard drops into that life with a thud, and he seems to have two personalities, both of which pose a threat to Daron.

Policewoman Andrea Parker is the heroine of Tara Taylor Quinn's *Dare to Love*. Andrea has always been able to handle tough men—until she meets Doug Avery, one of the officers she has to train for the DARE program. He's rude, crude and arrogant, but somehow Andrea can't throw him out of the program—or out of her life.

Ginger Chambers, well-known to readers of American Romance, comes up with an intense, dramatic conflict in her first Superromance novel, *Till September*. Twenty years ago, a man drowned to save Robin Farrell's life. Imagine her guilt and confusion when she finds herself falling in love with Eric Marshall, his orphaned son! How on earth can she tell Eric that *she* is the woman he blames for his father's death?

There's a Superromance novel to fit every reader's taste this month, with settings ranging from small-town New England to exotic Bali. So find a cool breeze, a quiet corner, and welcome summer with Superromance!

The Editors

TARA TAYLOR QUINN

DARE TO Love

Harlequin Books

TORONTO • NEW YORK • LONDON
AMSTERDAM • PARIS • SYDNEY • HAMBURG
STOCKHOLM • ATHENS • TOKYO • MILAN
MADRID • WARSAW • BUDAPEST • AUCKLAND

ISBN 0-373-70600-6

DARE TO LOVE

ABOUT THE AUTHOR

Tara Taylor Quinn became acquainted with the DARE program, a special unit of the police force, when she recently attended a graduation ceremony where her eight-year-old daughter was involved as a dancer. The master of ceremonies talked about the vigorous training the recruits engaged in, as well as the dedication it took to succeed in the program. Tara, a born romance novelist, immediately realized that any of the graduates could be classified as hero material, and *Dare to Love* was born.

Tara makes her home in Arizona with her husband and daughter, Rachel.

CHAPTER ONE

ANDREA PARKER FORCED a smile when she entered the eighth-floor hotel suite. The men waiting inside did not smile. Six superb male bodies, in the prime of life, roamed the room like caged tigers.

"Good evening, gentlemen."

Clutching DARE Bear beneath her arm, Andrea stepped carefully into their midst, asking herself if she really wanted to do this, if there wasn't some other way to atone for past negligence.

Several half-mumbled replies fell stiffly into the silence. The men stopped pacing. They stood in various positions throughout the room, watching her warily from hooded eyes.

Andrea ran her fingers through her short blond bob as she passed the conference table and headed toward an armchair. She felt like she was on display, like the regulation shorts she was wearing, which only moments before had been standard attire, now were far too short.

She sat down, perching DARE Bear between her legs on the cushioned chair, and braced herself for the thoroughness of the men's suspicious scrutiny.

"Come. Have a seat." Her voice was gentle and welcoming.

She waited as all but one man slowly complied. In her peripheral vision Andrea saw this last figure move to a round table along the back wall of the room. She wasn't surprised by his actions; she understood that he was merely keeping his back covered. But the weeks ahead would certainly be easier if he would trust her enough to come forward like the rest.

The men were all there of their own free will. They'd all agreed to the intimacies that were about to follow. But that didn't necessarily mean they'd be easily tamed.

"I'm Andi Parker." She spoke to the room at large.

Someone had turned the air-conditioning up full blast since Andrea had been in to unlock the room an hour before.

"Welcome to DARE, gentlemen. I know you've all heard unsettling things about this session, but I hope the next two weeks will be rewarding for all of us."

"Was it for you, the first time?" a sandy-haired man, the shortest of the group, asked.

"Yeah, but it was as bad as I'd heard it would be, too."

"Was it worth it?" The question came from a big redhead with a booming voice. He sat on the couch with his arms folded across his chest.

"Every minute of it."

"Did you ever regret your decision?" a tall, skinny man asked, watching her through narrowed eyes.

Andrea didn't like being on the hot seat. "Lots of times, but never enough to want to change it. I hope it's the same for all of you. My job over the next two weeks is to smooth your way as much as I can."

She smiled at the five men sitting around her. One by one, they looked away.

"The first thing you need to know is that any personal confessions that may come about during the course of the next two weeks will remain completely confidential." The tension in the room seemed to escalate. She wasn't surprised. She was going to be becoming emotionally intimate with these men. Men didn't usually like that.

But it was time to get started. Her gaze came to rest on the dark-haired loner at the back of the room, whom she planned to call forward. Shock sent adrenaline flowing from her neck down to her toes. The man had an attitude a mile long. He was wearing skintight black jeans, a T-shirt with the sleeves ripped out, black boots and a black leather wristband with silver studs. His nose looked like it had been broken at least once, he had a jagged scar running outward from his left temple and his biceps were bulging. But it was his eyes that knocked the breath out of Andrea. The cynical, aged, disillusioned look shocked even her. Had she not been a cop, in a room full of cops, she would have been frightened. Who was this man? Why was he in the suite? And where was her sixth officer?

"May I help you?" she asked, her voice quiet but authoritative. She set DARE Bear behind her.

The man shrugged, his arms folded lazily across his chest. "I doubt it."

He met her gaze head-on, his dark look challenging.

"Who are you?" she asked, her muscles poised to move quickly. She'd all but forgotten the other men in the room. She was a police officer first and foremost, and she sensed danger.

"Doug Avery. Officer Douglas Avery." The words were laced with the challenge she'd read in his eyes. Andrea heard the "you wanna make something of it?" almost as surely as if he'd said the words aloud. And for a split second, she did want to make something of it. She wanted to accept his challenge and throw one right back at him. Then she remembered who she was, the job she was there to do. She caught her control just before it slipped away.

"The Doug Avery who appeared out of nowhere to save a sergeant's life last year?" she asked, her surprise carefully cloaked. She'd assumed one of the five men in front of her was the highly acclaimed Officer Douglas Phillip Avery. Though he was only thirty years old, the man's professional record was filled with commendations. He was reputed to be afraid of nothing. He was also the only Columbus, Ohio resident in the room besides herself. Until that moment, Andrea had been looking forward to meeting him.

Avery shrugged again. His eyes were still dull and cold, and Andrea's stomach filled with dread. No matter what kind of record he had, no matter how good a cop he was, he was going to have to make a mammoth attitude adjustment before he'd even begin to fit into the DARE program.

Doug Avery didn't look like he would instill trust in anyone, let alone elementary-school children. His very presence seemed threatening. He was the furthest thing from soft that Andrea had ever encountered. He wasn't role-model material. She wanted him out of the program.

"Would you please join us over here, Officer Avery?" she asked.

Her imperious tone of voice was not lost on him, Andrea noticed, for his eyes narrowed and his chin lifted just a fraction. He pushed himself away from the table and loped slowly forward, and Andrea half expected him to continue walking right past her and out of the suite. She would have liked nothing better.

He plopped down in the chair directly to her right, stretching out until he was half sitting, half lying in it. His head rested on the back of the chair. His fingers unsnapped and resnapped the strip of leather at his wrist before his hands came to rest along the cushioned armrests. He gave every appearance of a biker settling back for an afternoon of televised sports.

Andrea looked away. "Kids can't be scared straight anymore, gentlemen...."

She tried to continue her opening session as if nothing had happened. But as she launched into the speech she'd rehearsed, she caught a whiff of Avery's musky after-shave and felt another unsettling jolt in her stomach, lower down this time. A softer jolt. A sweeter one. A much more dangerous one. Stunned, Andrea paused to catch a breath. She could hardly believe what was happening to her. She was getting turned on by a hoodlum.

"You're going to have to reach out to your students...." She pulled DARE Bear back up onto her lap, holding him close against her. She hadn't felt desire for a man in more than four years. The feeling had no place in her life—it was that simple. She didn't look Doug Avery's way again.

"...care about your kids, gentlemen, or you'll lose lives."

The big blond man seated in the armchair to her left choked and tried to turn it into a cough. Andrea didn't think he had something stuck in his throat—more like in his craw. She looked at him, all too aware of the opposition she would be facing over the next two weeks as a training officer in the Drug and Alcohol Resistance Education program.

The pencil in his fingers snapped in two.

"You must be Sven Johnson," she said, placing DARE Bear on the table beside her. She leaned over to shake the man's hand.

The big officer, obviously of Swedish descent, engulfed her small hand in his and nodded. He met her gaze squarely, honestly. He would do fine. Her skin felt hot as she imagined Doug Avery's eyes behind her, boring into her.

"You like children, Sven?" she asked, her voice carefully modulated.

"I wouldn't be here if I didn't. I've been working with a camp for latchkey kids in Cleveland for years. But aren't you overdoing this caring thing just a little? No offense, ma'am, but we aren't the ladies' circle here."

She saw him glance at DARE Bear and then look quickly away.

"We're not out to amuse children here, guys. We're out to affect the rest of their lives. Most of the kids you're going to be facing during your career with DARE are as street-smart as you are. You can't convince them that someone cares if you don't. It's that simple."

The air in the room was growing thicker. Andrea could almost feel the men struggling to draw breath into their lungs. She ached to turn her head, to find out how Doug Avery was reacting to her words, but she couldn't allow herself to look his way—not until she could trust herself to remain completely unaffected by him.

"Tenderness is nothing to be ashamed of."

The rest of the men sat stiffly, bouncing a knee or thrumming fingers on a thigh while attempting to appear completely relaxed.

"Which one of you is Steve Cummings?" she asked, letting them off the hook for now.

Fifteen minutes later she'd matched names and file data with all the faces. And with one exception, she was satisfied with her new team. The men were understandably defensive, but they were good guys.

"Now, before you all go, I have an introduction to make," she said, knowing that she couldn't stall any longer. She sat her teddy bear up on the arm of her chair, spreading its arms wide until the DARE emblem on its stomach was clearly displayed. The men all glanced away.

"This is DARE Bear," Andrea explained, persevering. "He's the DARE mascot, a symbol, something tangible to represent the warmth and security that will hopefully empower your children to make the right choices. You'll receive a replica of DARE Bear when you graduate from the DARE training program and you'll be expected to take him with you into your classrooms. Smaller versions are given to students as incentives, or rewards for classroom participation. Get used to him, guys. You're going to need him.''

Andrea studied the men around her, trying to gauge their reactions. And as she met the eyes of each, as she saw their tense nods, she felt a small thrill of victory.

But the thrill was short-lived. Her glance landed on the sixth officer in the DARE program, the man she'd been working so hard to ignore for the past fifteen minutes. He too was nodding, but not in agreement or even in understanding of the dictate she'd just issued. His chin was nodding down against his chest, a reflexive muscle reaction. The man was sound asleep!

All traces of fleeting attraction fled as rage coursed through Andrea's veins. Children were dying every day, in some cities every hour, because they didn't have access to programs like DARE, because there weren't enough trained officers to go around, because there weren't enough places in the training seminars to accommodate the qualified policemen who wanted to be DARE officers. And Douglas Phillip Avery the Great was using up one of those priceless places to catch up on his beauty sleep. The man needed more than an attitude adjustment. He needed to get out.

Calmly setting DARE Bear aside, she stood up and shook hands with the other five officers. ''It was good meeting you, guys,'' she said as she followed them to the door. ''I'll see you for breakfast tomorrow morning at eight o'clock. If you need anything in the meantime, I'm right next door.''

DOUG AWOKE WITH A START and sat up as the door clicked quietly closed. Immediately wide awake and on guard, he realized even before he opened his eyes that the meeting had ended. *Damn.* He'd completely missed the last part of the session. That must have gone over well. He flung himself backward in the chair, staring at the ceiling.

As much as he was dreading the next two weeks, the next year, he did intend to get through it—awake. He had to do well with the DARE program to secure a position on the Drug Task Force. And nothing was going to stop him from getting that job—not a classroom full of kids and not Miss Compassionate herself, either.

Doug didn't believe for a minute that the warmth Officer Parker imparted was anything more than a carefully calculated plan of action. He didn't believe in it any more than he believed that she'd reached out and touched him with her smile at the beginning of the session. He was just tired. And Officer Andrea Parker was a pro.

"Oh, you mean you weren't bedded down for the night?"

Doug's head popped up. He'd thought he was alone. He must be more tired than he thought. The past three weeks of moonlighting had really taken their toll. But a special-forces officer had been putting Stan's job on the line, and Doug owed Sergeant Stan Ingersoll.

Officer Parker approached his chair as if *she* was the one who had the sixty-pound, seven-inch advantage. "So, tell me. Did you have important dreams to get to,

Officer Avery? More important than the program you volunteered to serve?''

This broad was something else. Didn't she realize he could take down grown men, men that were twice her size, with one hand?

He looked up at her, letting her play her power games as she stood over him. "I don't dream." So why in the hell did he want to see that damn smile again? Just to convince himself that his reaction to her wasn't real, that was why.

"No? Then would you mind telling me why you chose to waste an evening's session, one evening out of only fourteen allotted us, on sleep?"

Doug shrugged. "I guess I was tired," he said.

"You were tired? And that makes it okay? What about all the information you missed?" Her voice was still soft, but it was filled with disgust.

"What about it?" The woman took this whole DARE thing too seriously.

"I'm just curious, Officer." She stepped back. "How do you plan to do your job if you don't know what it is?"

"Anyone can stand up and lecture to a bunch of kids all day." Doug rested his elbows on the arms of the chair and gave her a quick scan. Her slim, athletic body was really kind of sexy.

He refused to listen to the little voice inside of him that asked why, if this was all so easy, he was dreading it so much.

Andrea Parker's breasts heaved up and down beneath her T-shirt once, twice, as she apparently tried to control the anger that was coursing through her.

She sat down on the couch opposite Doug, leaning forward with her elbows on her knees and pinning him with a searching glare. Her breasts were hanging temptingly between her arms. Doug concentrated on them so he didn't have to meet her eyes.

The woman planned to cramp his style. He didn't plan to let her—no matter how attractive she was. Doug had made it a rule from the very beginning never to associate with his fellow police officers, male or female. He didn't go out for beer with them or sit around doughnut shops with them or even shoot baskets with them after shift. And he most certainly didn't date them.

"I'd like you to do something for me."

Andrea's softly spoken, husky words brought Doug up with a start. Did the woman know he was attracted to her? And did she actually want him to do something about it? Here? Doug had thought she couldn't stand him. He'd seen the revulsion in her eyes the minute he'd identified himself to her earlier. Of course, some people got their kicks in strange ways. He studied her silently, wary of what was to come.

"I want you to go back to your sergeant and resign from the program." Her words were still soft, her voice still sensitive, but Doug saw the determination in her big blue eyes. He saw it, but he wasn't fazed by it. There was nothing this woman could say to change his mind about the course of the next few years. He let her continue, anyway.

"You obviously don't want to be here. You weren't even interested enough to stay awake for the first session. Why waste everybody's time, including your own? Why take up a spot in a program that's desperately needed when you'll never graduate anyway?''

Doug was beginning to wish he'd stopped her, after all. She was really starting to piss him off.

"And what makes you so sure I won't graduate?" he asked. His words were softly spoken, too, but there was nothing friendly about them. If Stan had been there, he would have recognized the stoic expression on Doug's face. He would have recognized it and given in to it. Doug Avery was one determined man.

Andrea's eyes burned with determination, too, but Doug knew she was no match for him. He watched her reach for her teddy bear. Even with that bit of stuffed fur, she was no match for him.

"Catch."

"What the hell...?" As the bear sailed toward him, Doug ducked, wondering if the idiotic woman had lost her mind. And *she* was supposed to be his *mentor* over the next two weeks? Not that Doug needed, wanted or intended to have a mentor—but, hell, if they were going to try to force one on him, couldn't they have chosen better?

The bear landed on the floor behind Doug's chair. He knew it had to be back there somewhere, because he'd felt the whoosh of air as it flew over his bent head. But he wasn't about to turn around to check on a stuffed toy.

"You just failed the first test, Officer Avery," Andrea Parker informed him as she retrieved her bear. She didn't return to her seat, forcing Doug to turn around after all. She was standing by the door, the bear held close to her heart as if she were apologizing to the damn thing for mistreating it.

"According to your records, you're an exemplary police officer, but not everyone is cut out to be a DARE officer. It takes a special kind of man, one who's not afraid to touch a teddy bear, to succeed in the DARE program. Now, I'm not *asking* you to withdraw from the program, I'm strongly *advising* that you do so."

She turned to leave, but Doug didn't intend to let her get in the last word. He knew damn well that had it been in her power to do so, she'd have just kicked him out of the program herself. Without ever knowing why he'd fallen asleep during her session, without any idea of the plans he had for his life—plans that hinged upon his service in the DARE program—she was ready to get rid of him. Just like that. He'd been judged and found wanting.

So what else was new?

He waited until her hand was on the doorknob. "Officer Parker?"

She turned around, looking, Doug thought, a little hopeful. "Yes?"

Her attitude ticked him off again.

"I was just wondering—is your stuffed toy good in bed, too?"

His words were like a gunshot in the silent room. He knew they were crude, but he didn't take them back. It was the kind of thing she expected from a man like him.

Andrea Parker opened the door and walked out without another word.

Doug was left with the startling vision of pink color tingeing her cheeks. And the bitter taste of shame in his mouth.

CHAPTER TWO

"ONE WHO REFRAINS from sexual, inappropriate or insensitive remarks." Andrea read the line aloud, as if speaking the words of policy #90-03 somehow gave them the power to solve her problem. Fuming she threw down the DARE policy and procedures manual and paced across her room in the Hetherington Hotel in downtown Columbus. The man didn't belong in the DARE program—it said so right there. He didn't meet the criteria of a prospective DARE candidate. Not only was he the coldest bastard she'd ever met, he was crude, too.

So what was she going to do about it? she asked her reflection in the regulation mirror mounted next to the regulation television.

Convince him to leave, that's what, she answered herself, turning her back on her silent nemesis to continue pacing the generic, earth-toned room. He had to resign from the program. There was no other option. The kids in the DARE program were all she had left. She wasn't going to risk their lives by sending Dirty Harry to their den. She just wasn't.

But what if he continues to refuse to resign?

The familiar churning started in Andrea's stomach again as she stopped to peer out her eighth-floor window. She had always liked butterflies, had always thought they were beautiful, fragile, harmless little creatures, until four years ago when an unfriendly team of them had taken up residence in her abdomen.

From her vantage point, she looked out over the lights of downtown Columbus, but she didn't see the collage of twinkling colors in front of her. She had to do something. She had to take control of the Avery situation once and for all. Control was the only thing that would calm her butterflies.

Andrea had no idea how or why Douglas Avery had been admitted to the DARE training program in the first place, but she knew that no screening system was perfect. He was proof of that fact. Somehow he'd managed to get through the rigorous DARE screening, and now it was her job to make certain he didn't slip through any more cracks.

If he wouldn't leave the program willingly, she'd take matters into her own hands. She still had two weeks before Doug Avery would be let loose in a classroom. With the little she'd seen of him so far, she didn't think it would be too hard to collect enough evidence against him to enable her to go to her superior and request the man's dismissal. She just had to keep a close watch on every move he made, and Officer Douglas Avery would very likely hang himself.

Andrea turned from the window, her stomach a little more settled, and crossed to her briefcase. Removing a blank ledger book, she took out a pen, settled at the small table beneath the window and wrote, Officer Avery, Douglas.

Two pages later, she slid the ledger back into her briefcase, pulled on her nightshirt and brushed her teeth. Padding back to the kingsize bed, she slipped beneath the covers, satisfied that the children were safe once again—Doug Avery would never step foot inside a sixth-grade classroom.

She was almost asleep, drifting off with a satisfied sigh, when the phone rang. With a strangled groan she looked at the clock and then turned her back, piling pillows on top of her head to muffle the persistent ringing. She'd been so preoccupied with Doug Avery before she'd gone to bed that she hadn't even noticed the remarkable silence while she'd been blessed with it.

Sixteen...seventeen...eighteen. She counted the rings. They weren't going to go away. With a muttered curse, she threw off the pillows and reached for the phone. If she didn't answer it now, it would just ring again in about an hour, and every hour after that, as well. She knew. She'd ignored the summons before. One way or the other her caller was going to get her.

"Hello, Ma," she said. The receiver felt cool against her heated skin.

"How'd you know it was me?" Her mother's voice always reminded Andrea of a Saint Bernard—huge but harmless. Gloria Parker had the temperament of her French-Italian ancestry. She yelled a lot, always spoke her mind, and loved intensely. Her loyalty was as much a given as her nagging. And Andrea loved her dearly.

She pulled the covers up to her chin, dragging the phone cord with her as she resigned herself to the conversation she knew was about to take place.

"You always call after opening session," she said. And because she understood the main reason why her mother called—out of love for her daughter—Andrea always answered her phone. It was her mother's secondary reason for calling that had her pulling her hair out.

"So, how'd it go?" Gloria showed no outward scars from the past four years, only a neurotic need to hear about each new battalion that joined the fight against drugs.

"Good. There's a lot of potential here."

"They all going to be able to love the kids?"

Andrea twirled the phone cord around her index finger beneath the covers. She had a sudden vision of Doug Avery's dark features, his shadow of a beard, his piercing black eyes, but she blinked it away. That problem was already being dealt with. "No one's going out that can't, Ma. You have my word on it."

"You really feel like they're right for the job?"

"I really do, Ma. One of them started a program for latchkey kids in Cleveland. He's been running it for years and it just keeps getting bigger." Andrea related what she'd read in Sven's file earlier.

"He runs it himself? He doesn't just hire someone else to do it for him?"

"He has volunteer staff, but apparently no one spends as much time with the kids as he does."

Gloria harrumphed in satisfaction. "You settled into your room okay? You got the safety bolt locked?"

"Yes, Ma." Andrea didn't even have to check. She was a cop. She always kept herself safe.

"You hung up your clothes so you don't have to call down for an iron? You know it always takes forever to get an iron."

"Yes, Ma. My clothes are all hung."

"Don't take that tone with me, Andrea. I'm only trying to help."

"I know, Ma. I'm sorry. I guess I'm just a little tired. The room really is great. And the guys are going to be fine, too. I already introduced them to DARE Bear."

"They didn't ignore him, did they?"

Andrea remembered the stuffed toy flying through the air, landing on the floor with a dull thud.

"Nope."

"So, any of 'em single?"

Andrea pushed back the covers and sat up, needing air more than she needed to hide from her mother. It wasn't working, anyway. Gloria Parker was the one thing in Andrea's life that she still hadn't figured out how to control. Probably because her mom was more right about some things than Andrea wanted to admit.

"Yes."

She cringed when she heard her mother's satisfied *harrumph*. She could almost hear her mother's blood begin to pump in anticipation, could almost feel the palpitations of the older woman's heart.

"So..." Gloria drew the word out to four syllables.

"So what, Ma? They aren't married. Did you ever stop to think that maybe it's 'cause they don't want to be?"

"Then it's up to you to change their minds, Andrea."

"All three of them, Ma?" Andrea asked, a grin spreading across her face.

"Now, Andrea Lee Parker, don't you get smart with me." Her mother's tone was working up to battle pitch.

"I'm sorry, Ma. But did you ever stop to think that I don't care if they're not married? What if I don't like any of them? You don't even know their names, and you're ready for me to bear their children. They could all be fifty years old and bald, for all you know." She could feel the tiny lines of frustration forming across her brow even as she spoke. By the time her mother was done with her she'd have so many lines on her face she'd look fifty years old herself.

"You're twenty-nine, Andrea. You can't afford to be so choosy. If you don't hurry up and find a husband, you're going to end up an old maid."

"I've already had a husband, Ma, remember?"

Gloria snorted loudly, expressively. "That sorry excuse for a man didn't deserve you, Andrea. He didn't know what a treasure he had. And you're a bigger fool than I thought if you let him keep you from finding a man to father my grandchildren."

Andrea smiled at the double-edged compliment, warmed in spite of herself by her mother's fierce loyalty, and maybe even by the older woman's tenacity. Deep down, she understood that her mother was just trying to help her find forgiveness.

"I've got time, Ma," she said, knowing that all the time in the world would never be enough to convince her to marry again. She always seemed to let down the people she loved.

"I can hear your clock ticking from here, Andrea Lee. It's not safe to have a first baby much past your early thirties."

Andrea sighed, refusing to think about the babies she would never have—the babies she had once wanted more than anything else in life. She hadn't even been able to handle being a big sister. She wasn't going to risk failing at motherhood, too. "Times have changed, Ma. Women are having babies, even first ones, in their forties."

"You are not going to make me wait another ten years to have babies to play with, young lady. Do you want to have to pull me up off the floor every time I get down to tickle their tummies?"

Andrea thought of her mother's considerable girth and grinned in spite of herself. Only Gloria could be tickling infants that didn't even exist.

"There's always artificial insemina—"

"Andrea! That's enough. A baby needs a father. It's your duty as its mother to provide it with one."

Andrea gave up with a resigned chuckle. Now she was failing the baby before it even existed. See, she was no good with those she loved. And why was it that she could hold her own with six cops at a time, yet still couldn't win a single verbal skirmish with her mother?

"I'll keep my eyes open for potential daddy material, Ma. Now how's Scotty?"

"He's just fine. Found himself a girlfriend. At least there's one child of mine who knows his duty."

Andrea laughed out loud, the first genuine amusement she'd felt since stepping into the suite next door earlier that evening. "Ma, he's only thirteen. You're not starting on him already, are you?"

"I'm not starting on anybody, Andrea Lee. I only want for you what you always wanted for yourself. One of us has to keep trying." Her mother's tone was becoming strident again.

"I said I'd keep my eyes open, Ma, and I will," she said, crossing her fingers. Someday she'd convince herself that her mother was wrong about things, that she *could* be happy without a family of her own. And then she'd convince Gloria.

"Just make sure you do more than look when the time comes." the warning in her mother's tone of voice was clear.

Again a vision of Doug Avery flashed before Andrea's eyes. She thought of her initial reaction to the man, of her urge to accept the challenge he'd offered, of the brief instant of stunning desire she'd felt.

"Tell Scotty I love him."

"I always tell him. Don't you think it's time you tried to tell him again yourself?"

Andrea stared at the beige-colored wall in front of her. "You heard his counselor, Ma. It's best to let him come around in his own time."

"And you think some stranger knows him better than his own mother? Scotty's ashamed, Andrea. I've told you that a hundred times."

"He hates me, Ma. He told me so himself. You're just going to have to accept that this is one thing you can't force."

"I'll talk to him." Her mother's determination carried over the several miles of telephone wire.

Andrea focused on a tiny crack in the wall. "Don't, Ma. Let him be. This is between me and him."

"Andrea..."

"I mean it, Ma. I'll never forgive you if you start badgering him about this. He's been through enough."

A resigned sigh traveled across the line. "I'll leave it for now, Andrea, but I'm telling you you're wrong."

Andrea's gaze followed the crack up to the ceiling. "I know."

"You get some sleep now, Andrea. If you go to breakfast with circles under your eyes, you'll scare off all three of my potential sons-in-law before I even have a chance to meet them."

Andrea smiled and sank back against the pillows. "Yes, Ma." Someday she'd argue with her mother again, when she felt confident enough to win. First she had to stop believing that Gloria was the one person she couldn't fool.

She settled the phone back into its cradle with a sigh, wondering if the Monday she had just had was any indication of the two weeks to come. Sometimes being in control was as hard to deal with as losing it.

She lay on her back, then turned over onto her stomach, cradling a couple of pillows beneath her head. But the bed was so much bigger than hers. And the more she thought about all the empty space beside her, the more alone she felt.

Scotty's laughing blue eyes flashed beneath her closed eyelids, gazing up at her adoringly, trustingly. Andrea sat up. This was the time to get dressed, go outside and take a walk. Walking always seemed to help.

But she wasn't at home. She was stuck in the middle of downtown Columbus, in a hotel swarming with her peers. She didn't doubt that the Hetherington Hotel's many lounges were filled with her fellow DARE officers, the teams of trainees and their off-color jokes. But Andrea was not in the mood for jokes. And the way she was feeling, she didn't want to run the risk of bumping into any of her fellow police officers in the elevators. Which meant she was stuck right where she was.

She got up to take an aspirin, passing DARE Bear as she trudged back to the huge, empty bed. He was grinning at her from his perch on top of the silent television, and she reached out, wanting to grab him, cuddle him against her, take him back with her to share her lonely bed. But she continued on without stopping and lay down alone, Doug Avery's parting remark stinging her ears: "Is your stuffed toy good in bed, too?"

"DAMN!" Doug glanced at his watch as he listened—again—to the annoying busy signal, and hung up the phone with a little more force than was necessary. Opening the fly of his jeans so he could tuck in his clean T-shirt, he swore again. He had hoped to get through to the woman before he had to see her again, and breakfast was due to start in less than sixty seconds.

If he didn't go now, he'd be late, and he wasn't about to give Ms. Andrea Parker any more reason to look down her perfect nose at him—even though, judging by her busy telephone, she was going to be late herself. The apology for his off-color remark would just have to wait, maybe indefinitely.

He was just pulling out one of the two vacant chairs left at the round table set for seven when Andrea walked into the small breakfast room. She was wearing blue jeans and a short-sleeved, button-up shirt with two pockets in just the right places. He wished to hell he hadn't noticed.

He looked at his watch. She'd made it with about two seconds to spare. *Wouldn't you just know it.*

She was wearing that smile again, too. His stomach lurched.

Hunger pains. That's all it was. He'd had them enough to know, hadn't he? But, hell, why couldn't the woman smile like everyone else he knew? A simple lifting of the corners of the mouth, add in a few facial lines, you've got a smile. But not Andrea Parker. No, her smile lifted right up off her face and electrified anyone in its path. She had no right going around giving everyone the illusion that she really cared, that she'd be there if she was needed. Doug had learned a long time ago not to believe in illusions.

He was going to have to call Stan. Maybe they could reassign him to another team, another mentor, another session.

"Hi, guys. Everybody sleep okay?" Andrea asked, sliding into the last empty chair. It was two down from Doug. He was thankful for small mercies. If he moved his own chair a little and leaned back just the right way, he didn't even have to see her.

He hadn't called Celia in a long time, hadn't slept with her in even longer. Maybe that was his problem. He'd just been too long without a woman. Maybe he should give Celia a call.

The men around him all nodded or grunted in reply to Andrea's cheery greeting. Doug remained silent. First thing in the morning was not a good time to chip away at the defenses of a bunch of strong, confident men. Hell, no time was a good time. Didn't the woman have any sense at all?

"What's for breakfast?" she asked the silent group, apparently undaunted by their evasive eyes and grouchy expressions.

"Eggs. They're scrambling yours, since you weren't here to order," the big Swede answered. He was sitting right next to Andrea, so it would have been downright rude of him not to reply. Doug felt a moment's empathy for the guy, but mostly he was just glad it wasn't him.

A couple of black-suited waiters appeared at the door, carrying large trays of dishes covered with metal lids. No more was said around the table as breakfast was served. Doug got scrambled eggs, too—not that he minded. He wasn't picky about *what* he ate, only *that* he ate.

"Anybody here a Browns fan?" Andrea asked.

A couple of the guys grunted an affirmative.

"Did you catch that pre-season skirmish on Sunday?" she asked without missing a beat.

Here it comes, Doug thought, pushing back his black leather wristband. The food on his plate no longer held much appeal. She was going to start playing with their heads now. *Go ahead, Officer Parker. Touch me.*

He figured the odds were that the lady didn't even know what sport the Browns played. He'd seen it happen a million times—women in bars or sports clubs, or even in line at the supermarket, trying to get close to a guy by bringing up sports. And most of the time—all the time, in Doug's experience—they knew only enough about the subject to embarrass themselves.

A couple of the officers were not quite as sharp as he was. They fell for her ploy and began to discuss NFL football with her—specifically, the Browns' chances of making it to the Superbowl this year.

She paused when the question was thrown at her, and Doug was tempted to lean forward enough to see her face. He would've liked to watch her squirm.

"I'd say we have an outside chance of going all the way," she said.

That's it babe, now let's hear you back that up, Doug thought, spreading a glob of grape jelly onto his toast.

"Their quaterback's healthy, he's throwing well, they're a veteran team, the coaching staff is finally solid and the rookie nose guard they got from the first-round draft pick is going to make their defense the strongest in the NFL. If they're on, yeah, I think they can do it."

A piece of soggy toast stuck in Doug's throat, sinking slowly down to his stomach. The woman knew football. The woman really knew football. She not only knew what she was talking about, but she sounded as interested in the subject as any guy. She hadn't been stringing them along, humoring them, playing with their heads, trying to win their trust. She'd just been making conversation—ordinary, everyday, nonthreatening conversation.

Doug felt an unwelcome twinge of respect for her. And a fair amount of relief. And he suddenly knew that he'd better start watching himself. He couldn't afford to get soft. Life ate up the softies, and, only if they were lucky, spit them back out.

Most of the major NFL contenders had been picked apart by the time breakfast was over. Andrea not only knew team stats, she knew which coaches had been fired from where and rehired by who. She knew what teams had a good running offense and which ones could rely on passing. And when one of the guys mentioned a rookie whose record she knew nothing about, she asked as many questions as a reporter for *Sports Illustrated*.

Doug still didn't feel that she qualified, in any way, to be any kind of a mentor to him. He wasn't so easily swayed. But by the time the breakfast dishes had been cleared away and the table wiped clean, he wasn't quite so resentful of Andi Parker. He settled back in his chair lazily, slouching down just enough to be comfortable while still keeping his muscles poised and ready to spring into action.

He watched Andi's hands as she juggled some papers in front of her. They were slender hands, with long, slim fingers. Her nails were short but smooth, as if she wore them that way on purpose, not because she bit them. Doug had never liked long nails. They could hurt a man, just when a woman's fingers were making him feel good. When he started to imagine Andi's fingers forming a soft cocoon around him, he shook his head in self-disgust. He was definitely going to have to make that call to Stan or to Celia—probably both.

"Okay people. Let's get to know each other. Who wants to start? I know—let's go around the room and tell our names and where we're from. And maybe add what we like to do best. Doesn't that sound like fun?"

Doug's head shot up. *What in hell?* Had the woman lost her ever-lovin' mind? She'd raised her voice by a couple of octaves at least, and was talking to them in that tone of voice reserved for babies and cute puppies. He felt his hackles rise. There was no way in hell he was going to recite his name like some damn kindergartner in Show-and-Tell. And he damn sure wasn't going to tell anyone where he was from—ever. He gathered his curriculum and stood up. It was time to make that call to Stan.

"Leaving us so soon, Doug?"

Her words were spoken to his back as he headed for the door. And though the volume of her voice was as carefully controlled as always, her tone cut clear through to his gut. She wasn't talking cutesy now. She was dead serious, and sounding a little victorious as well.

He turned around.

"You realize that these sessions are not optional. If you leave now, you're out of the program."

Her threat was not negotiable. Doug sat back down. The guy to his immediate right, Steve something or other, sent him a sympathetic glance.

Andi tapped the eraser of her pencil against the papers stacked in front of her. "Okay, who wants to begin?" she asked, using that sing-song voice again, as if she'd never been interrupted.

She looked to her right. The ends of her short blond hair brushed against the back of her neck. "How about you, Sven? Can you tell us your name and share with us where you're from?"

Sven shrugged, looking almost as insulted as Doug felt. Doug's glance moved around the table to the four other men seated there. There was Keith Randolph, the big redhead; a tall, skinny guy called Jim; Daniel, the shortest of the group; and Steve, with whom Doug figured he probably had the most in common. Like himself, Steve looked as if he'd had his nose broken a time or two. Right then, all four of them were wearing expressions similar to the Swede's.

Andi glanced around the table too, eyeing them all with such a sickly sweet, phony smile on her face that Doug could barely stand to look at her.

"Well, then, how about if I begin? We'll all feel more comfortable then, right?" She wasn't giving up.

Is this lady for real, Doug wondered. The men moved in their seats, as if unable to get comfortable. All but one of them had their arms crossed against their chests. Even Doug could read that particular body language.

"Let's see. I'm Andrea Parker," she said, still in that singsong voice, and then she giggled.

Doug swore under his breath.

"I was born and raised right here in Columbus, Ohio, and what I like to do best is, gee, um, oh, I guess, eat?" She paused, as if waiting for a laugh.

Was the woman honestly trying to be funny? Doug was at a total loss and growing angrier by the second. No one talked down to him and got away with it for long—not anymore.

"Now, who wants to go next. Keith? You look brave, how about you?" she asked, still talking in the same insipid voice.

The redhead shook his head and looked away, refusing to meet her eyes. His chin was jutting out about a mile.

One by one, she looked at all of the others and got similar reactions. Chins were jutting all over the place. If the broad didn't do something soon, Doug decided, she was going to find herself the recipient of a full-scale walkout.

"Not feeling too good right about now, are you, gentlemen?" Andrea asked, her voice soft and even again.

The guys looked at her, wary but curious. Even Doug found himself watching her, wondering just what was going on.

"Please remember how you felt just now each and every time you walk into a classroom full of bright, offendable sixth-graders. If you try to be their best friend the minute you meet them, or pretend that you're their equal, despite your age differences, you might as well turn around and walk right out the door. The most important thing to remember *at all times*, when dealing with your kids, is to be completely honest with them. Don't try to be funny if you're not, don't pretend an interest in something you know nothing about, don't claim to be good at something you don't do well, and above all, don't ever talk down to them. You'll lose not only your credibility, but possibly several lives as well."

She was good. Doug had to hand it to her. It had all been an act, but for a minute there even he hadn't been sure. She was damn good. He, for one, was never going to walk into a group of people again without being aware of how his actions could affect each and every one of them.

More interested than he had expected to be, he suddenly wasn't quite as anxious to make that phone call to Stan. It could wait at least until lunchtime.

"Now relax, guys," Andi was saying. "While we do all have to get to know each other rather well in an awfully short time span, we don't have to immediately crowd each other's space. The lecture you'll be attending this afternoon covers the first of the seventeen DARE lessons you'll be presenting in the class-

room. It deals mainly with the necessity for rules and
laws, and with basic human rights. You should all be
able to recite those in your sleep, so we don't really
have specific material to cover this morning.

"I'm going to suggest instead that we get acquainted out on the basketball court that's located
behind the swimming pool. But only if you all understand up front that while I like the game, I'm not good
at it, and don't have any particular desire to get any
better. And if, when we split up into two teams,
someone picks me anyway."

The weight in Doug's chest lifted for the first time
since he'd packed his bag and left his apartment the
day before. He could relax for a while. No one was
going to probe his psyche on a basketball court.

Doug had heard the usual rumors about the men-
tor-trainee relationship, about the closeness among
DARE officers, and he'd been dreading the training
almost as much as he'd dreaded the year he had to
spend in elementary-school classrooms. He wasn't sap
material.

But he was getting a reprieve, and judging by what
he'd seen that morning, he might even be able to convince Andi that some guys just weren't the sensitive
type.

He leaned his chair back on two legs and reached
behind him for a couple of plastic stir sticks lying on
a coffee cart.

"How about this side of the table," he said, pointing to Steve, Keith and himself, "plays against that
side, and we draw straws to see who's stuck with

Andi." He broke one of the sticks in half. "Shortest straw loses."

There was general agreement all around. Sven drew for the other team, and left Doug with the longer stick in his hand. Doug looked across and saw Andi smiling as the groans emitted from her side of the table. He could no longer deny that her smile was doing things to him that had never been done to him before. It made him feel kind of like warm mush inside. He didn't like warm mush, and he was relieved that she wasn't on his team. He needed to stay the hell away from her.

It didn't strike him until they were all out on the court, dressed in shorts and T-shirts, that he'd figured it all wrong. Not the staying-away-from-her part—that definitely would have been smart—but the playing-on-the-opposite-team part. A player never guarded or was guarded by his own teammates. A player did not spend the game face-to-face—within kissing distance, for God's sake—with his teammates. A player only did that with members of the opposing team, and Andi was on the opposing team.

They were playing man-to-man basketball instead of zone. Doug was an inch under six feet, but he was still the shortest man on his team. Andi was the shortest on hers. Her team assigned her to guard him.

And every time she raised her arms in the air and bobbed up and down in front of his nose, placing her breasts so close to his face he could almost kiss them, he got a little hotter. He had to use all the control at his disposal to keep his body limp in all the right places. Her long, smooth, bare legs brushed up against his and he had to remind himself that she was not a woman free for him to pursue. She was a police officer—someone in his new life who could never get close enough to learn about his old one. She was also the woman who was planning to take things from him that he had no intention of giving.

They were in the last minutes of their impromptu game, and Doug had almost made it through without making a fool of himself over his training officer. His team was ahead by two points and they were at their basket again, ready to clinch the game.

Sven and Jim were both guarding Doug's teammate, Steve. Steve tossed the ball up in desperation, trying for a wild shot. The ball rimmed the basket and then fell out. But Doug was there, catching the rebound, ready to make the easy shot.

He raised the ball up over his head, and Andi jumped up in front of him, trying to block his aim. Doug wasn't worried about her—she didn't have a chance in hell of stopping him. He waited a fraction of a second to get his shot off, just long enough for one more bob from Andi, one more close-up view before he forced himself to forget she was a woman. Up she came, and she was close, so close.... Too close. Her nipple brushed his chin, and Andi had the basketball.

"Hey, man, wake up!" Steve called to Doug, chasing down court to guard his man.

Dazed and humiliated, Doug raced down the court in turn. Empowered by a healthy dose of male ego, he beat Andi to her basket. He planted himself firmly in her path, careful not to foul her, but determined not

to let her score against him either. She came sailing
down the court and rammed straight into him.

"Uh!" She grunted, losing the ball and landing on
her backside on the court. "You're supposed to
move," she said with a disgruntled look. "Wasn't that
a foul or something?"

Steve stole the bouncing ball just before it went out-
of-bounds, and the rest of the men chased him up-
court.

"It's a foul, but not a defensive one," Doug said,
automatically checking to make sure his wristband was
in place as he reached a hand down to help her up.
"My feet were firmly planted, and you'd have been
called."

"Oh. I knew there was a reason I didn't want to
learn to play this game," she said, letting go of his
hand to run up-court and assist her teammates. She
got there just in time to see Steve sink an easy hook
shot.

The game was over, which was a very good thing as
far as Doug was concerned. He could never have hidden the heavy bulge in his shorts, a result of his colli-
sion with Andi, from a bunch of streetwise cops.
Foregoing the good-natured congratulations going on
behind him, Doug headed off to his hotel room and a
long, cold shower.

He stood under the stinging spray with only one
thought racing through his head: who said making
love with her meant he had to get close to her? He and
Celia had shared a satisfying relationship for years,
and she'd never asked for a thing Doug couldn't give
her. Andrea didn't have to be any different. He'd just

been letting all this DARE screening get to him. Having sex wasn't like going out for beer. You could do it without giving anything away.

It didn't dawn on him until much later that night, as he lay sleeplessly, pondering the unusual day, that he'd just played his first game of hoops, ever, as "one of the guys." And aside from a little frustration, he'd enjoyed it.

CHAPTER THREE

"'NIGHT, MA."

"Sleep tight, dear."

Andrea slowly replaced the receiver in the cradle and then lay back against her pillows. She didn't know what was the matter with her. She'd just spent the past fifteen minutes giving her mother a rundown on two of her trainees—two of her *single* trainees. She hadn't voluntarily talked to her about a man since her divorce.

And she'd just led her mother to believe that she had two possible sons-in-law on the horizon. She, who knew there would never be another son-in-law in her mother's life, not unless Gloria herself gave birth to another daughter.

And now, in spite of her stalling, she was still left alone in the dark with too many thoughts to run from. She knew her unrest had more to do with something she'd felt during that morning's basketball game than with the uncomfortable bruise it had left on her right hip. She just didn't want to acknowledge what that something was.

There was absolutely no logical reason for her suddenly to feel this challenging need to discover what, if anything, lay beneath Doug Avery's cold, hard shell.

Nothing had changed. The man had done nothing to indicate to her that he belonged in the DARE program, and plenty to indicate that he did not.

Yet each time she was with him she sensed a tightly leashed vital energy that, if properly channeled, might just make him the best DARE officer the country had ever seen.

Something had to have made the man so crude and hard. Babies were not born that way. And if she did her job right, she would find that something, bring it to light and then determine whether or not there was anything left inside Doug Avery to offer to children.

And there was more.... Her mind quickly skittered away from what that "more" might be, but her traitorous thoughts kept coming right back to it. With the silence settling around her like a thick, dark curtain, it got harder and harder for her to push the unsettling subject away. She shifted in bed, then jerked back with a hiss. She'd forgotten her bruised hip.

Doug's body was rock solid. It was no wonder she'd fallen so hard.

Andrea's skin tingled as she remembered the instant when her body had slammed into his. For that split second, she'd felt his masculinity pressing against her intimate parts. He'd offered his hand to help her up and she'd been tempted to look at his crotch....

No!

She must stop this. She had to stop. She simply couldn't allow herself such thoughts—not about Doug Avery, not about anyone.

She was alone now. That was as it should be. She'd had her chance, and she'd blown it. It was time to sleep, to rest her body in preparation for the next day. Her only concern was performing her job perfectly. And vital to this particular job was keeping a tight rein on Doug Avery's actions. She'd actually forgotten the ledger.

She got out of bed and collected the account she'd started the night before. Thinking of the kids, and of one little boy in particular, she forced herself to be objective and recall the officer's transgressions that day. There was his lack of contribution to the innocuous conversation at breakfast; the display of temper when he'd almost stomped out of the morning's session; the way he'd just walked off after the basketball game, leaving his team standing there accepting congratulations without him. The man was a loner, and loners didn't attract friends, especially in children.

Andrea was about to close the ledger, put her pen away and climb back into bed, but in all fairness, there was more she had to write. At the bottom of the page, she made a little plus sign. And then another. Doug Avery had swallowed his anger and sat back down without insolence when Andrea had warned him that he was on the verge of being thrown out of the program. For some reason, the man wanted to be there. It meant a lot to him. That had to count for something. And beside the second plus, she wrote, At least he played the game.

That settled, Andrea returned to her bed, punched her pillow a little harder than was necessary and settled down to do her mind's bidding. She would sleep. She *would* sleep.

Sometime after midnight she slipped out of the bed that hadn't yet coaxed sleep from her body, gathered DARE Bear from atop the TV, cuddled him to her breast and took him back to bed. He kept her company until sleep finally claimed her.

"*DO NOT*, I repeat, *do not* stand up and lecture your kids. Their minds will wander, they'll miss something. You have to involve them in every aspect of their learning." Andrea looked out to the sea of faces and spotted her team of six among the other DARE trainees. They all seemed to be absorbing her words.

All except Doug Avery. Andrea couldn't really say whether Doug was paying attention or not. She refused to look at him directly. Her reactions to him on the basketball court the day before were still too recent, her resolve not to feel them again too shaky for her to take a chance on putting it to the test.

"In other words, guys, do as I say and not as I do," she continued, lightening her tone once she was certain her point had been made.

"Now, before I give you my own inspired ideas for getting the kids to participate, do any of you have any suggestions?"

A hand or two popped up, and then two or three more.

"Make crossword puzzles, with the day's facts as clues."

"Play a board game where teams have to recite facts to progress."

"Have them do group reports and read them to the class."

Andrea continued to take suggestions, adding her own comments where she thought appropriate, pointing out hazards as she saw them. All in all, she was pleased with the attention the men were giving the exercise.

And then, in the back corner of the ballroom-cum-lecture room, she saw a hand go up, a strip of silver-studded black leather attached to the masculine wrist. For a moment her heart stopped. In her mind's eye, she saw again that scrap of leather moving down toward her on the basketball court, felt the strange, instant excitement as a firm grip took possession of her hand. And again she felt the urge to find the man inside the shell of Doug Avery, to bring him out, to get to know him.

"Doug?" she called. He didn't move from his slouched position. His legs, covered with the inevitable black denim, were stretched out in front of him and crossed at the ankles. His arms rested against his massive chest.

"Listen." The one word was spoken inflexibly, as if his was the only answer.

He still had an attitude problem.

"Listen to what the kid knows," he went on. "It'd probably save everyone lots of time. Then channel that knowledge onto a course that helps the kid find his own answers. When push comes to shove, those are the only ones he's going to have faith in anyway." His piercing brown eyes looked straight at her, as if daring her to argue.

But for once, Andrea had no desire to argue with him. He sounded as if he was speaking from experience. He also sounded right. Still, the children could be led through proper channels only if they trusted their guide, if they felt that their leader cared where they were going and where they ended up.

Andrea still didn't think Doug Avery could inspire that trust. Not only was he crude, and slightly sinister-looking with his crooked nose and jagged scar, but his whole attitude suggested that he was self-sufficient and expected others to be the same. That was the attitude that led kids straight to hell.

DOUG HAD HIS FIRST one-on-one session with Andrea later that evening. He'd seen her at dinner, sitting with a couple of other training officers, but hadn't spoken to her directly since the previous day on the basketball court. Not that he minded. Speaking wasn't what he wanted to do with her.

The thoughts he'd been having about her since the game had everything to do with doing, and nothing to do with saying. He wanted her long, silky legs wrapped tightly around him. He wanted to watch her face on his pillow after some hard loving. Above all he wanted to believe that sexual attraction was all he felt for her, that making love with her would cure the uneasiness he felt inside every time she entered a room. He *needed* to believe it.

He did not want to share his thoughts with her, to show her his soul.

He walked into the suite that had been assigned to his team, the one where he'd first seen her, feeling more uncomfortable than he did walking a beat among gangs and druggies. The suite was empty. He'd beat her to it.

Doug slouched down in the seat Andrea had occupied that first night—not because she'd occupied it, but because he could view every other part of the room from it. It made him feel better, somehow, more in control, to have the whole room under his command.

He knew that a couple of the other guys had already had their first one-on-one's. Right now, he sure would have liked to know what to expect out of the next hour. How was she going to be coming at him? How best could he avoid her? Was there any chance he could get her into bed instead?

Did he really want her to be that kind of woman?

With his elbows resting on the arms of his chair and his fingers propped in a steeple below his chin, he watched as the door swung open and Andi came into the room. She was wearing white jeans and a bright blue polo shirt that detailed the delicate shape of her breasts above her trim, womanly waistline.

And she was smiling. Did the woman ever enter a room without that damn smile? Doug glanced away, ignoring the curious pool of warmth he felt deep inside as he got caught in that smile again, and also ignoring the stuffed bear in the crook of her arm.

"Hi, Doug. You're on time," she said, taking the seat opposite him. She ran the fingers of one hand through her stylishly cropped blond hair. He really liked her hair. Its shortness was sassy, not harsh.

"You sound disappointed," he said.

"Nope. Not even surprised." She settled her stuffed toy on the table beside her. Doug was glad to have it out of the way.

"I knew you'd be on time. You're very methodical about doing what you have to do to accomplish the goal you've set for yourself." Her voice was warm, husky, as well modulated as ever.

So it's finally arrived—the time when she plays shrink. Let her play her games, he thought, determined not to let her get to him. *She can't take anything I don't give her. Nobody can.*

She seemed to be waiting for some kind of reply to her statement. He nodded.

"That's an admirable quality."

He nodded again, trying to picture her in a shower—or better yet, naked in the woods in a downpour. It was the only thing he could think of to take his mind off the probing look in her eyes.

"I'm just not sure why," she continued. She crossed one knee over the other. Her hands rested comfortably along the arms of her chair. Her whole confident, controlled demeanor was beginning to bother him.

"Why what?" he asked.

"Why you've set this goal for yourself."

Doug shrugged. "Why have any of us?"

If he'd hoped to slow her down with that one, he was disappointed.

"Usually out of compassion for the children." Her watchful eyes gave him no peace.

"That's as good a reason as any."

"Is it your reason?"

She was getting close to invading his space. Doug felt his defenses shoot up. *Calm down, man. You don't want to blow this.* His muscles tightened, ready for action, but he forced himself to stay right where he was, lying back in the chair. "Maybe."

"You don't seem the compassionate type."

She was challenging him. He wasn't going to let her trap him so easily. He'd long since stopped needing to prove himself to anyone.

"You're into stereotyping?" he asked.

They were no longer just talking about the reasons for his stint with DARE. They were like two tigers stalking each other, each waiting for the other to make that crucial mistake that would give the other control.

She kicked off her shoes, white leather slip-ons that she wore without socks, and curled her feet up under her. She leaned closer to the table on which her toy was perched.

"I just say it like I see it," she said.

A part of Doug approved of how she gave as good as she got, but the bigger part of him knew it was time to end their charade. She may have the upper hand as far as DARE was concerned, but he had the final say about what he was going to reveal about himself, and to whom.

"Well, what I see here are two healthy adults who could be using this room for something much more mutually satisfying than—"

"Officer! Let's stick to the business at hand, hmm?" she said without raising her voice. "Unless, of course, you'd like to resign from the program and save us both a lot of time?''

What did it take to make the woman understand that he was not going anywhere?

"Sorry, no can do," he said. He unsnapped his wristband and snapped it again before letting his arm fall back to the chair.

The stuffed bear with the DARE emblem kept staring at him, as if the damn glass eyes could see everything Doug wanted to keep hidden. He decided that maybe there was a purpose for the thing, after all. He could use it for target practice. He'd bet he could take out one of those eyes with a single shot from fifty feet.

"Is your mother still alive?"

Andrea's question startled Doug back to the business at hand.

He turned slightly in his chair, lifting his ankle to rest it across his knee.

"I have no idea," he said. He thought briefly of the woman he'd known, of her softness. He hoped she was still alive. He wanted her to have had a happy life all these years.

Andi's eyes took on a peculiar light—softer, warmer. "How long has it been since you've seen her?" she asked.

Doug shrugged. "I don't know. Twenty, maybe twenty-five years."

Her blue eyes opened wide. "But you're only thirty now. You're telling me you haven't seen her since you were a little boy?"

Doug nodded, wondering why she was making a big deal about it. Lots of guys grew up without mothers. "I was five when she took off."

"She deserted you?" Andi asked, a hint of criticism in her voice.

Doug was getting ticked off again. Andi Parker had no business judging a woman she'd never met.

"She didn't desert me. She merely did what she had to do. She had a chance to escape an abusive situation that was going to kill her sooner or later, and she took it."

"Was it your father she was running from? Did he hit her? Is that what you're saying?"

Doug could feel the muscles in his neck begin to clench.

"He hit her when he was in a good mood. It wasn't nearly so pretty when he wasn't."

"And yet she just ran off and left you there with him?"

Doug couldn't believe her naiveté. The woman was still a police officer. Hadn't she learned anything during her years on the force?

He couldn't believe her nerve, either. His childhood was his business. He sat up in his chair, his hands ready to push off.

"The guy who offered to take her away from it all, to give her a chance at a better life, didn't include a snot-nosed kid in the bargain. She did what she had to do. That's what life's all about—each man for himself, the strongest wins and all that. Besides, she wouldn't have been doing me any good by staying just so I could watch the bastard kill her."

Andi leaned forward. "But what about you? What happened to you after she left? Did he hit you, too?"

Doug shook his head. He'd had enough. None of this had anything to do with teaching kids to stay off drugs.

He looked her up and down, slowly, deliberately. "Doesn't your old man ever worry that you might be doing more with us guys than just talking, while you're here alone with us in a hotel room each night?" he asked.

He'd meant to unnerve her, to shake her up, to throw her off track. He hadn't meant to be interested in her answer.

She didn't blush. But her eyes were no longer boring into him. "I don't have a man, and if I did, he'd either trust me or be history."

"You're not married?" he asked. He shouldn't have been so pleased to hear it. Besides, there was no reason for him to continue this line of questioning. He'd accomplished his goal—they were no longer talking about him. He wanted to hear her answer anyway.

"Not now," she said, meeting his eyes with her own electric blue gaze. And for the first time, Doug looked back. Really looked back. The woman had something...substance, maybe. He kept looking.

"Were you ever?" he asked, knowing darn well that he was overstepping his bounds.

"I was, yes."

"What happened?"

"He didn't like being married to a cop."

"The jerk."

"Yeah."

"You got any kids?"

Her eyes became shuttered. Doug saw it, the barely perceptible shadowing, the hint of agony. Her husband must have gotten custody along with the divorce. A cop was hardly single-parent material.

"No."

That wasn't the answer he'd expected. Had he imagined the pain he'd seen so briefly, then? Or was it something else? Maybe she was unable to have children. . . .

"So what's the real reason you want to be a DARE officer?"

She slid the words in so casually that Doug almost missed them. Or rather, he almost missed the fact that they'd just returned to the roles of trainee and mentor.

But even being caught off guard wasn't enough to make him betray himself. Each man for himself—he'd learned the lesson well. And it worked. It had pulled him out of hell and turned him into a respected, even decorated member of the force. How much he liked or didn't like Andi Parker had no bearing on things at all.

He looked at his watch. Their time was about up, anyway.

"Look, lady," he said, pushing out of his chair. "You're good at what you do. I'll admit I had hesitations about the training program at first, but I'm already convinced that it's not only a necessary part of DARE, but a vital one. You can take credit for that. You'll have my full participation. Let's just leave it at that, shall we?"

Andi got up too, facing him. She still hadn't put her shoes back on. Her head only came to his shoulders.

"Will you answer just one more question for me?"

Her bare toes were more of a distraction than they should have been. He'd never, not once, had a kinky thought about toes. Doug put his hands on his hips.

"Probably not," he said.

"Do you really believe it's always each man for himself?"

Finally, an easy answer. "Absolutely."

She slipped into her shoes and wrapped her arms around her midriff, cradling herself.

"How old were you when you left your father's home?"

She'd said only one more question. "Sixteen."

"So you had to live with his abuse for more than half of your life. . . ."

Her words hung between them, seeking confirmation. Doug simply shrugged.

"I'm sorry."

She looked at his implacable expression for another second, then walked around him and left the room. But not before he'd seen the tears in her eyes.

No one, not even his mother, had ever cried for him before. It gave him the strangest feeling—like he was special or something, important enough to draw tears other than his own. Doug had absolutely no idea what to do about that.

And he had no idea what to do with the tiny beige teddy bear she had forgotten to take with her, either. With a shake of his head, he turned his back and left the suite, leaving the nosy glass eyes staring after him.

CHAPTER FOUR

"HELLO?"

"Yeah, is Celia around?"

Doug lay nude across his kingsize hotel bed, wondering what derelict Celia had taken in this time. He didn't recognize the guy's voice.

"She's here. Who's this?"

Doug frowned. The male voice on the other end of the line was almost challenging. None of the drunks Celia rented rooms to had ever before been sober enough to fight a flea.

"Tell her it's Doug. She'll come to the phone." He was getting a little defensive himself. After the evening he'd just had, all he wanted was a little uncomplicated sex to sooth his raging nerves. He didn't need more complications; Andrea Parker and her stupid teddy bear presented enough to last him a lifetime.

Doug listened while the man spoke to someone, presumably Celia. He hadn't bothered to cover the mouthpiece.

"Some guy's on the phone. Says his name's Doug. Says you'll talk to him."

Doug heard a feminine murmur, followed by the distinct muffling of the phone and an unintelligible masculine reply. What the hell was going on?

He sat up, his adrenalin pumping. Had Celia finally trusted one too many down-and-outers?

"Doug?"

"Yeah, babe, you okay?" he asked, relieved when Celia's familiar, high-pitched tones came over the line. She didn't sound scared.

"Sure, Doug. I'm fine. Just fine."

He lay back down, searching for a clear picture of the woman on the other end of the line. He had some fond memories of midnight snacks and late-night sex shared with the buxom brunette. But he was having a hard time envisioning dark hair instead of blond. And Celia's full, rosy lips were being superceded by a megawatt smile.

"You know, it's, uh, been a long time. I really didn't think I'd be hearing from you again," she said.

"Yeah, well, I've been doing some extra stuff for Stan. You know how it is." He rolled over onto his back, staring at the shadowy shapes on the ceiling.

"You never called. Not once in all these months."

He didn't need this. Celia had never given him a hard time before. Why the hell did she have to start tonight of all nights?

"I'm sorry, babe. I meant to. But you know how I get when I'm working on a case."

"Yeah, I know, Doug. I understand."

That was more like the old Celia—full of tolerance, never laying guilt where he couldn't take it. But she was different, too.

"So, you busy tonight?" he asked, trying to convince himself that he was imagining things, that if he just acted normally, so would the rest of the world.

"It's kinda late." She'd never refused him before—ever.

"It's only eleven o'clock. I could be there in half an hour." Doug didn't know why he was pressing so hard, except that he felt like something safe was slipping away from him and he couldn't seem to do anything about it.

Celia sighed, sending frissons of warning through him.

"I'm not alone, Doug."

He rubbed his hand across his eyes, scraping it over the day's growth of whiskers. He'd known, of course. But surely she didn't want to do this. They were too good together. She just needed to make him pay for having neglected her for so long. He could understand that—she had her pride.

"So send him away."

The line was quiet. Deathly quiet. And that's when Doug knew things had really changed. The guy who'd answered the phone had had a reason to sound defensive—apparently more reason than he had had. She'd found someone else.

"I'm sorry, Doug," she finally said, her voice more sad than regretful.

"It's okay, babe." He slid up to sit against the headboard. "It's my turn to understand. He treat you right?"

"Yeah. He's a good guy, Doug. You'd like him."

He doubted that. "You be happy, okay?"

"I will, Doug. I am. If you'd just quit running long enough you might find a little happiness yourself one day." Celia's voice was softer, more caring than he'd ever heard it before.

"I'm already happy," he said, adjusting his aching genitals. "Call me if you ever need anything, you hear?"

He didn't bother to hang up the phone after Celia's goodbye. He lay there in the darkness, restless and awake as the night ticked slowly by, his only company the dead receiver resting on the bed beside him.

GLORIA PARKER DROVE down the highway like a bulldozer plowing a field. The only concession she made to the other motorists sharing the road with her was the heavy hand she laid on her horn every time one got in her way. Scotty was at Liz's house for the afternoon. Gloria had a whole hour to fill, and she didn't want to waste one minute of it.

She knew exactly where she was going, and pulled into the parking lot in record time.

The dresses were all gorgeous, as usual, but for the first time, Gloria did more than window shop and worry. She opened the door and peeked inside, as excited as a child in a toy shop. Everywhere she looked there was white lace and satin and pearls. Gauzy veils lined the walls. Taffeta billowed out around perfectly shaped mannequins that seemed like they belonged in a fairy tale.

Andrea was going to look beautiful in one of those dresses, more beautiful than the models who wore them. And she would be happy again—finally. She would finally quit punishing herself for a crime she hadn't committed. She would have the babies she'd always dreamed of having. Gloria's baby girl was going to be happy again, even if Gloria had to move the world to make it so.

She let the door swing shut without going in. She couldn't go in, not yet. Not until she could shop for real. But she hadn't been able to resist the peek. Something was up—she was sure of it. Andrea had spent too much time extolling the virtues of two of her trainees that last time they'd talked.

Gloria wasn't fooled. She knew her daughter wasn't interested in either one of the men she'd talked about. And that was why she was so certain that Andrea had finally met the man that mattered. Her daughter was hiding something. And sooner or later, she would find out about it.

"TRY IT, MAN. It's better than sex." The words held conviction and a hint of a dare.

"Naw. I gotta get home. My brother's on the warpath again." The second voice was weary, aged and scared.

"That's why you need this, man. A couple of swallows and you'll be able to take anything the bastard dishes out. You'll even be strong enough to give him a little back for once, if you want to." The first voice again, cajoling this time.

"Nothing's gonna make it any easier to face that jerk if he's in one of his moods. Nothing."

"This will, man, I swear it. You'll be feelin' better than a wet dream. You're invincible. There ain't nothing you can't do. Come on. I ain't even gonna charge ya. It's yours. Take it."

Andrea's eyes were glued to the stage, her throat thick with checked emotion. She was no longer a training officer watching an exercise in role-playing, she was on the streets of any one of a hundred cities, with two of the millions of kids living with the horrible fascination of drug use.

It had never been so real before, so tangibly painful.

"Thanks, man, but I better not. It'd kill my ma if she ever found out, and besides, it's just my luck I'd get some bad stuff. How'm I gonna help my ma if I'm six feet under? She's outta work again. Which reminds me, I gotta find some dinner for the little kids. You think D'Ambros put out his old bakery goods yet?"

"Not till six . . . and it ain't bad stuff, man, I swear it. I wouldn't give you nothin' bad. We're buddies, man, you know that. I took some of this stuff last night just before the Black Sox rumble. I took three punches and didn't feel one of 'em. Broke some guy's nose, too. You should'a seen it, man. I was awesome."

"It didn't hurt at all when they blasted you?"

Tears swam beneath Andrea's lids. She didn't want it to happen.

"I didn't feel a thing, except great. You'll see, man, it'll get you through anything."

The owner of the second voice, Doug, reached out for the imaginary pipe, raised it to his mouth, took a long drag and held it, letting the narcotic fill his lungs. The floodlight glinted off the silver studs of his wristband.

Andrea bowed her head as the trainees left the stage. The auditorium full of police officers was deathly silent.

"It's two months later, same time, same place."

Andrea's gaze flew back to the stage. Doug and Steve were back in place in the middle of the empty stage, a single floodlight their only illumination. They were dressed identically in the same ripped jeans and stained, too-small T-shirts, but the expressions they were wearing bore no resemblance to the weary yet strangely trusting glances of moments before. Andrea had no idea what was going on. She'd thought they'd completed their exercise.

"You get me more of that stuff, man, unless you feel like dying tonight."

The voice was Doug's.

"What's wrong with you, man? This is Steve, remember? I'm the one who showed you where Old Man D'Ambros throws away his dayolds. I taught you how to steal fruit from Sherman's Market. I gave you Cindy Lou when we was ten and you wanted to try sex. Remeber Cindy Lou, Dougie?"

"I remember what my bastard brother's gonna do to me when he finds out I hid Ma's stash again. I gotta have those pills, *now.*"

"Maybe if you talk to him, maybe he'll listen."

Doug laughed harshly, humorlessly. The sound chilled Andrea. She had to remind herself that he was role-playing, fulfilling an assignment. His bitterness felt so real.

"Oh yeah, he'll listen, while he's pounding my brains into the porch. Trouble is, I won't be able to talk no more by then, and neither will you, *Stevie,* if you don't come up with some stuff."

"I don't have it, man. I swear to God, I don't have it. My supplier's gone dry. There was a big bust down by the waterfront last week."

"Don't give me that bull, man. You're holding out on me, keeping it all for yourself. You got to like it just a little too much, didn't you? But I'm not going to let you do this to me."

Doug stepped closer to Steve, grabbing a fistful of the other man's T-shirt. "Now, you gonna get me that stuff, or do I have to hurt you first?"

Steve lifted both hands to Doug's arm, struggling to free himself from his grasp.

"Calm down, Doug. You're losing it, man. I haven't taken any of that stuff for weeks, not since I saw what it's doing to you. You need help, man. You gotta get some help."

Doug pushed Steve, causing the other man to stumble backward. He spat at Steve's feet.

"You're really low, man, you know that? Telling me *I* need help. I need help beating a little weasel like you into the ground. You're the one who sold me on 'em, remember? And you were right. Those pills are keeping me sane, man. They're all I got. When I'm high I can feed the kids, take care of Ma *and* put up with the bruises. I can't make it without them and you know it."

Doug started to walk away, but he turned back.

"You say we're buddies, Steve. You say we been thick. But what kind of guy would hold out on a buddy? You're no friend—you're a damn pig, just like the rest. And I'll tell you something else. I'm gonna get my stuff, with or without you. I'm gonna get it. Just watch me."

Steve moved forward, back into the middle of the floodlight. He reached out a hand imploringly, holding onto Doug's shoulder as Doug turned to walk away again.

"Please don't do this, Dougie. You got hope. You're smart. You got a chance to get out of this hellhole, to have a real life, but you're not gonna get anywhere if you don't stop this. Smoke some pot, man. Cool out. And then get some help."

Doug whirled around, appearing to throw his forearm up and to smash Steve's face. Steve reeled, fell backward, then slowly started to rise.

"*Never* tell me what to do again, you hear me? You have no idea what I need."

"Sure I do. Listen to me—"

Doug's fist shot out, making contact with Steve's jaw. Steve's head jerked backward once, twice, before he fell to the stage once more.

"You have no idea what it's like!" Doug was shouting now. "You go home to a little old lady who doesn't even kill the roaches in her kitchen. She may be looney, but you never have to wonder when you go to bed at night if you're going to wake up with your arm pinned to your shoulder blades or a knee breaking your back."

Steve didn't get up this time. He lay still on the stage, limp and lifeless.

Doug stood over him for a frozen second, looking down at the body of his friend. Then he reached down and pulled a plastic bag from Steve's front pocket.

"You don't need these, man. I do," he said, and turned and strode away.

The spotlight remained on the supine body in the middle of the stage.

Andrea swallowed the lump in her throat, glad she was not visible in the darkened auditorium. The afternoon's session had been intended to impart new understanding to the trainees surrounding her. But Andrea had a feeling that she'd learned the biggest lesson of all. The bitterness, the despair she was feeling couldn't possibly be the products of a cold, heartless man.

DOUG PULLED the too-small T-shirt over his head, dropping it in the trash can in his hotel room. Thursday's dinner was supposed to be a barbecue, an informal event conducive to socializing. Doug didn't feel like socializing. He had to get out.

He was on his third beer in Harry's, the first tavern he'd come to after leaving the Hetherington Hotel, before the tension in the back of his neck finally slackened. He slouched down on his stool, resting his arms on the bar in front of him.

"You ready?" the craggy bartender barked out from the other end of the bar.

Doug nodded once, picked up a couple of bills from the pile in front of him and pushed them across the bar in the direction of the weathered old man.

"How many you got on me, Avery?"

"Three, if you hurry." Doug turned, watching the man who was settling onto the stool beside him. He was a little surprised to find that he was glad to see his acting partner.

Steve flagged himself a beer and tipped it, not bringing his bottle back to the counter until it was empty.

"Make that two," Steve told the bartender with a grin.

"You eat?" Doug asked.

"Naw. Barbeques aren't my thing. How about you?"

"This is dinner," Doug said, motioning to the empty bottles in front of him.

"I figured you were at some dame's place, laying it on real nice and smooth, all ready to respect her in the morning," Steve said, looking at the various whiskey bottles lining the wall in front of them.

"She preferred someone who wanted to *be* there in the morning," Doug said, not minding that Steve knew that. After what they'd been through together that afternmoon, it seemed fitting somehow.

"You know her long?"

"Five years on and off, give or take a couple."

Steve finished his second beer and motioned for a third. "You're probably better off."

Doug peeled the label off the half-empty brown bottle in his fingers. He thought of Andrea, of her smile. He remembered the brush of her breast against his chin.

"Yeah." He took another sip of beer. "How 'bout you? You got someone keeping your bed warm while you're gone?"

Steve shook his head. "Nope." He took a long swig of beer. "I tried three times. The last one wanted to be a farmer. I didn't."

Doug grinned. "So, is she farming?"

"Yep. She married some guy with twenty head of cattle and a beat-up little house out in the middle of Boondock City, USA."

"You sorry?"

"Not for her. We lived in Chicago, inner-city Chicago. She couldn't take the ugliness anymore. She needed a nice simple life straight from TV land, and she got it. But I miss my kid."

Doug turned on his stool until he was facing the other man. "Kid? You got a kid?"

Steve looked at Doug and then back at the display of bottles in front of him. "Yeah. A little girl. She's got dark hair just like her dad, and she's got my temper, too."

"No kidding." Doug was grinning straight out. "You got a kid. That's great, man! How old is she?"

"Six. She started school this year. She's good at it, too. She's gonna be a lawyer someday."

"A lawyer, huh? Well, congratulations! A damn lawyer. You're a lucky man."

Steve flashed Doug a lopsided grin. "Yeah, I am, aren't I?"

The two men finished their beers, ordered one more apiece and then decided that maybe they should have some food after all. They walked back to the hotel in

companionable silence, went to their separate rooms
and ordered up separate sandwiches from room service.

In his room, Doug fell asleep in the armchair he'd
settled into, his sirloin sub half eaten and a late-night
talk show blaring out of the television. The grin he'd
worn earlier was still faintly visible on his face.

ANDREA SAT AT THE TABLE in her room, a glass of
club soda beside her and the television murmuring
quietly behind her. She opened the ledger she was
keeping on Doug Avery and immediately wrote about
his unexcused absence at the barbeque that evening.
She'd watched for him all evening, trying to tell herself that her disappointment in him was purely professional; that she hadn't been looking forward to
spending time with him in the informal setting; that
she hadn't worn her skintight black jeans just to see if
he'd notice.

And all evening long, as steaks were being grilled
and officers were throwing each other, fully dressed,
into the pool, she kept hearing the words he'd said to
her just two days before. "Each man for himself. Absolutely." She'd do well to remember that.

Andrea chronicled the day's woes and then spent
another hour writing about the skit Doug and Steve
had done that afternoon. For those few minutes up on
stage, Doug Avery had finally shown Andrea a brief
glimpse of the depth she had sensed in him. It took
compassion, large doses of it, to emulate the suffering of another, and Doug had done so with incredible
intensity.

Andrea believed that Doug could be a top-notch DARE officer if he only could acknowledge that compassion. And she knew it was up to her to help him try.

She scooted down in her chair, leaning her head against the upholstered back, and tried to imagine a softer Doug—one who was strong and sure, but tender, too. She closed her eyes, suddenly realizing how draining the day had been, how tired she was. And she drifted off to sleep, joining an incredible new lover as they traveled together along the sensuous road to ecstasy. In her dream he was as naked as she, except for the skinny black strip of leather with silver studs that encircled his wrist.

CHAPTER FIVE

DOUG WAS LEAVING a networking session with his other team members at ten o'clock Friday night when he saw Andrea heading out toward the hotel pool alone, a towel in her hand.

"I'm going for some air. I'll see you guys in the morning," he said, slipping away from his teammates as they headed to the elevator.

He slid into an alcove until Andrea turned the corner, and then he followed her outside. Quietly, he leaned his body against a cement column, watching as she entered the deserted pool area. She dropped her towel on one of the empty lounge chairs near the Jacuzzi. Her short terry wrap barely covered her thighs. She really was a beautiful woman.

Looking around her, as if to make sure she was completely alone, she dropped the wrap. Doug felt like the adolescent he'd portrayed on stage the day before as his body hardened, and still he kept watching her. Her legs were not particularly long, but they were firm and perfectly shaped. Her thighs were exposed in the French-cut one-piece suit she was wearing, and they too were smooth and sleekly muscled.

Doug's jaw clenched, and he forced himself to look away before he did something he'd be ashamed of. He

wanted her. He'd even go so far as to say he intended
to have her. But he wanted her to be a willing participant—a knowing participant—not an inadvertent
sideshow for some insensitive pervert.

He waited until she was completely concealed by the
bubbling water of the Jacuzzi before he stepped forward. He saw her turn in his direction as he approached, but the shadows surrounding them were too
dense for him to see her features clearly. She didn't
speak—not to say hello, but not to send him away, either.

Doug remained silent as well, satisfied that what
was waiting to be said between them would be said
best without words. In fact, he'd prefer it that way.

He unbuttoned the fly of his jeans, pulling the stiff
material away from his swollen body as he slid the
zipper down. The rasp of the taut metal could be heard
even above the bubbling water. It was like a siren, a
warning call.

Doug kicked off his shoes, shrugged out of his pants
and T-shirt, and then, dressed only in his bikini-cut
briefs, stepped down into the Jacuzzi.

The water covered him to midthigh, but he didn't
immediately sink down to conceal the rest of his body.
He was watching a still-silent Andrea, close enough
now for him to see her round blue eyes trained on the
bulge between his legs. He allowed her to look for a
minute, and then he slid down to the bench beneath
the water, close enough to touch her if he chose to, but
not too close. He wanted to make their eventual coming together as pleasurable for her as it would be for
him. He didn't want to rush her.

The water was hot, stinging his skin, yet its very warmth enveloped them in a cocoonlike intimacy that made being there with her seem more private than a public pool should have allowed.

He looked over at Andrea, content for the moment to share the intimacy with her. She smiled a confused, awkward little smile and then looked away. It was the first time Doug had ever seen her anything but completely controlled. The sight stunned him.

It also made him feel kind of protective, which he didn't like at all. He was only looking for mature, adult satisfaction here.

Angry with himself for getting soft, he looked away.

"You shouldn't be here, Doug," Andrea said. Her voice was as gentle as usual, but it was trembling, too.

He studied her through narrowed eyes. "Not if you don't want me here, I shouldn't. I was under the impression you did."

Her gaze flew to his, alarmed and hesitant at the same time. "Where did you ever get that impression?"

"It's there every time we're in a room together. It's been there all week."

"But we don't even like each other."

"I think we do. Even though you want me out of the program, I think you know I'm a good cop. And I respect the job you do, the way you handle yourself with the guys."

"I have a lot of respect for you, too, Doug. I do. A whole lot. You've got nerves of steel, and honor and courage. I'd trust you with my life in a dangerous situation. But that doesn't mean you're right for the

classroom. And it certainly doesn't mean I want...
this." She raised her hand out of the water, gesturing
to encompass the hot tub, the night, him.

He wanted to lick the beads of water from her forearm. "Don't you?"

"No."

Doug didn't reply. He just watched her, holding her
eyes with his own, forcing her to be honest.

She met his gaze for a couple of seconds and then
looked away, out over the deserted swimming pool
beside them.

"I don't. I know I don't."

"Who're you trying to convince?" he asked, remaining where he was, keeping his hands to himself.

"Okay. I like your after-shave. But that means less
than nothing. I can't lose my perspective here, Doug.
Too much is at stake. I have to be able to evaluate you
as you are, not as I want you to be." Her tone of voice
begged him to let her do the right thing, even as her
eyes expressed her regret.

"And afterward?"

Her gaze flew to his. "Afterward, we go back to the
real world, to our own lives."

His eyes narrowed. "You're saying we don't see
each other again?"

"We've never run into each other before."

"Oh, but that's going to change. You can count on
it," he said.

Before she had a chance to reply, he rose from the
Jacuzzi, leapt the couple of steps to the pool and dove
in cleanly, with barely a splash. He would give her the

rest of the two weeks, but he wasn't done with her yet, not by a long shot.

DOUG ENTERED the auditorium-cum-lecture room with tight lips the next morning. He wasn't looking forward to the hour or so ahead—he already knew everything they were going to tell him, probably better than they did. But the session was mandatory.

He looked for Andrea as soon as he entered the room. She was looking for him, too. He knew it as soon as her eyes met his. He also knew, no matter what she said, that they weren't finished with each other yet. She had to know it, too. She was too smart a lady to ignore the obvious.

Andrea pulled her gaze from Doug's as soon as she took her place at the head of the room. She told herself she hadn't been looking for him specifically, but she knew she was lying. She had been looking. And she'd been pleased with what she'd seen. He was wearing the inevitable tight jeans and a T-shirt that molded his muscular upper body to perfection. His features still showed years of rough living, but Andrea was used to them by now. Too used to them, she thought wryly, as her nipples tightened in response to his laconic grin.

She'd spent the better part of the night telling herself that she was going to give her all to teach Doug to care—but not for her. And she wasn't going to care for him, either—not in a personal way. She was just doing her job.

She stepped up to the microphone, forcing her mind away from Doug and the minutes she'd spent with him in the Jacuzzi the night before. She had a job to do, a lesson to teach, the most crucial and personally painful lesson of all. She knew every fact like she knew her own name—but she hadn't once, and she was going to spend the rest of her life atoning for it. She would teach people to see the signs, so that maybe the next time a child would have a chance before the damage was done. She *wasn't* going to be sidetracked by an inappropriate attraction to a James Dean look-alike.

"Pot smoking, glue sniffing, beer snitched from someone's refrigerator—these are all factors in the early stages of chemical dependency. Children do not start out as druggies. They start out just wanting to experiment, to feel grown-up, to fill empty weekend hours or long summer days...."

Andrea spoke to the room at large, but she was talking to Doug. She covered the four stages drug users usually pass through on the road to hell, sparing the people in front of her nothing. It was ugly, it was frightening and it was fact. She wanted Doug to be shocked enough to care.

"The books will all tell you to start watching for these signs in late-elementary-aged children, or early junior high. They're wrong. Can I have the lights off, please?"

Doug's mind wandered as he listened to Andrea. She didn't know the half of it. But she didn't need to, he supposed. She was giving them enough to get the job done.

He glanced up when the auditorium was plunged into darkness and felt cold all over as the first slide flashed up onto the screen behind Andrea. One after another came pictures of kids—clean-cut, innocent-looking kids in different stages of drug abuse. There were guilty faces, deals being made, furtive glances, vacant looks, belligerence and gross contortions on faces that should have been naive and sweet. All the slides were of children less than nine years old.

Doug watched as long as he could without feeling anything, and when his gut was as hard as a rock, he slumped down further in his seat, rested his chin on his chest and waited for the session to end.

"Lying, self-hatred, a different set of friends, dropped activities, especially sports, lower grades, asking for money—all of these are visible signs that a youngster may be on his way to chemical dependency. Please watch closely for them. They more than a knowledge of the four stages of chemical dependency could be the tools that save a child's life. . . ."

Andrea finished her slide presentation, feeling relieved, as she always did, that it was over, that she'd made it through again, that there would now be almost two hundred more people in the world looking out for the children who might be led astray.

She called for the lights to be turned back on, her eyes immediately seeking Doug's. Had he joined her campaign? Did he understand? Was he ready to fight for the lives of Columbus's children?

She glanced his way and almost buckled, bracing herself against the podium in front of her. She should have known. She damn well should have known. She'd started to feel again. Last night, down by the pool, she'd actually considered making love with Doug

Avery. And where she cared, she lost perspective. She *knew* that.

She took one last look at Doug, forcing herself to face the facts as they were, not as she wanted them to be. Doug's chin was resting on his chest—just as it had during her opening session. The bastard was asleep.

DOUG WAS JUST getting out of the shower when he heard the pounding on the door of his hotel room. Thinking it must be Steve coming to harass him into taking another trip to Harry's Tavern, he wrapped a towel loosely around his waist and went to open the door.

He didn't know who was more shocked, he or Andrea, as he stood there dripping wet. His first thought—that she'd come around even sooner than he'd expected—was squelched after one look at her face. Even the short, spiky edges of her hair looked angry. What in hell was he supposed to have done now?

"Uh, come in," he said. She was still wearing the uniform she'd had on for her lecture that afternoon.

"Put some clothes on first."

Doug shrugged, left the door ajar and went back into the bathroom to pull on the briefs and jeans he'd carried in there when he'd gone to take his shower. He flicked a brush through his hair and went out to face the music, whatever it might be.

Andrea stood in the doorway, counting to a hundred while she waited for him. Her attempt to calm herself failed miserably as he came from the bathroom looking exactly like a man prepared for love. He was lazy masculinity and the promise of strength all rolled into one. Andrea felt her pulse pounding, her limbs weakening. And then she remembered why she was there. She thought of Scotty.

Doug Avery was like poison spreading through her veins, robbing her of her competence. She wasn't going to allow it to happen again.

She stepped just far enough into the room to block his way. "I want you out," she said, her voice soft but laced with steel. "Now."

Doug pushed past her, his naked chest scorching her arm as he headed toward the pair of chairs on the other side of the room. He dropped down into one.

"You came to my room, lady. If someone has to leave, it should be you."

Andrea kept her eyes away from the dark hair spreading over his solid pectorals. It was just a chest. Men had them. She shut the door and followed him over to the chairs.

"Don't get smart with me, Avery. I'm in charge here and you're out."

He smiled, but the expression didn't reach his eyes. They were narrowed, and piercing her with something she didn't understand.

"Are you?" He dared to challenge her authority even now.

She couldn't believe she was attracted to such an insolent boor. She gritted her teeth to keep from yelling at him.

"That's your whole problem, you know that? You're so busy being Mr. Tough Guy that you can't do things any way but your own. Well, I'm here to tell you once and for all that your ways don't work here, Avery." She couldn't believe any officer worth his salt could sleep through two sessions of a critical training exercise and not even feel remorse.

"Is that why you're here?"

His smile was still lazy, still more of a challenge than an expression of humor, but there was something else there, too. He was teasing her. *Damn him.*

"Why else would I be here?"

His gaze ran lazily up and down her body, and then moved to the king-size bed beside her. He shrugged his scarred naked shoulders. "Oh, I don't know. Maybe you've decided not to wait for the session to be over. Maybe you're as impatient as I am to explore the possibilities."

Andrea was still reeling from the shock of seeing that scar. It looked like his left shoulder had been sliced with a big knife. After her fatal glance at his crotch in the Jacuzzi the other night, she'd kept her eyes trained on his face. She hadn't noticed the scar. But she couldn't look away from it now.

The man was cocky, he was insolent and crude, he was far too sure of himself. But he risked his life on a daily basis for people he didn't even know, people he had sworn to protect. And the scar was proof of the fact that he didn't always win.

"P-possibilities?" she heard herself ask, suddenly more scared than angry. She was losing her perspective. Doug Avery was an honored police officer. He wasn't the scum of the earth. Why couldn't she get a hold on him, on this job? Why did this one man matter so much?

"Come on, Andi. Why does the fact that we're attracted to each other upset you so much?" His voice was warmer than she'd ever heard it before. Suddenly she wanted him to hold her, to make all the confusion go away.

She had to get a grip. "It doesn't upset me, because it doesn't matter. It's a non-issue and I don't want to talk about it again. What's important here are the children whose lives are depending on the success of this program."

His chin jutted out, his lips tightened into a thin line and then he nodded. "Okay, I can give you that, for now. But rest assured that when this training is over, you and I will talk again."

"You and I need to talk right now. It's been almost a week, Doug, and after today, I think it's more than obvious that you don't belong in the DARE program. I have to insist on your resignation."

The mask that slid down over his features was almost frightening. The scar on his temple stood out starkly. He was once again the cold, hard stranger she'd met five days before.

"You're overstepping your bounds, Officer. As I understand it, you don't have the authority to *insist* that I do anything. You are here to guide and to instruct, not to discipline. I suggest you keep that in mind."

Andrea studied her shoes, concentrating on the calming exercises she's learned at the academy. In through the nose, out through the mouth, each breath a conscious effort. If she didn't keep her control, she'd be lost.

She needed to sit down, but was afraid to show him any weakness.

"You're right, of course, and I'm sorry." She saw the surprise flicker across his features. "But, please, can't you see that you're not right for this particular assignment? It's nothing against you, as a man or as a police officer. There's no shame in the fact that not everyone is cut out to work with little kids."

He stood up from his chair, coming over to stand within inches of her. Andrea could smell the hotel soap he'd used, the shampoo scent in his hair. His heat was burning her up.

He wrapped his hand around her neck, forcing her to look up at him. His touch was insistent without causing her any real pain. "Let's get one thing straight right now. I am *not* leaving DARE. I will graduate next week, and by fall I will be working in the classroom."

Andrea knocked his hand away. She'd never come up against such stubbornness in her life.

"Why?" she asked, looking up at him as if she could somehow read in his eyes what his mouth wouldn't tell her. What was it that was driving him, that was making him so insistent on remaining in a program where he clearly didn't belong? Did he have a reason, or was he just playing the macho hero, unable to admit that there was something he couldn't do?

His eyelids lowered, shuttering himself off even more from her probing gaze. "Why not?"

"Because you seem to think that class time is bedtime. And I somehow don't think that you use bedtime to study."

"You're still harping on that? So I made a mistake. Are you so all-fired perfect?"

"A mistake? How many times can you repeat the same mistake and still have it be just one?"

Doug turned away from her, shoving his hands into the back pockets of his jeans as he walked toward the window. His wristband strained against his arm.

Andrea's glance rested on the taut flesh his fingers outlined, and then on the implacable back above it, as she waited for an answer. She wasn't going to let him walk away from this.

Doug turned back to her, his expression laced with disappointment. "I figured you were better than this, Andrea. I figured you were above the usual games, the dishonesties, the making of things what they aren't. Obviously, you're so against an attraction between us that you've resorted to making mountains out of molehills. I fell asleep on Monday, and it was wrong. But I will not leave the DARE program because of that. Nor will I be continuously persecuted because of it. Now, if that's all you wanted, please leave."

"What about today?" Andrea shot back, doing her best to ignore his tone. "Was falling asleep today just a continuation of the same mistake? Or wasn't it a mistake at all?"

"Today?"

"Yes, today. I looked over as I finished my lecture. You were sleeping."

"I was." It was more a statement than a question.

"I saw you, Doug. When the lights came on after the slide presentation, you were sleeping."

Doug studied her face for several seconds, his expression serious but otherwise unreadable. She didn't know what he was looking for. But she had a feeling that something was happening, something over which she had little control, something that was going to matter.

He nodded once and then walked to the door, opening it for her. "I can assure you that it won't happen again, Officer. Now if you'll please be so kind as to give me my room back, I'd like to finish dressing for dinner."

Andrea watched him for another second and then left, careful not to touch him as she walked past. She knew she'd just failed. She just wasn't sure at what.

CHAPTER SIX

DOUG DIDN'T MAKE DINNER, after all. He'd meant to go down, to meet Steve and a couple of the other guys. He'd been on his way to the dining room, but his feet had carried him past the turnoff to the hotel's restaurant and right on out into the night.

And once he was out there, he'd kept walking. He hadn't had to go far—just two miles. Two miles from downtown Columbus and the elite Hetherington Hotel, filth and squalor were the mainstays, hungry children and homeless people were everywhere and hopelessness was a way of life. It was the birthplace of "each man for himself." It was the neighborhood in which he'd grown up.

A couple of muscular teenagers watched him as he approached a crumbling street corner. They wore black leather jackets, even on this hot August night. Their heads were shaved, except for the ponytails that hung down their backs. They were leaning against a streetlight that hadn't lit up the night since before Doug had been born. Their waistbands bulged. Doug knew they were concealing weapons. They watched him approach, checking him over for a possible take.

He reached down, as casually as he could, and removed his wristband. He approached the corner just as casually, his spine straight, his body ready for action, his heart frozen. He wasn't afraid. He'd survived the first twenty years of his life here. He knew how.

Doug raised his hand to flick his hair back out of his eyes as he walked past the punks. He saw them straighten, ready to saunter over, to follow him, to intimidate him before they made their move. Their eyes flashed to the wrist he'd raised as he slid his fingers through his hair, and suddenly Doug was walking past them—alone. The guys were once again leaning against the light post, looking for action someplace else.

Doug passed an old man humped over on a broken stoop, probably drunk, possibly dead. He walked on. A couple of kids were rooting through a dumpster in the alley behind D'Ambros's. Doug watched them for a minute, then started walking again.

He'd come here for a reason. He'd come here to remember not to care. Andrea Parker had disappointed him. A man didn't get disappointed unless he allowed himself to care. That was another lesson he'd learned long ago—right about the time his mother had left him alone with his old man.

Doug wanted to make love with Andrea. He wanted her to want it, too. But he didn't want to care for her, or to want her care. He didn't want her opinion to matter to him. It couldn't. He couldn't get soft. His whole life would be in vain if he got soft. He'd be right back where he'd been twenty-five years before.

He reached an old brick building with graffiti spray painted all over it. The steps leading up to the building were cracked and broken. An iron post was the only remains of the railing that used to run along them. He stopped and stared, seeing the dim light filtering through cracked windows, and knew that it was not from lamps, but from naked bulbs hanging from ceiling sockets. Nobody here owned lamps. If they had, they'd long since sold them to a second-hand furniture store, or had stolen them so someone else could.

He heard a baby wail, a young child laugh and a woman yell.

He sat down on the sidewalk, leaning back against the old building, and let the memories wash over him. A teenage girl left the building, dressed in skintight clothes, walking on impossibly high heels and made up like a clown. Doug watched her saunter past without even noticing him. She had a destination. Doug didn't want to think about where it was. He knew he could stop her—this time. But he knew that she'd be back out again tomorrow night, or the night after that.

He felt a pang of regret, and then a sharper one—anger, maybe. And then he shook himself. This was life. He knew it better than most. It had quit bothering him long before he'd even known for sure where girls like that were headed. He didn't want it to bother him now.

He forced his eyes away from the girl's swaying back and saw the hole broken into the side of the steps leading up to the building. His stomach lurched as his eyes assessed the size of the hole—the smallness of it. He'd remembered it as being much larger. That was his hole. The one he'd found. It had been his refuge, his hiding place, his only security in a childhood from hell.

Doug remembered crawling into that hole and hiding beneath those steps the day his mother had left for good. He'd heard her say she wished she knew where Dougie was so she could tell him goodbye. He'd watched her get into that beat-up station wagon and drive away anyway.

The hole had seemed huge then. He'd never had any trouble scrambling into it. But now the sight of it made him sick to his stomach. It was so small. Christ, he couldn't have been much more than a baby to have fit in the damn thing.

Doug swallowed, and then swallowed again. But he couldn't seem to choke back the feeling that was shooting up from someplace inside of him. He couldn't care. He couldn't allow himself to care. He'd have been dead long ago if he'd allowed himself to care.

He turned his head away and his gaze fell on the girl who'd walked by him earlier. She was standing a couple of blocks down, leaning against a bus-stop sign. He stood up and headed toward her.

She watched him approach with a welcoming smile pasted on her painted lips and a weary, hesitant look in her eyes. She didn't back away when he stopped right beside her. She didn't flinch when he pulled his hand from his pocket and held it out to her.

"Take it." He couldn't keep the anger from his voice. It was the only way he could speak at all.

The girl looked down, saw the size of the bill he was

handing her and snatched it from him as if she was afraid he would take back his offer.

"Where you wanna go?" she asked, cracking the wad of gum she was chewing.

Doug shrugged one shoulder and tipped his head. "Back there."

She pushed away from the sign and headed in the direction he'd indicated, not checking to see if he was following her. "You gotta place here?" she asked as she climbed the broken-down steps.

"No."

She stopped halfway up the stairs. "Then why're we here?" Her eyes narrowed. "You ain't a cop or somethin', are ya?"

"I know where to find one. Now get in there, take that crap off your face and lock your door," he said harshly.

She stared at him for a moment as if he'd sprouted an extra head or two, looked down at the amount of money in her skinny fingers and then bolted into the building.

Doug listened as the door slammed behind her, and listened some more until he heard the second door—the one that meant she'd entered her apartment—slam, too.

And then he turned back toward the Hetherington Hotel, more frightened than he'd ever been in his life. How was he going to live with himself if he was getting soft?

"Hi, Ma. How was your weekend?"

"Your pop and I went to Barbie Leone's wedding.

You should have seen the flowers, Andrea—they were glorious. And the food! Sarah Leone outdid herself this time. She colored the pasta to match the bridesmaids' dresses!''

Andrea lay back on her bed, the phone at her ear, picturing the scene as her mother described it. She tried not to remember when Barbie Leone was born, that she'd baby-sat for Barbie for years, that she'd once thought Barbie would one day be baby-sitting for her.

"And did I tell you Scotty has a new girlfriend? He and Lizzie—that's her name—they danced all night. Everybody was talking about what a cute couple they made."

"Did anybody say anything?" Andrea asked, tense as always when she heard about Scotty.

Gloria paused, and Andrea heard what she didn't want to know from her mother's silence.

"It wasn't much, Andrea, I swear. Just about everyone was positive. They can't help but see that he's grown into such a nice boy."

Andrea knew better. She knew that people saw what they wanted to see, and that everybody loved a scandal. But she wasn't going to tell her mother that. Gloria had suffered enough. She deserved her illusions.

"So, was Barbie beautiful?" Andrea asked, trying for a lighthearted tone.

"Oh, sure, she looked nice, but not nearly as beautiful as you'll be when your time comes. She's just a kid, you know. She hasn't got real beauty yet."

Andrea smiled. "Yeah, Ma. I'll be a ravishing eighty-year-old bride, huh?"

"Now don't get me started, Andrea Lee. I promised your father I'd just call to see how you're doing, that's all."

"The training sessions are going fine. We're right on schedule. The guys are working hard and the hotel's been very accommodating. So, if that's all, I guess I'll talk to you later, huh?"

Andrea pulled the phone away from her ear and waited. She might not be up for one of the all-out battles she'd waged with her mother over the years, but she could still get a good rise out of her now and then.

"Andrea!" The disgruntled tones reached her ear even at arm's length.

"Yeah, Ma?"

"Don't you dare hang up on me without telling me how you're making out with your team."

Is there any hope for you with any of the three bachelors yet? Andrea translated silently.

"They seem to be soaking it all up," she said of her first five trainees. She wasn't even going to *think* about the sixth while she was talking to her mother. Andrea sometimes suspected that Gloria Parker had some kind of secret telepathy that gave her access to her daughter's thoughts.

"Does any one of them stand out from the rest?"

No. Andrea refused to grant him entrance. But could her mother read her subconscious, too?

"Uh, yeah, one does," she heard herself saying. "His name is Sven. Sven Johnson. He's a big blond

Swede and just about the nicest guy you'd ever want
to meet. As a matter of fact, there's probably not another man alive that a girl would be as happy to take
home to meet her mother."

What was she doing? She barely knew Sven.

"How does he feel about babies?" Gloria asked.

Andrea remembered the program Sven had set up
for latchkey kids in Cleveland. "He loves them."

She didn't hear her mother's satisfied sigh, but she
supposed Gloria must have released one.

"And you—how does he feel about you?"

Andrea knew she was getting in too deep. But she
also knew that she had to keep her mother from finding out about Doug. Yet when it came right down to
it, she couldn't allow herself to build up her mother's
hopes. Not when Gloria's hopes were just for Andrea's happiness.

"It's only been a week, Ma. Besides, he just broke
up with a girl in Cleveland, and I don't think he's over
her yet. As a matter of fact, they might just get back
together, so don't get your hopes up."

"Yeah, well, just don't you close your eyes to possibilities, Andrea Lee. My back's been hurting me all
week, you know."

*Yeah, I know, and pretty soon you won't be able to
crawl around on the floor....* "Have Pop rub it for
you."

ANDREA ADMIRED Sven Johnson. She listened as he
gave his public speech Monday afternoon, and felt an
all-over glow as the man pontificated on everything
that DARE stood for. Here was a man who would save

the children. Boys and girls would not be led astray with Sven Johnson around. And Andrea wouldn't be led astray, either. Her nerves weren't tingling a bit.

She sat in her seat at the back of the auditorium and let the feelings of peace and goodwill settle upon her. She'd done her job well. Her trainees were getting the message. She was proud of that.

"That's all but one of your trainees, isn't it?" whispered the man to her left. Dave O'Dell was a training officer, too. Andrea had worked with him several times and found him to be a superb DARE officer. She'd heard that his wife was with the DEA.

"Yeah. They're a great bunch of guys," she said.

"What about Avery? I've heard he's a tough nut to crack."

Andrea shrugged. She could tell Dave that she didn't expect Doug to graduate, that Doug was not just tough but impossible to crack. She could tell him about the ledger that she was rapidly filling up, about her fears for the children if Doug were ever set loose in a classroom. Dave would understand. He'd probably even help her with a report of his own if she asked him to.

"It's not over yet." She heard her words even before she was aware of having thought them.

"He's a great police officer. I heard he was the undercover that exposed Stan Ingersoll's bad apple last week."

Andrea's heart started thumping. "Undercover?" Doug had been working on a series of car thefts from local dealerships. She'd read his reports on it. They were in his file.

"Yeah. Ingersoll had some guy pimping, and apparently the guy started to like the business a little too much. He started running things for real. Word is that Avery worked his own day shift, and then was up nights running a scam on the guy. Avery brought him in last Monday, just before showing up here."

Andrea swallowed the lump in her throat. *He'd been sleeping because he'd been working doubles to save his sergeant's butt.* Why hadn't he said anything?

Why hadn't she asked? Why hadn't she at *least* asked?

But what about Saturday? What about sleeping through that session? Even Doug Avery couldn't be working undercover during DARE training.

Dave nudged her arm with his elbow. "There he is."

Andrea glanced back up to see a man standing in full dress uniform in the middle of the stage. She was ready to tell Dave he was mistaken, that Doug wasn't scheduled until the following morning, but then she saw the man on stage reach up to adjust the microphone. And she caught a glimpse of silver-studded black leather on his wrist.

Her breath caught as he stepped forward to introduce himself. He looked dependable in his navy blues. More than that, he looked impressive. The uniform she'd always thought rather plain bore no resemblance to its usual self with Doug's body inside of it.

Andrea squirmed in her seat, pulling the sweaty material of her own set of blues away from her thighs. She ran her fingers through her hair, thankful that she could hardly do damage to its short, sassy style, and hoped that Dave had no idea that she was suddenly feeling like she was sitting on hot bricks.

Her butterflies were back full force, and Doug's ten-minute speech loomed before her like a week-long specter.

"Kids do drugs. Good kids do drugs. Honest, moral, sensitive kids do drugs." Doug's words filled Andrea's mind as his voice boomed out across the auditorium.

And suddenly she was listening to the man, not re-acting to his body. For the first time she was hearing from the man inside of Doug, the one she'd sensed was there, the one she'd despaired of ever finding. She'd feared him dead.

"It's not the drugs that do the damage, ladies and gentlemen, it's the adults that make babies and then refuse to be parents. Children are innocent. They have no weapons to fight the cruelty in this country. But thousands of them are sent out into it anyway, with-out a clue how to cope. They aren't mature enough to think clearly, they haven't yet developed the ability to separate their thoughts from their emotions, or even to control their emotions. All they know is that they feel. They *feel*. And if they receive nothing but crap from the bodies that gave them existence, if taking chemical substances is the only way to make them-selves feel good, my money's on the substance every time...."

Doug's speech absorbed Andrea. She listened to it for a full five minutes before she even remembered she was supposed to be evaluating it. He *knew*. He knew what they were trying to do here. He knew about the stages of chemical dependence; he knew how drug abuse started, how it got worse; he knew how pushers were born. And she knew he couldn't possibly have been sleeping during her lecture that weekend.

He told a couple of stories about kids he'd known. They were tragic stories, with tragic endings, but the most tragic part of all was the fact that with a little outside guidance, with a caring hand, they might never have happened at all.

Doug's voice drifted off, leaving the auditorium silent, but teeming with an almost palpable sense of responsibility. Andrea reached up to her cheek and was startled to find tears there, streaming slowly down her face.

DARE needed this man. It needed his intensity, his strength, his never-give-in attitude. She couldn't let him fail now. She was going to have to find a way to teach him how to soften up, to make himself accessible to the tender affections of the children who needed him, without giving up who and what he was. And she was going to start with the apology she owed him....

"God, he's good!" Dave's whispered words followed Andrea as she headed to the front of the auditorium.

Doug saw her coming. And she was the last person he wanted to see. He'd just spilled half his guts out on the stage and was still trying to figure out how to clean up the mess he'd made of things. He'd practiced his public address half the night, and it had been good. But it hadn't been the speech he'd just given.

He wasn't sure what was happening to him, but he knew two things: he didn't like it, whatever it was; and it had something to do with Andrea Parker.

He fell in with several other trainees who were heading toward the door of the auditorium. Safety in numbers. The old adage came back to him, guiding his choices as did all of the other hard-learned lessons from his past. They'd been keeping him alive for thirty years.

"Doug!"

He heard her, but chose not to stop. The talk droned around him. And then a light, feminine hand settled on his forearm.

"Doug," Andrea said breathlessly.

He slowed down, falling away from the crowd. If she was going to be that determined, he might as well get it over with. "Yeah?"

"It's time for another one-on-one. I'd like you to meet me in the executive suite after dinner, if you don't already have other plans."

He thought about having other plans. He considered another trek downtown. But a vision of the girl he'd sent home the other night flashed before his eyes, and he knew he'd rather risk a meeting with Andrea than go back down there.

"What time?"

"Is seven o'clock okay?"

"Fine." Doug turned and walked away, deciding he'd rather order room service than face the congeniality of his colleagues in the dining room.

CHAPTER SEVEN

"I'M SORRY."

Andrea stopped Doug with the words as soon as he entered the executive suite two hours later.

"For what?" He sounded defensive.

She stood up from the corner of the couch where she'd been curled up for the past half hour. Her regulation shorts and DARE T-shirt were slightly wrinkled, but otherwise she knew she was as well groomed as she'd been when she'd inspected herself for a final time before coming to this meeting. It was wrong, but she'd wanted to look good for Doug Avery. She'd wanted to look like a woman.

"For misjudging you the other day. I don't know what you were doing when you appeared to be sleeping, but it's obvious you didn't miss a word of that lecture."

He nodded his head in acknowledgment of her apology and then proceeded to the other end of the couch, slouching down in the corner, his jeans stretching taut against his hips. He fiddled with his wristband for a moment, and then let his arm drop to the couch.

"So what's this all about?" he asked, gesturing between the two of them.

Andrea tried not to notice the biceps bulging from the sleeves of the black cotton T-shirt he wore. They were not the issue here. Somehow she was going to have to convince herself of that fact.

"I just thought it was time we talked again. I've had sessions with the rest of your teammates. It's your turn."

He shrugged, folding his arms across his chest. Andrea's stomach sank. She'd been hoping to open him up, not close him off.

"Your speech today was pretty intense."

The cold mask she'd come to know settled across his features. The jagged scar at his temple stood out as he clenched his jaw. Again he acknowledged her words with a single incline of his head.

Andrea was waiting for some sexual innuendo, some little zinger designed to throw her off. So far, he'd come up with them every time she got too close. She hoped she was prepared not to let it succeed this time.

"I was wondering where you did your research— besides Saturday's lecture, I mean. Some of the stories you told had to be true."

"Maybe."

"So, where did you meet those people?"

"Around."

"Do you still know them?"

"Nope."

He wasn't giving an inch, but he wasn't evading her question, either. Andrea grasped onto that fact with everything she had inside of her.

"So do you think there's hope for any of them?"

"The kids, you mean?"

"Yeah."

"Before or after?"

"I think we both know there's hope before they get hooked or we wouldn't be here. What about afterward?"

Again he shrugged, and slipped further down into the couch, stretching his long legs out in front of him. Andrea was beginning to suspect that sometimes Doug's lazy posture was just a cover for his sharp mind.

"Yeah, there's hope. Not much. But there's hope."

That was more of an admission than Andrea had ever dared expect.

"Have you ever seen anyone make it?"

"You mean after they're hooked?"

Andrea nodded. She was afraid to say too much in case she shut him down.

"Yeah, I've seen one or two. 'Course, I've seen hundreds who didn't."

She had, too. Which is why it took a special person to notice the one or two that did make it back after an addiction to drugs.

"What would you do if you ever came across a kid personally who had a habit?" Andrea asked, holding her breath. This was what it all really boiled down to. Was it really each man for himself, or would Doug stick his neck out to help someone else?

"Kick the stuffing out of him."

Andrea released her breath and smiled. Doug cared. Whether he knew it or not, he cared. He wouldn't just walk away.

He was watching her through narrowed eyelids, but even so, Andrea noticed the instant his mask slipped. She saw the warmth seep into his eyes as the muscles around his jaw unclenched.

"What are you smiling at?" he asked.

"I think that beneath all of your gruffness you're a good man, Officer Avery."

He looked startled and somewhat skeptical as his dark brown eyes met her open stare. Andrea felt herself being swallowed up by the depth of his gaze, by the potential in him that she was only now beginning to discover.

"And I had you figured for a smart lady," he retorted, but the edges of his lips twitched with just a hint of a grin.

"Why don't you do that more?"

"What?"

"Smile."

"Is that what I'm doing?"

"Looks that way to me."

"Then maybe you need to have your eyes examined. And have your IQ looked at while you're at it."

He sounded like he was trying to be sarcastic, but he looked too pleased. Andrea shared a grin with him for a few dangerous seconds, and then sobered.

"Why are you so afraid of talking to me?"

She asked the question boldly, expecting a sexual comeback.

He crossed his ankles. "Who says I'm afraid?"

"Aren't you?"

"No."

"Then why do you run every time the conversation gets a little thick?"

"I'm not going anywhere."

Andrea digested that in silence. He was right. He was still hanging around. She wondered why.

"So why won't you tell me about your research for your speech?"

He lifted a hand to his hair, running his fingers through the lush brown strands. "It's not important."

"How do I know that if you won't tell me? Are you doing some kind of work with troubled kids that you don't want me to know about?"

The possibility had just hit her, but she didn't think it was nearly as farfetched as it sounded.

"Nice try, but nope."

"So that story you told about the kid escaping a chemically imbalanced mother—you just made it up?"

"No. It happened."

"And the other, the one about the sexually abusive brother—was that real, too?"

"Even I couldn't make up something like that."

"And you just met these people through your work on the streets?"

"Don't we all?"

Andrea supposed that at one point or another all cops came across stories as tragic as the ones Doug had told. But his stories hadn't been told by an impartial bystander. They'd come from the heart. That's why they'd been so painfully real, so able to move everyone who listened to them.

She was beginning to wonder if maybe those kids he'd talked about had been people he'd known. Maybe he'd gone to school with them. Maybe they'd even been his friends. How else could he have known the details he'd given that afternoon? Some of that stuff never made it into police reports.

It suddenly dawned on her that if Doug had a first-hand knowledge of the pressures these kids faced every day, he was probably more qualified to be a DARE officer than any of the other two hundred trainees in the hotel.

"I'm glad we had this talk," she said. She'd pushed him far enough for the time being. She'd lose him forever if she tried for too much too soon. Men like Doug Avery just didn't crumble.

"Then I'm glad, too," he said softly, reaching across the couch to brush his fingers against her cheek.

Andrea knew that he'd just crossed the imaginary boundary she'd erected between what she could and could not allow. She could tell by the watchful yet hungry look in his eyes that he knew it, too.

But his gaze was so full, so tempting, that she was mesmerized. Doug was the most intense individual she'd ever met, and she was responding to him in a way she couldn't seem to control. There were no half measures here, no cute little comments to defuse the moment. There was nothing a giggle would do except come out on a sigh of longing.

Her gaze was locked with his and she leaned into his simple caress as naturally as if she'd willed the action herself. He cupped his hand around her neck and pulled, guiding her across the couch until her lips touched his.

His very first kiss was hot and strong and full. Everything she'd come to expect from Doug was in that kiss, and the minute Andrea felt his mouth upon hers, her memories of the past, her concerns for the future seemed to disappear. He took and he gave with the same intensity with which he guarded his heart. He hinted at secrets, at mysteries yet to unfold. He made her hungry for more . . . and more. . . .

Kissing Andrea was like nothing Doug had ever experienced before. She was so fresh, so brimming with passion, yet so innocent all at the same time. And, God, was she generous. She opened to him, allowing him anything he asked for, giving more than he demanded.

She allowed his tongue to explore the velvety sweetness of her mouth, but she teased it with her own, promising him a coupling that would be heaven for both of them. She didn't wait for him to give her pleasure; she took it.

With a groan he barely recognized as his own he pulled her across his lap, settling her bottom firmly against his tense zipper. He slid his hand beneath her T-shirt, and almost laughed with sheer male approval when he discovered that she wasn't wearing a bra. He boldly took possession of her naked flesh, claiming his right to do so.

She pulled her mouth away from his lips, burying her face in his neck, but instead of stopping things, instead of stopping him, she nibbled at the juncture between his neck and shoulder.

"You're so hot," he said into her hair, his voice low and husky with passion. His fingers held her breast while he ran his thumb back and forth across her thickened nipple.

She moaned something unintelligible and brought her mouth back to his, rotating her hips against his crotch, nearly sending him over the edge before he'd even begun his ascent.

His hand moved to her other breast, delighting in its mysteries, its heaviness, the miraculous contrast between its outer softness and its tight, hard center.

It occurred to him that he'd left his wallet—and his protection—in his room. He wondered if she was on the pill, and why he was reluctant to ask. He thought about shooting his seed inside of her, of having it embedded within her, taking root, becoming life.

He rolled her over more roughly than he meant to, settling her on her back on the couch. His desire became liquid fire as her legs dropped open for him, making a cradle for his body. Her hands slipped under his T-shirt, running through the hair on his chest, pulling softly, passing lightly across his nipples. And as he reared back, afraid she was going to drive him over the edge too soon, he spotted an abandoned DARE training agenda on the floor.

It must have fallen out of someone's notebook. Here. In this room. And suddenly Doug was disgusted with himself. Andrea was no animal, there for his rutting pleasure. She was everything good and pure and beautiful that embodied womanhood. And she deserved better than a quick lay on a couch in a community suite where any one of five other guys could walk in and catch her unaware.

And with that realization came another: he was having sex and he wanted more than a climax. He was thinking beyond the moment; he was more concerned about the woman he was lying on than about the body beneath him. Something was happening inside of him that had never happened before.

It scared the hell out of him.

But when he gazed down at Andrea's passion-glazed eyes, when he saw the utter abandonment on her features, he couldn't just stop what he'd started. He couldn't leave her frustrated, dissatisfied. He sat up again, pulling her up into the corner of the couch, and slid his fingers inside the elastic waistband of her shorts.

With a few quick motions, he had her writhing beside him. He watched her climax. Her expression was one of wonder, and then peace, and Doug knew that if he died that night he'd have lived a complete life.

Her lovely blue eyes started to fill with consternation as they began to focus on him, as she realized what had happened. Doug leaned over to kiss her again. He didn't want to see any regret in her eyes. He didn't think he could bear it.

So with one last, long, sensual kiss, he stood up.

"Good night, sweet princess," he whispered against her closed eyelids, and left her, still fully dressed, on the couch.

"HEY, ANDI, you wanna have dinner tonight?"

Andrea turned around in the corridor outside the

Santa Maria meeting room to see Dave O'Dell striding toward her. His wasn't the voice she'd wanted to hear, which is precisely why she smiled warmly at her colleague.

"Sure, Dave. You offering to take me away from this place?"

"I figured we could both use a little R and R. How does Mexican sound?"

"Like I'm ready to go, anytime you are."

The food was wonderful, the atmosphere relaxing and the company quite pleasant, but still Andrea didn't enjoy herself. Dave was witty, a perfect gentleman and safely married—Andrea's ideal dinner companion—but she wanted more. Or more precisely, she wanted different.

"Three days to go before Sunday's ceremony. You think your guys are going to make it?" Dave asked over coffee.

"Every one of them," Andrea said without hesitation.

"Avery really seems to have come around, hasn't he?"

Andrea shrugged. "It took him awhile to loosen up, but I think he's going to make one hell of a DARE officer. We've been going over the seventeen-week curriculum they'll be taking into the classroom, and he's like a sponge soaking up water."

"Yeah, I noticed him reading over some stuff at dinner last night. And one of my guys was telling me about some ideas Avery had for building self-esteem in some of the more downtrodden kids. He had some pretty remarkable insights. I was impressed."

Andrea felt a thrill of victory as she listened to her colleague clarify what she was beginning to suspect herself. After much deliberating, she'd thrown away Doug's ledger the night before, and she was more than a little relieved to hear that her perception of the situation wasn't completely off. Doug was still a little too rough around the edges, but it looked like he was going to win his battle.

If only she could win hers as well. She'd told herself after the unfortunate incident the other night that she had to stay away from Doug Avery, that her interest must remain purely professional, that her lapse that night had been completely physical—a healthy adult woman's reaction to four years of sustenance.

She kept telling herself that the subtle changes in Doug meant nothing to her personally, but she wasn't sure she believed it. In the two days since their evening in the suite, she hadn't had a chance to put herself to the test. Doug was keeping his distance so successfully that she didn't have an opportunity to keep her own. And the more he avoided being alone with her, the harder it was for her to remember that she wanted him to.

Andrea was silent during the cab ride back to the hotel. Dave didn't seem to notice, as he spent the entire twenty minutes talking about how much he missed his wife. Andrea was happy for him, happy that he was one of the lucky ones to have found a mate for life. But she wasn't envious. Not at all. Mating for life wasn't for her. She wasn't going to care again. She'd

had her chance, she'd lost perspective and the two
people she'd loved most had suffered.

She was still reminding herself of that fact a few
minutes later, when she and Dave passed by the lounge
on their way to the elevator. She glanced in casually,
not expecting to see anything earth-shattering. And
the sight of Doug Avery bent over a woman, saying
something to her beneath the din of boisterous conversation and loud music, shouldn't have bothered her
a bit.

But it did.

DOUG HAD A CALL from Stan Ingersoll indecently
early on Thursday morning. His sergeant wanted to
meet him for breakfast.

At seven o'clock, Doug rode the elevator down to
the lobby, curious about Stan's visit. The older man
usually left him alone when he was on assignment. He
hoped Stan was not planning to try to talk him out of
the DARE program. His mind was made up on that
one.

"Hey, old man, you're looking as shiny as ever,"
Doug said, approaching from behind and swiping his
hand across the top of Stan's bald head.

Doug knew Stan hated it when he did that, but he
also knew he was the only person in the world who
could get away with teasing the sergeant. Which was
why he did it.

"And you're still just a smart-ass little punk, Avery," Stan said, his eyes brimming with fondness.

Stan was a big burly man, always dressed in starched
blues and always correct. He reminded Doug of a

marine sergeant. He was married to a meek little woman who brought out his protective instincts, but she'd never been able to give him the son he'd always wanted. And Doug had never really had a father. He figured the facts suited the two of them just fine.

"So what's up?" he asked, heading toward the coffee shop. Stan preferred to eat, not be waited on.

"I need your John Henry on the final report. It's going before the board today. They're anxious to take action and get this one wrapped up before the press has a field day."

The two men took seats at the breakfast counter. "Are they going to need me to testify?"

Stan dumped two packets of sugar into his coffee. "It doesn't look like it. Now that he's talking, they've got enough on him without you. But I told them where you are, just in case. They'll call if they need you."

Doug nodded, glad to see that Stan was looking a lot more relaxed than he had the last time he'd seen him. He'd like to have five minutes alone with the bastard who, for a few quick bucks, had almost ruined Stan's life.

"So how's it going?" Stan asked as soon as they'd placed their orders for bacon and eggs.

Doug slouched down, resting his forearms on the counter in front of him. "It's going."

"You gonna make it?"

"What do you think?"

"It doesn't matter what I think this time, buddy. This one's up to you."

Doug nodded and ran his finger along the edge of his coffee cup.

"You wanna know what I think?" He looked sideways at Stan, uncomfortable when he saw the other man's clear dark eyes gazing at him piercingly. "I think I'm going to make the best damn DARE officer this state's ever seen. That's what I think," Doug said. He hated the defensiveness he heard in his voice. But when he was with Stan, it was sometimes hard to think of himself as more than the loser he'd been when Stan had first found him. He could never quite get past the fact that the sergeant knew what he really was. Which was one reason why he swore to himself that no one else would ever know.

Stan sat silently sipping his coffee, waiting, Doug knew. That was Stan's way. He'd wait until Christmas if he had to, and eventually Doug would talk—he always had.

A middle-aged waitress brought their breakfasts, set a basket of jelly packets down between them and left. The two men ate in silence until both plates were clean, and didn't talk until they'd been cleared away.

"I think I'm pretty damn qualified to impart the importance of alternative choices," Doug finally said as Stan started on his second cup of coffee.

He nodded.

"I won't just be mimicking lessons I learned in a classroom. I can teach these kids about life. I can teach them the difference between my life and theirs."

Doug fiddled with his wristband, until he saw Stan glance at it, too. Stan knew what it covered. Doug picked up his coffee cup.

"You gonna tell 'em about it?" Stan asked casually.

"That won't be necessary," Doug said. His tone brooked no argument.

Stan didn't argue. But he didn't look completely satisfied, either.

"I think I might be able to save a life or two just the same," Doug said.

Stan reached across to squeeze his shoulder, the closest he'd ever come to showing Doug real affection.

"I think so too, son. I think so too."

CHAPTER EIGHT

ANDREA MANAGED TO AVOID Doug until Friday afternoon. She was scheduled to review his interpersonal communication skills before dinner. She'd been alternating between dreading and looking forward to the session all week. When she was dreading it, she knew she could handle it. It was when she found herself looking forward to it that she considered turning Doug over to one of the other mentors.

She was feeling somewhat in control when she slipped a note under Doug's door early Friday morning, asking him to meet her out in the atrium alongside the pool late that afternoon. She'd put Monday night's foolishness behind her. She wasn't going to dwell on her response to Doug's touch; she wasn't going to believe in the incredible passion she'd thought she felt in his arms. She'd just been geared up, and overtired.

And since he hadn't tried, even once, to seek her out all week, she could only assume that the episode had meant as little to him as it had to her.

She dressed for the meeting in denim shorts and a polo shirt, careful not to do more than freshen her light makeup and run a quick comb through her hair.

She wasn't going to go to any extra effort to look good for Doug.

She'd chosen the atrium on purpose. The tables in the glassed-in room were set far enough apart to afford privacy, yet the place was public enough that nothing as intimate as a caress could pass unnoticed by the other occupants. The topics she and Doug were to discuss had been predetermined by DARE procedure. She was in control.

Until Doug came striding through the atrium dressed in golf shorts and a sports shirt. His lean, muscled legs were covered with crisp dark hair, his chest was straining against the cotton of his shirt and he was smiling. The scar at his temple was barely visible.

His gaze met hers across the room and Andrea was flooded with an instant replay of the mind-numbing sensations she'd wallowed in four nights before. And if the look in his eyes was anything to go by, he was remembering, too. She felt the onslaught of a major panic attack.

Doug settled into the seat across from Andrea, glad to be with her again. He'd missed her.

"So where do we start?" he asked.

She looked up at him briefly, and then concentrated on the papers in front of her. Her features were stiff. Her hands were trembling. Doug wanted to reach across and hold them until they were steady. He wanted to slide his hand beneath her short, sassy hair and rub the tension from her neck. He wanted to tell her she had nothing to fear from him.

He knew then that he'd just wasted the better part of a week for nothing. The fact that Andrea made him feel like more of a man than any woman ever had before should be something to celebrate, not worry about.

"You're at the grocery store." Her voice broke into his thoughts. "The cashier gives you your change. You get out to your car and discover that she gave you a dollar too much. What do you do?"

Doug smiled, and settled down further in his seat. "How far am I parked from the door of the store?"

Andrea glanced up from her papers. "About half-way down the parking lot."

"Is it raining?"

She rolled her eyes at him. "No."

"Then I'd take it back."

She smiled. "What if it had been?"

"Raining, you mean?" He smiled back.

"Yeah."

"How hard?" He held her gaze with his. She didn't look away this time.

"Hard. Really hard."

Adrenalin started pumping through Doug's veins. "Is there lightning? Am I in danger of being struck?"

Andrea's gaze broke away from him. She looked out toward the swimming pool. "No."

"Then I'd have to say I'd still go back," he said. He watched her, waiting for her to meet his gaze again.

"What if I'd said yes?" The words were so soft Doug almost missed them.

"I'd have taken my chances."

She looked back at him then, and her eyes were filled with such conflict that Doug wanted to take her in his arms right then and there. He wanted to erase her doubts, to show her how good it could be between them.

"You'd have gone back anyway?"

"Yep."

She looked relieved, just briefly, but it was enough to convince Doug that they hadn't just been talking about the weather.

"If you had to choose between the good of one and the overall good of many, which would you choose?" She read the next question on her list, but she sounded more like a woman getting to know a man than a mentor training an officer. She leaned forward, as if his answer was important to her.

Doug had to remind himself that she'd run through this same exercise with every other man on his team.

"I suppose it would depend on how crucially the one was in need, how much harm would be done to the majority and how closely I was involved with either."

She pushed her papers aside and leaned on the table. "Let's say you're closely involved with the one. It's a friend of yours. And a lot of harm would come to the majority."

"Is it a matter of life and death for any of them?"

"No."

"Is the need of my friend legitimate?"

She considered his question carefully. "Yes."

"Would the majority be put in physical jeopardy?"

Again she thought about it. "No."

"Then I guess I'd have to do whatever I could to help the majority overcome the harm."

It took her a second, but then she smiled, wrapping him in invisible bands of warmth. "You'd help the one."

"Wouldn't you?"

She fiddled with the papers in front of her. "I'd like to think so."

A waitress came by and offered them drinks. Andrea ordered iced tea and Doug asked for a beer.

"How much weight do you put in material wealth?" she asked after their drinks had been delivered.

Doug shrugged. That was a tough one. He knew what answer she was looking for. He knew what the "right" answer had to be. But he didn't want to lie to her.

"A lot."

Her face fell. "You do?"

"You have to understand. I've lived without. Where I grew up things were worth only what you could get for them if you could find someone to buy them. I've seen what that does to people—being forced to sell off their only possessions for about a quarter of what they're worth. It dwindles them down to nothing. No goods, no home, no pride—nothing. People need money to make it in this world. I decided a long time ago I want to make it."

"At the cost of someone else?"

"What do you mean by that?"

"Would you step on a little guy just to get bigger?"

"I never said I need to be big, I only said I'm going to make it. I don't think it has to be a matter of one guy making it at the expense of another. It's all a matter of how much effort someone's willing to put forth, how hard someone tries. If a guy's not willing to take care of himself, if he wants to reap the bene- fits of others, if he wants something for nothing, that's when he might get stomped on." He looked at her in- tently before asking, "And how about you? Is physi- cal comfort important to you?"

She stirred some sugar into her tea. "Yeah. I guess it is. I'd hate to live without air-conditioning, central heating and groceries in the fridge. But I'd rather drive a Ford than a Jaguar."

"That's just 'cause you have the inside track on theft figures."

"Maybe. Or maybe it's that I know I'll never make enough money to afford the Jaguar, anyway."

Doug liked her answer. He liked her honesty.

"So what *is* important to you? What would you sweat over not having?" he asked.

Her forehead creased as she considered his ques- tion. "My family. They're important."

"More important than your job? Than DARE?" He didn't think so.

"Yes."

He felt his gut clench. He'd never really had a fam- ily. He'd never consciously wanted one before, either. Not until he heard Andrea declare her loyalty to hers. He wondered how different his life might have been if he'd had someone looking out for him that way, if he'd had someone to look out for.

"What about you? What's most important to you?" Her eyes were soft, her voice as gentle as always.

Doug wanted to tell her something that would keep that look in her eyes. He wanted to please her. He told her the truth.

"Being able to take care of myself."

Her eyes fell back to the papers in front of her.

A couple of officers walked through the atrium on their way to dinner. They waved, but didn't stop. Andrea continued with her questions.

"How old were you when you went on your first official date?"

"Define 'official.'"

"You ask her, you pay, she says thank-you at the end."

"She always says thank-you at the end."

"Answer the question, Doug," Andrea said, but she was blushing.

"Would you like to order something to eat? I'll buy."

"Answer the question, Doug," she said again, a playful warning in her voice.

"Answer mine first and then I'll tell you."

"Okay. Yeah, I'm hungry. Let's have something to eat. Now, how old were you when you went on your first date?"

"Do you think you'll thank me for buying you dinner?"

"Doug!"

"Do you?"

"Of course I'll thank you. My manners are exemplary. And you aren't going to sidetrack me from my question."

"I wouldn't dream of it. Thirty."

"Thirty what?" Her brow creased with confusion. It wasn't something Doug had seen very often. He kind of liked it.

"That's my answer—thirty."

"What kind of an answer is that? You're thirty now. Are you trying to tell me—" Her voice broke off as her eyes lit with comprehension. "Oh no. No way, buddy. You're not going to convince me that you've never been on a date before."

Doug took quite a bit of satisfaction from the fact that she wasn't denying that they were now on an official date. "I've certainly been places with women, I've even picked up a tab or two when it served my purposes, but by your definition, I've never been out on an *official* date. Until now, that is." He couldn't resist challenging her again, just for fun, just to see if she'd let his label stand.

"You never went to a prom? Or to a Christmas dance?"

"Nope, never did." *Yep, it stood.*

"Why not? You got something against dancing?"

It was more that the kind of girls Doug would have liked to have asked out wouldn't have been caught dead with him. But he wasn't going to think about any of that now. For the time being, life was looking pretty good.

"It's not my favorite thing to do. What about you? How old were you?"

Andrea grinned. "I was fifteen, I was a full six inches taller than he was and I had to call my dad to come get me."

"The guy get too fresh?"

Andrea smiled. "No. But he'd forgotten to tell me that he'd had his license suspended and that he'd borrowed the car he was driving from his brother-in-law. He'd also neglected to say that his brother-in-law hadn't given him permission to do the borrowing. Anyway, the brother-in-law reported the car stolen. We were picked up at Columbus's rendition of Inspiration Point. Pop had to come bail us out."

Doug grinned at the picture she painted. "You were out at Alum Creek."

Andrea's face filled with color. "Yep."

Doug was liking her more and more. "Bet you caught hell for that one."

"Ma yelled a lot. But I yelled back. I was, after all, an innocent bystander to the whole thing. It just took until three in the morning to convince my mother of that."

Doug wished he could have been a fly on the wall for that one. No matter how hard he tried, he just couldn't picture Andrea yelling at anyone—and half the night, no less.

They ordered dinner, manicotti with meat sauce, and when Doug charged the tab to his room, Andrea thanked him politely. She asked him to stay for coffee, telling him that she still had a few more things to go over.

"Do you believe in monogamy?"

Doug didn't even blink when he heard the question. But he would have bet his life that it wasn't written on that piece of paper in front of her.

"In this day and age I'd be a fool not to."

"So you only believe in it because of the health issue?"

His answer was important to her. Doug sensed it as surely as he knew he didn't want to live long enough to have her find out about who and what he'd been before he'd become a police officer.

"Not entirely. I was in my last relationship for several years. I was never unfaithful to her because I chose not to be."

He hadn't chosen Celia all that often either, these past months, but Andrea didn't need to know that. He'd never thought much about being faithful to one woman before. It had never seemed to matter. But he'd bet his life that if he ever got into Andrea's bed, he wouldn't leave it for another woman's.

"Y-you were married?"

"No."

"You lived with her then?"

"No."

"Oh." She wouldn't meet his eyes.

He didn't like her hiding from him again, especially after they'd just come so far. He reached across to still her fingers as they flipped the edges of her papers.

"Andrea." He waited for her to look across at him. "We had an understanding that was mutually satisfying. It's been over for a long time."

Andrea nodded, swallowing at the same time. Doug was beginning to realize that the lady had a few barriers of her own that needed to be broken down, and he figured he might just be the man to do it. She wanted him. He was sure about that much. The rest could wait.

He'd learned how to be patient a long time ago.

"HI, POP. It's Andrea. How ya doing?"

Andrea stood beside her nightstand, twirling the phone cord around her fingers.

"Andi! You okay, hon?" Her father sounded worried.

"Yeah, I'm okay. I'm fine. I just haven't talked to you in a few days."

Andrea knew the call was out of character. But sometimes a woman just had to call home for no apparent reason.

"Well, you know I always like to talk to my only daughter. Seems like I don't get much chance when your mother's around. She took Scotty and Lizzie to the movies this afternoon."

"To the movies, huh? But they're only thirteen. I had to wait until I was fifteen to go out."

"It's not really a date when your mother's with you," Pop said, obviously mimicking Scotty. "Besides, your mother had already told him he could go and you know how she gets when she's made her mind up about something."

Andrea sank down to the edge of the bed, still fidgeting with the phone cord, but smiling, too.

"That's right, Pop. I don't know how you've put up with her all these years."

"Yes, you do, girl. And you love her too. Now, do you have any particular news to report?"

She sighed. "Not really. Things are wrapping up here. I should be back at my apartment sometime Sunday evening."

"Come on, Andi. Make up something or your mother will be ranting at me all evening for not taking my duty to you seriously." Pop was joking, Andrea knew, but she was just so tired.

"I went on a dinner date this week."

"You did? Really?" She hadn't expected her *father* to be excited at the news. Andrea felt guilty. The only date she'd been on had been with Dave O'Dell. All the other dinners she'd had that week had been business.

"I did. But before you go getting all excited, you should know that he's married."

"Andrea! What's the matter with you, girl? Your mother and I didn't raise you to take what doesn't belong to you." Her father's voice was no longer teasing.

It was a sign of just how mixed up Andrea really was that she hadn't realized how her comment would sound to her father.

"Pop! It's okay. I only meant that it didn't amount to anything—that it can't, because he's married, not that I'm seeing a married man. He's *safely* married. He's a mentor here just like me and we talked about his wife all night."

"Now that sounds more like my girl." Andrea was relieved to hear Pop return to his normal, easygoing self. Upsetting her father was the last thing she'd had in mind.

"I just thought you could tell Ma the first part without telling her the rest. You know. Give her a little something to keep her calm for a week or two."

There was a pause on the line. "You want me to get her off your back? Her meddling's starting to get to you again?"

Andrea smiled and ran her fingers through her bangs, letting them fall back across her forehead. She could always count on her father. "Would you mind, Pop? I know she means well, but I could really use a break if you could manage it."

"I'll see what I can do, hon. Now, do you want to tell me about him?"

"Oh, Pop. There *is* no him."

THE PHONE RANG in Andrea's room an hour later. She was just drifting off to sleep and considered letting it ring, but she knew she couldn't. She never could get by the fact that someone might really need her.

"Hello?"

"Andrea? It's me. I have to talk softly because your father forbade me to call, but I just have to know about him. Your father thinks you've met someone and he wants me to leave you alone to see what develops, but he doesn't understand how women are, he never has. Women need to talk about these things, and I knew when I'd heard you'd called that you needed to talk to your mother. I'm just sorry I wasn't here for you earlier. So quick, before your dad catches me, who is he?''

Andrea flopped back against the pillows, flinging an arm over her eyes. She was too tired to deal with her mother. When was Gloria ever going to see that she could learn to be happy without a husband and children?

"His name's Steve, Ma. He's been a police officer for several years, he likes what he does and he's good at it. He doesn't take crap from people, but he's still sensitive enough to listen to those in need. You'd like him."

"What's he look like?"

Andrea tried to get a clear picture in her head. Maybe if she did this well enough, her mother would finally leave her alone, just long enough for her to catch her breath. Then she could arrange to have Steve dump her.

"He's cute, in a rugged sort of way. His nose has been broken more than once, but it gives him a roguish kind of look."

"Is he good to you? You know there are a lot of men out there who would be intimidated by a lady police officer, especially one as good as you are, baby."

"Oh yeah, Ma. He's great. He respects what I'm doing here. He's really supportive." He had to be. He wanted to be a DARE officer. Other than that, she wasn't sure Steve even knew her last name.

"Does he like kids?"

Andrea thought of the report she'd read on Steve almost two weeks before, and of the conversations she'd had with him over the course of the session. "He's got a daughter," she said when she finally remembered. "He's really proud of her, and seems to miss her a lot. Yeah, he really likes kids. He's a good father."

Andrea couldn't do it. She just couldn't lie to the woman whose only motivation was to see her happy. "He's been married three times, Ma."

"He's been divorced three times?" Gloria asked, not nearly as enthusiastically.

"Yeah, three times, and to be perfectly honest, Ma, I'm not completely sure he's really over his last wife. She's remarried and all, but he's still not at peace with things. As a matter of fact, he's not from Columbus either, Ma, and you know how long-distance relationships are—they almost never work out. So, now that I think about it, I guess I won't be seeing Steve again after Sunday." Andrea held the phone away from her ear, waiting.

"Andrea Lee Parker, if you ever do find a man, and he does want to marry you and give you babies, I hope you have a daughter who drives you in circles until you're dizzy...."

Andrea heard the click loud and clear, but it was another ten seconds before she realized that her mother had actually hung up on her. Astonished, she looked at the receiver, as if it somehow could explain what had just happened. Then she reached over and put it back in its cradle.

"MIND IF I RIDE?"

His voice came unexpectedly from behind her. Andrea jumped, and her foot slipped from the pedal of the exercise bike. "Feel free," she panted.

She tried to concentrate on regaining her footing, but she was aware of every move Doug made as he slipped up onto the bike beside her. He was wearing cutoff sweats and the inevitable T-shirt. Andrea decided that his looks should be registered as a lethal weapon.

"Do these things work?" he asked. He was studying the control panel between his handlebars. The break in his nose was more obvious from the side.

"Just...punch in...your weight. It'll tell you...what to do."

She continued pedaling, finding her rhythm again. She'd probably never see him after tomorrow.

She saw his legs in her peripheral vision as he began pedaling. Up, down, up, down. The muscles in his thighs were clearly defined, tight and hard. She pictured him on her bed, using those muscles to move up, down, up....

"How long do you normally ride?"

Her shocked gaze flew to his. He was punching things into his control panel. *Oh. Yeah. The bike.*

"Half an hour."

"Would you have dinner with me tonight?"

Andrea lost her rhythm again. The lights on her panel started to blink, indicating that she was losing her speed.

"Tonight?"

"I thought maybe we could get away from here and spend a little more time alone together before tomorrow."

Tomorrow. Tomorrow they'd be going their separate ways. Tomorrow he'd be gone. The threat he posed would be gone, too. And so would the excitement.

"I'd like that...."

DOUG DRESSED FOR DINNER before he went to his last training session. Andrea was giving the lecture and they were planning to leave the hotel from there.

He hadn't been kidding when he'd told her he'd never really had anything that could be termed a first date. He'd never had predate jitters, or even prepared himself specifically for a woman. But here he was, thirty years old and feeling like he was getting ready for his high-school prom.

He had one decent outfit besides his blues, and he pulled it out of his duffle bag, disgruntled when he saw how wrinkled the dress slacks and blue oxford shirt were. He phoned down for an iron, and then had to ask the maid how to use it when it arrived. He practiced on a couple of T-shirts, threw the first one away and figured the scorch marks on the second wouldn't be that obvious, since it was black.

He didn't recognize the man who looked back at him from the hotel-room mirror when he was finally ready to go. But it wasn't because the clothes were ones he seldom wore, or because he'd brushed his hair until every strand was in place. He'd drawn the line at wearing a tie, so it wasn't even that he looked all that different. It was something about his face—about his eyes—that he didn't recognize. He looked almost happy.

"THE HARDEST THING to accept as a DARE officer is the fact that you can't help them all. You have to know when to draw the line...." Andrea's words fell on a silent room.

What the hell? Doug slouched down in his seat in the front row of tables in the meeting room. His chest was growing tighter by the second. These people had just spent two weeks telling him about choices, about survival, about hope. So what in the hell was this?

"Not all people in this world are good people. Not all children are good children. Not everyone wants to be helped. Sometimes the conditioning has been going on for so many years that by the time we get to them it's just too late. Sometimes the realities a kid would have to face, the memories of things that have happened to him, are too much. You must be aware of the existence of these young people. You must be able to know when to trust, yet also be aware of the fact that you can't always. Above all, you must protect the first group from the second."

Doug couldn't believe his ears. He recognized Andrea's gentle voice, but what was she saying?

"The pushers in the schools are not slimy men who watch for innocent children on the playground. They are students themselves. Many of them are so bitter they can't be made to feel guilt or remorse for the kids they lead astray. They care only for their next fix. They'll lie, they'll playact, they'll agree to anything, all the while planning that next snort, or pill, or hypo-dermic.''

She was right there.

''This is when the barriers have to go back up, Of-ficers. Beware of the hard-core druggies. By *each one* of them, there will be more than ten good kids led astray each year. You cannot afford to waste your compassion on them. In most cases, they won't even know it if you try. By the time they get to this state, their brains are so fried they can't even think straight. They need more than a friend. They need more than you are qualified to give them. They kill innocent children every day and don't give a damn. Don't ever forget that.''

Doug sat in his seat while the session was being wrapped up, but he didn't hear a word of what was said. His heart was turning to stone. She'd told them all to never forget. And dammit, she was right. He never would forget. He might not remember for an hour or two, but ultimately, he would never forget. He unsnapped his wristband, as if he needed the physical reminder to remember all that he'd been.

He'd been a fool to think he could leave it all be-hind, to think that maybe he'd paid his dues, that he deserved to share some part of his life with a woman like Andrea. But her words cut through him like a knife. He could never make her his. He could never make her a part of what he was.

He couldn't have her. He'd probably known it deep inside all along. It was probably that knowledge that had stopped him from taking her the other night.

But he didn't have to watch the admiration in her eyes turn to disgust, either. He'd stay away from her. He'd get out now, before she had a chance to learn who Doug Avery really was.

Refastening his wristband, Doug left the meeting hall, went to his room and changed back into the jeans and T-shirt that fit him like a second skin. And then, without a word to anybody, he slipped down the back stairs and out into the night. He went back to the only home he'd ever known, to the place where he really belonged, and spent the evening coming to terms with the reality of Douglas Phillip Avery.

DOUG HAD BEEN NINE when he'd first realized that drugs were the most important thing in his life, and eleven the first time he'd nearly killed a guy to get a single fix. By the time he was sixteen, he'd tripped on every hallucinogen known to the ghetto, sometimes more than one at the same time. He was well known to the pushers, and later on, to the dealers. And finally, he'd had the reputation of being a good source himself. He'd stolen from his father, from his neighbors, even from his friends, just to get another fix.

Doug was a druggie. He'd abused his body so badly that some of the damage was irreparable. He'd developed such a chemical dependence that even though he was straight, he would never be fully over his addiction. There were some drugs, legal drugs, that—were Doug to take them even once—could send him right back to where he'd been at seventeen, nineteen, twenty....

Doug walked the streets that were as familiar to him as his skin. But he didn't see the people that were loitering on them, as he had the last time he'd come down this way. Instead, he saw into the past. He saw the Rattlers, his brothers in crime, and the Scorpions, their archrivals. He saw the knives, the blood, the brawls. He saw the hopelessness.

He saw himself, leaning against a streetlight, ruler of the block, frightening anyone who got too close, so fried out of his mind that he didn't even know where he was. He saw Chuck, the buddy Steve had portrayed on stage the other day. He saw Chuck's body, a few years older, contorted with convulsions. He saw Chuck's funeral. His old buddy had never made it out. But he'd been right about one thing. Doug *could* make it out—he *had*.

And that's when Doug saw the hope. He'd survived. He'd been there. He'd lived in hell with the worst of them, but he'd made it out.

He wasn't in Andrea's league. He'd done too much, seen too much. He'd been what she despised. But he did have a purpose, an important job to do.

Doug left his old neighborhood behind and headed back toward the Hetherington Hotel. He was what he was. But there was good in that. He could go out into the schools. He knew what the kids needed, what he'd needed. He knew how to beat it. He was going to get to the next generation of drug users while they still had a chance. *He would make a difference.*

ANDREA FIGURED there was some kind of irony in it. She wondered if her mother would see the humor. She had finally accepted a date with a man about whom she didn't feel indifferent. She'd actually been looking forward to it. And she'd been stood up.

She punched her pillow for the hundredth time, telling herself she wasn't pretending it was Doug Avery's face, telling herself she didn't care that he hadn't even had the decency to cancel their dinner together. She lay on her stomach. And she lay on her back. And finally she got out of bed.

It didn't take her long to slip into a pair of jeans and a faded DARE T-shirt. She didn't care who she saw in the elevator, or how many revelers there were in the hallways. She had to get out, go for a walk, use up her energy so she could sleep.

She didn't care who she saw, until she saw him. She was walking out in the gardens by the pool, trying to convince some of the tranquility surrounding her to seep into her bones, but even in the subdued lighting she knew it was Doug coming toward her. And she knew he hadn't seen her until it was too late for him to escape. She stood in his way and waited to see what he'd do.

"Oh. Andrea. Yeah, sorry about tonight. Something came up." He stopped in front of her, pushing his hands into the pockets of his jeans. He looked more preoccupied than sorry. Something strange was going on.

"That's all right. Did you eat?"

"Uh, no. I guess I'll just order room service." The scar at his temple stood out as he looked at her and then looked away.

"They quit serving at ten."

"I can always go to the coffee shop. They're open all night."

He was the Doug Avery she'd met two weeks ago. A closed book. Except there was something different about him, too.

"Would you like some company?" *Why was she doing this? Why couldn't she just let him go?*

He looked back at her, his jaw tight. Andrea wished she knew what was going on behind those inexpressive brown eyes, hoping against hope that she was about to find out.

"No. Really, I'd rather not. But thanks. I'll see ya later."

He stepped around her and strode down the path.

Andrea didn't bother to brush away the tears that trickled slowly down her cheeks. There was no one there to see them anyway.

CHAPTER NINE

GLORIA GOT UP BEFORE dawn Sunday morning. Church wasn't until ten, and if she was very quiet, the guys would sleep in at least until nine. That gave her just enough time to get across town, take a peek at the DARE trainees at their culmination breakfast and get back before anyone was the wiser.

She brushed her teeth at the kitchen sink so no one would hear, pulled on the gardening dress she kept hanging in the pantry and slipped out the back door. So far so good.

She'd waited to hear from her daughter again, waited for Andrea to tell her why she'd really called the other day, but her firstborn had remained frustratingly silent. Something was going on. Gloria could sense it. And she'd never forgive herself if she didn't do what she could to help her only daughter find happiness.

Gloria found the ballroom where the breakfast was being held with surprising ease. She felt a twinge of discomfort as she realized that she was hardly dressed like a patron of the hotel, and she didn't look like one of the staff, either. She'd have to make it quick.

The door to the ballroom was open, allowing her a clear view of the officers seated inside. She spotted

Andrea's table right off, and had identified Steve and Sven within a matter of seconds. Three other members of Andrea's team were easily dismissable, being either too old or too obviously married.

And then she saw him.

Gloria's breath caught in her throat as her avid gaze landed on the sixth member of Andrea's team. Seated directly across from Andrea was the most powerful-looking man Gloria had ever seen. And her daughter was stealing surreptitious glances at him so often it would have been embarrassing if it wasn't so darn wonderful.

Gloria felt her own knees get a little shaky as the man glanced up at Andrea. He had enough sex appeal to make ten babies.

Gloria saw one of the waiters watching her and decided she'd better leave while the going was good. She'd gotten what she came for. She wondered if a little girl with dark brown hair and dark brown eyes would look good in a calico print. Or would solid yellow be better? She'd definitely need dresses. With Andrea's slender build, no one would be mistaking Andrea's daughter for a boy....

ANDREA'S STOMACH WAS a mass of butterflies that afternoon as she watched the DARE trainees file into the auditorium for their culmination ceremonies. She always felt this sense of hopeful anxiety as she got ready to send another team of qualified people out to do damage to the drug activity in the schools, but never had she felt the importance of the next minutes so personally.

Was Doug going to show up? He'd been silent all through breakfast. Andrea couldn't understand it. What had happened to the rogue who'd ridden the exercise bike with her just the day before?

She relaxed, though only slightly, when she saw him take his place between Sven and Steve. He looked marvelous in his blues. He also looked determined. He didn't glance at her.

The speeches seemed to take forever. Though they usually inspired Andrea, she barely heard a word this time. DARE T-shirts were passed around to all of the trainees, and finally the moment Andrea had been anticipating—and dreading—arrived.

"Ladies and gentlemen, you have all successfully completed the rigorous course set before you. You all have the knowledge you need to fight one of this country's most hideous crimes. It's now up to you how well you do your jobs."

One by one, the trainees were called to the stage by Sergeant Miller, the man in charge of the DARE training program, and one by one they filed back to their seats. Andrea didn't see any of them. She only saw Doug. She watched as he rose when his name was called. In her mind she walked across the stage with him, willing him to hold out his arms when the time came.

And she felt her eyes moisten when he took his DARE Bear from the sergeant and held it up for his peers to see. Doug had done it. He was now, officially, a DARE officer.

He glanced her way and a smile flickered across his face, though it didn't reach his eyes. Nothing seemed to reach his eyes. He was again the cold stranger she'd met two weeks before, with one major difference—he was holding a teddy bear. Had he reverted back to each man for himself? Or was it just her he was shutting out?

"SERGEANT, MAY I HAVE a word with you please?"

"Of course, Andrea, come on in. What's up?"

Andrea entered Sergeant Miller's office Monday morning with less control than she would have liked, but determined all the same.

"I'd like to be assigned to Doug Avery's classroom, sir."

Miller never missed a beat. He picked up a pen, scribbled his signature on a form and passed it to Andrea.

After she'd put it in her pocket, he spoke. "Do you have doubts about Avery's capabilities?"

"No! No, sir, I don't. It's just that Officer Avery had a harder time than most in coming to terms with himself and his new position. He had some disturbing philosophies that needed to be changed. I just feel that we'd be shortchanging the children if we don't make sure he's not still reluctant to turn his back for fear of being stabbed."

Miller nodded, as if satisfied. "You're on him for seventeen weeks. We'll talk again after his first students graduate."

"Yes, sir," Andrea said. She shook Miller's hand and went to turn her assignment in to bookkeeping. She hoped she hadn't just made the biggest mistake of her life.

IT DIDN'T LOOK TOO BAD. Really. What could possibly be threatening about patches of sandy earth and a swing set? A couple of people walked by. *Little people*. Impossibly little people. They stared at him.

Doug broke out in a cold sweat. He shouldn't be here. He didn't belong.

He ran a finger inside the collar of his navy uniform shirt, the one he'd ironed for the first time in his life that morning. The top button was fastened, and Doug felt like he was strangling. He couldn't do it.

Another surge of kids walked past, eyeing his cruiser and him with open curiosity. Hadn't anybody taught them that it was impolite to stare?

A bell rang. The children, all squeaky clean and dressed in miniature versions of the current fashions, started to run. A couple of girls squealed, their fresh young faces filled with laughter. Doug watched from the relative safety of his car, his stomach knotting with dread.

Everything looked so innocent, so pure, so fresh— as if from a Norman Rockwell masterpiece. He would never have fit in here, even when he was their age, and he certainly was out of place now. Norman Rockwell would have been a flop if he'd ever tried to depict lives like Doug's. Doug couldn't believe what a fool he'd been. He wasn't needed here.

But he couldn't make himself leave, either. He'd spent the last week mentally preparing himself for this assignment. He had five schools to hit in five days. And he'd be hitting them again every week for the next seventeen. He had a job to do. An important job. He watched as two girls walked past, holding hands and giggling, and was once again seized with doubts.

A second bell rang, and Doug watched in amazement as the children cleared away, leaving the playground deserted and the sidewalk in front of him empty. In a matter of seconds, the brick building before him had swallowed up every last one of them.

Or had it? Doug caught a movement in his peripheral vision. He watched without turning his head, hoping to catch it again. Was there someone behind those bushes? He was sure he'd seen a flash of green.

He only had to wait about a minute before he saw the movement again. It had definitely been a flash of green—a lighter green than the bush. Doug felt his adrenalin begin to pump. This was what he did, what he was good at.

He had to remain patient for a few more minutes, and then suddenly a blond head peaked out from behind the bush. Alert eyes surveyed the playground, but they missed the parking lot—and Doug.

Apparently deciding that the coast was clear, a grubby boy appeared and dashed toward a side entrance to the school. Doug knew that he should report what he'd seen, that it was probably even his duty as a cop to check behind those bushes. But mostly he knew that he felt sorry for the kid. It looked like the boy had been wearing somebody's castoffs, like he needed a bath. Maybe he needed a friend. With one last look around, Doug picked up his brand-new briefcase and got out of his cruiser.

THE HALLWAYS WERE NARROW, with ceilings so low Doug felt like he was King Kong as he walked toward Room 116. Everywhere he looked there were primary colors and shapes made out of construction paper. Outside Room 102 there was a paper kite with the longest tail he'd ever seen. And on each segment of the tail there was a name written in black Magic Marker. Doug's chest tightened again. He was used to dealing with theft and back stabbing. Here they dealt with nontoxic glue and brightly colored paper. Even the floors were clean and new looking. Anything he might have to offer was tarnished and used.

But then he remembered the boy he'd seen running from the bushes. If there was one, there could be more like him in this fairy-tale building. Doug kept his eyes focused on the little black numbers above the doors, cloaking himself with numbness and a determination to do the job he'd come to do. When he reached Room 115, he looked straight ahead, preparing to commit himself to the next doorway.

He froze at the sight before him. Andrea was there, standing in the hallway, watching him. She was all decked out and official looking in her blues and shiny black shoes. Her sassy blond hair looked freshly cut. She looked wonderful.

He'd thought it would be easy to get Andrea out of his mind after the training course had ended. He'd finally managed to convince himself that his reaction to her had just been unfortunate timing, a matter of proximity.

And then she smiled. That's all it took. He wanted to wrap his arms around her and carry her away. He was turning into a sap.

".What're you doing here?" he asked as soon as he reached her side. He sounded gruff, even to his own ears.

"A mentor usually follows her trainees out into the schools."

Her chin was jutting, as if she was daring him to oppose her.

"So you check up on all of us?"

"Not quite." She looked across the hall at the door they'd both be entering. "I've been assigned to your schedule."

Doug didn't like the sound of that at all. "You're going to be working with me every day?"

"For a while."

"How long's awhile?" Why wouldn't she look at him, damn it?

"Seventeen weeks."

Doug was beginning to understand. "You don't think I can handle it, do you?"

Her gaze flew up to meet his then, and Doug couldn't doubt the sincerity in her beautiful blue eyes. "Yes. I do. I think you're going to do just fine. It's procedure, really. There aren't enough mentors to assign one to every new officer, so Sergeant Miller usually sends us to the ones who've worked the toughest beats out on the streets. The adjustment period is usually a little harder for them."

Doug was a little worried about the ease with which he bought her story. But he was more worried about

the lightning he felt in his gut as he realized that he'd
be seeing her every day, at least for the next few
months.

"Let's go in," he said, motioning for her to pre-
cede him.

"NAME ME a consequence of not using alcohol."

Doug's statement was met with total silence. He sat
on the tile floor of the classroom, resting his back
against the wall as he looked around at the myriad
faces surrounding him. He waited.

Andrea sat beside Doug, watching the scene unfold. They'd been in the schools for almost three
weeks and already she was addicted to Doug's teaching methods. This week he'd pushed all the desks to
one side of the room, saying that the sixth-graders
were too stuck in their student roles to really open up
to him.

After what seemed like forever, a big boy in front of
Doug raised his hand.

"Mike?" Doug nodded to the boy.

"I thought consequences were like what happened
to you when you did something bad," Mike Cooper
said.

"Yeah," several voices chorused.

"Okay. Let's talk about that." Doug spread his legs
out in front of him. The kids, all sitting Indian fash-
ion, scooted back on the floor to give him room.

"You got a big game coming up Saturday," Doug
said, addressing Mike. "Let's say you spend the night
with a friend Friday. You eat so much junk you think
you might barf and you stay up trying to scare each

other until dawn. What are the consequences gonna be?''

"I probably wouldn't play too good."

"Anything else? Anybody?"

"The team would lose for sure. Mike's the only good player we got," another boy called out. The classroom resounded with laughter.

Doug smiled briefly, and then his expression turned serious again. The room fell back into attentive silence. "So you got consequences. Negative consequences. Now let's take the same thing. You got a big game on Saturday. But this time you go right home after school on Friday, eat a decent dinner, watch a little TV and go to bed early. Then what?''

"I'd probably have the best game I've ever had," Mike answered with a laugh.

"Probably." Doug nodded. "And that would be a consequence of having been smart on Friday. A positive consequence."

A girl in the middle of the crowd raised her hand. "I get it," she said before she was called on. "So like, if we don't use alcohol, maybe a positive consequence would be that we won't, like, get in trouble for it, right?" She smiled shyly at Doug.

"Right," Doug said. Andrea wished he'd smiled back at her.

"And we'd have more brain cells," a bespectacled boy called out.

"We'd have more energy and drive and stuff," someone else said.

Pretty soon the entire class, with the exception of one grubby blond boy who had refused to join the rest of them down on the floor, was calling out benefits to be had by staying straight. Some made more sense than others, but they were all equally important simply because the kids were calling them up from within themselves. Just like Doug had suggested all those weeks ago, the kids were buying into the program by coming up with their own conclusions.

If only Doug were able to feel half the personal satisfaction Andrea did as she listened to the kids. If only she could be sure that he allowed himself to feel anything at all.

It was so hard for Andrea to believe that less than a month ago, the man had been trying to go to bed with her. The way he'd been acting for the three weeks they'd been working together, you'd think she was sixty years old and married.

And there were times when she wished she was. She kept telling herself that Doug was constantly on her mind because he was her responsibility—and because it was human nature to want what you couldn't have.

But when she lay alone in her apartment at night, remembering something Doug had said, or feeling weak inside as she thought of an expression she'd caught on his face, she had a hard time convincing herself that he meant no more to her than any other professional challenge.

And then, as the morning hours loomed close and panic started to set in, she'd console herself with the fact that she'd been alone a long time. She was still living in a healthy adult body with healthy adult needs. Her attraction to Doug was a result of neglected hormones. There was nothing personal in it.

She'd fall asleep believing herself, too. Until the dreams set in.

"OKAY, THIS IS IT, guys. If we don't get 'em now, we're sunk. I'll fake it to Brackwhite, you two head straight up the center and Avery, you get to the short outside so I can lob it over to you."

Doug nodded, going over the play in his mind. He'd been a member of the precinct's intramural football team for only a couple of weeks. He didn't want to let the guys down now when their first big win depended on him.

He left the huddle and jogged over to his place on the twenty-yard line. They should pull this off without a hitch. They'd better. He didn't relish the idea of walking into the locker room with the braggarts from Precinct 11. He'd probably need to punch out one or two of them.

"Twenty-six, forty..." Doug was listening to the quarterback's calls, waiting for his signal. He looked over to the sidelines, judging how far he could go and still be in bounds, and was startled to see a boy walking off in the distance. A slight boy. A slight, blond, grubby boy. Was that Jeremy? He hadn't been in class all week.

Before Doug could tell for sure who the boy was, he'd been blindsided by the nose guard from Precinct 11 and was eating grass. His ribs ached. He couldn't breathe. His head felt like he'd bashed it into a slab of concrete. He forced his eyes open long enough to see that he'd blown the play. And that the boy was gone. *Damn.*

"I HAVE A FAVOR to ask, baby."

Andrea sat at the kitchen table and watched her mother roll out dough for homemade pasta, marveling for the thousandth time that she went to all that trouble when there was perfectly good pasta for sale down at Gibraldi's market.

"What do you need?" she asked, munching on a carrot stick.

Gloria started cutting lasagna-size lengths of dough. "Remember I told you about that nice man who moved in next door?"

Andrea reached for another carrot stick. "The one with the two little boys?"

"Yeah. They're such good little guys, Andrea. They march behind Mark with these little bubble mowers every weekend, helping him cut his grass."

"What's the favor, Ma?"

"Well now, don't say no right off, Andrea. Just hear me out. You see, Mark won this mystery-weekend adventure for two. Well, he didn't win it, exactly, little Shawn did by accident. Anyway, Mark's not going to go, because he doesn't have anyone to go with."

Andrea quit chewing. "No, Ma."

"I told you to hear me out. It might be fun, Andrea. You arrive at this hostel in Cincinnati on a Friday afternoon and they stage this crime. You and twenty other guests have the place to yourselves, and all weekend to solve the crime. The winner gets a room for a whole week at the hostel."

"Oh, great. So what would I and what's his name do with that?"

"You'd give it to him, of course, since he's the one who won the mystery weekend to begin with. It might be fun, Andrea. Just think, a real policewoman playing at solving a crime."

"No, Ma."

"He's alone and lonely, Andrea. He's an architect and he works at home so he can watch out for his boys. He hardly ever has an opportunity for adult conversation. He *needs* this weekend."

"No, Ma." Andrea picked up another carrot and started crunching again.

"His wife left him high and dry. He came home one day to find the boys alone with a note from her. She needed to take time off from family life and go find herself. So he quit his job, moved the boys to a new city where there weren't constant reminders of their mother and is doing the best he can to give them a good life. Don't you think he deserves one simple weekend away?"

Andrea could think of someone else who deserved a weekend away, someone who'd been all work and no play for weeks, someone she'd love to have to herself for an entire weekend.

No!

What she'd love was to find a nice safe man she could spend some time with without risking her heart, someone with other responsibilities and obligations taking up his time so he wouldn't need much from her. And she needed to find him soon, so she would quit being obsessed with Doug Avery.

"Sure I do," she said, finally answering her mother's question. "I just don't see why I should have to go with him. Come on, Ma, the man doesn't even know me.''

But he definitely has other obligations that take up most of his time, was her next thought.

"That's just it, Andrea. I talk about you so much that he feels like he does know you. And it has to be you, because he doesn't know anybody else here yet."

Andrea wondered how Mark kissed.

"You mean he doesn't know anybody who's going to watch his boys for an entire weekend?"

Gloria had the decency to blush.

"Okay, Ma. You win. I'll go."

THE BOY WAS THERE again, hanging outside his apartment. He was there every morning, watching Doug from his world-weary, bitter, eleven-year-old eyes. Doug called out to him, but the boy didn't seem to hear. He just stared, daring Doug to make something of it. Doug put his briefcase down and started back toward him. He watched the boy, willing him to stay put, to trust him, but just as he was getting close, the boy vanished into thin air. He didn't run away, didn't go anywhere, he just ceased to exist. . . .

Doug sat up in his bed, pulling a corner of his tangled sheet up to wipe the sweat from his chest. He'd had it again. The dream had been visiting him on and off for weeks.

The damnable thing was that he knew who the boy was: Jeremy Schwartz. He was the boy Doug had seen coming out from behind that bush his first day as a DARE officer. He was the boy in class who refused to sit with the rest of them on the floor, who refused to

participate in the DARE program at all. Doug had
done his best for the kid. He'd tried to include him.
There was nothing more he could do.

But he didn't go back to sleep. No matter how sure
Doug was that he'd done all that could be expected of
him, the boy continued to haunt his dreams. And if
Jeremy didn't figure in his dreams, Andrea probably
would. The two seemed to take turns monopolizing his
nights, until he thought he'd lose his mind.

Doug figured he'd tasted every inch of Andrea's
body so many times these past weeks that he should no
longer be hungry for her. But he was tasting something in his dreams that he'd never seen in real life.
And he wanted to see her. To see her, to touch her, to
make love to her until neither one of them could possibly ever have a need again.

Instead, he satisfied himself with being close to her
every day, with soaking up her smile when she greeted
him, with remembering the soft, full feel of her breasts
the one and only time he'd ever been close enough to
touch them.

Letting out a long sigh, Doug headed for another
cold shower.

DURING THE FIFTH WEEK of the semester, Doug
started talking to the kids about ways to say no. It was
an easy week for him because he had the kids role-
playing, matching types of peer pressure with the most
effective ways to resist it. Other than offering a little
guidance, his job mainly consisted of being an audience.

He and Andrea were sitting on opposite sides of a classroom on Wednesday afternoon, listening to a boy trying to use a short-term excuse to solve a long-term problem, when the loudspeaker above the door started to crackle.

Doug looked up, startled. Ordinarily the system was used only for morning announcements and the daily Pledge of Allegiance.

"Teachers, boys and girls? This is Mrs. Menlo. I want you all to listen very carefully to me and follow my directions as quickly and quietly as possible. There's been a tornado sighted nearby and it's heading in our direction. I want everyone to line up, single file, and walk, *don't run,* out into the hallway. You're to remain seated along the nearest north wall until further notice."

Pandemonium broke out in the classroom and Doug knew a moment of sheer panic as he realized that, for the moment, *he* was the teacher. It was up to him to calm down twenty-six frightened children and get them safely out into the hall.

He headed for the door with the thought that he wasn't going to lose anyone and watched as the children scrambled for belongings, for escape, for each other.

And then an ear-splitting whistle cut through the tension. Everybody in the room froze, their eyes on Andrea.

"Mrs. Menlo said quietly," she said. "Now I want everybody to find a hand to hold and line up behind Officer Avery."

Doug was amazed at the effect her calm words had on the kids. Not one of them complained about having to hold hands—they actually seemed to welcome the contact. Andrea's understanding of what the children needed, her ability to give it to them, was something Doug still had a hard time grasping, even after seeing her in action for more than a month. What was even harder for him to believe was that her words had a calming effect on him as well.

He saw her grab his DARE bear on her way to the end of the line.

The children filed out into the hallway and walked, still holding hands, to the nearest north wall. They ended up in a little corridor near the janitor's closet. They were the only ones there.

"Okay, everybody sit."

"Officer Parker? Are we going to die?"

Andrea sat down at one end of the line, Doug at the other.

"It's not likely that anyone will be hurt, Mary—even if the tornado hits, which it probably won't," Andrea said.

Doug noticed that she hadn't actually answered the girl's question.

"How long are we going to have to sit here?" A boy in the middle of the line asked.

"Probably not long, but we'll stay here as long as it takes," Doug said, taking the easy question for himself.

"I have to go to the bathroom. I feel like I'm gonna throw up."

"Come here, Sara, sit by me," Andrea said, drawing the girl beneath her arm. She handed Doug's bear to the frightened girl. "Try not to think about it. You don't really want to be in the bathroom with all those windows right now, do you?"

Doug heard a soft "uh-uh" and breathed a sigh of relief. He wished he had a few more of the little DARE mascots. A tornado he could handle, kids out of control he wasn't so sure.

The children sat quietly for a while, but they soon grew bored with the forced inactivity. In spite of his and Andrea's instructions, their voices rose higher and higher, competing with their neighbors', until Doug wanted to gag a kid or two.

"How about a game of I spy?" Andrea's voice rose above the din.

"I'll go first."

"No way! You always wanna be first."

"We'll start at Officer Avery's end of the line and work our way down," Andrea said. She had the patience of a saint.

Doug was relieved to have the problem solved, until he realized that they were all waiting for him to begin. He had no idea what to do. He'd never even heard of the game. But he didn't want the kids to know that. He didn't want them thinking he was strange.

He saw comprehension dawn on Andrea's face as she looked at him, and knew that she was going to rescue him, just like she'd rescued the children.

"Officer Avery and I will be referees. Jimmy, you start."

The skinny boy next to Doug rattled off the famous verse ending with the color gray. Doug waited to see what was going to happen next. So far, the game didn't sound like much.

It didn't take long for him to realize that he was wrong. The kids all got into the spirit of the game, trying hard to be the first to guess what Jimmy had spied. They gave as much energy to their guessing as they had to their earlier panic. Doug started to relax.

Half an hour later they were playing another game, and this time Andrea and Doug joined in. They were going down the line saying words, and each person had five seconds to think of a word that started with the last letter of the previous word. Doug's turn came. He had to think of a new word that started with an *X*.

He never had a chance. Just as everybody's eyes turned toward him, their little hallway was filled with a frightening rumble. Several children screamed, a couple of them started to cry.

It all happened so fast that Doug never had a chance to think, only to react. He laid his body out across as many kids as he could cover, urging the others to stay as close to the wall but also as close to him as possible.

"Lie flat, and no matter what, keep your heads covered," he hollered. He knew he was frightening them, but there was no time for niceties anymore. The next few seconds could mean their lives.

He didn't know where Andrea was. He hoped to God she was doing as he'd instructed. He didn't know what he'd do if anything happened to her.

The rumbling started again, like a heavy wind was blowing things against the building or onto the roof above them. It got louder, then even louder. And just when the crescendo became deafening, Kyle Winslow darted away from the wall and took off down the hall.

Doug was after him in a flash, catching the boy just as he would have turned the corner and run for the side exit. Kyle flailed at Doug, landing a couple of good ones on his jaw and nose, and coming dangerously close to emasculating him with a wildly kicking foot. Doug finally calmed the boy by flattening him and lying on top of him.

"Stay put, you fool. Do you want to kill us both?"

He felt Kyle go limp beneath him, but he didn't dare let the boy get up.

The cacophony continued until plaster gave way someplace nearby and Doug heard the horrifying sounds of the building falling around him. He covered the boy as best he could, knowing that he and Kyle were in a dangerous area at the hallway intersection, but not daring to move.

He thought of Andrea, of the time he'd wasted in not trusting her to see in him the man he was becoming. And then he thought nothing at all as a piece of drywall came loose above him and splintered across his upper body.

CHAPTER TEN

THE DEAFENING ROAR lasted only a couple of minutes. But it was followed by a deathly silence that was almost as frightening. Andrea lay at her end of the hall feeling the heartbeats of the children plastered beneath her, listening for the breathing of those she couldn't reach.

Was it safe to get up? The children were going to need attention. Many of them were crying quietly. Some were probably in shock. From somewhere off in the distance Andrea heard a louder cry. It sounded like someone in another hallway was hurt. No one moved, too afraid of what might yet lie ahead.

Andrea heard sirens in the distance. Help was on its way. Which probably meant that the immediate danger was past. It was now just a matter of assessing the damage and getting the kids safely out of the building. She thanked God that their little hallway had remained intact. They had all come through safely.

"Stay put for a few more minutes," she told the kids at her end of the line. "I'm going to see how bad it is and then I'll be back to get you out of here."

She got up, releasing the children beneath her, and reached out to brush Sara's hair off her tear-stained cheeks.

"Try and relax, guys. I think the worst is over."

She walked down the line, repeating her instructions to the children as she went, all the while looking ahead for Doug. She couldn't see him anywhere. Had he already gone on ahead to assess the situation?

"Officer Parker?" The words were muffled by a pair of skinny arms.

"Yes, Jimmy?"

The boy looked up at her with worried eyes.

"Do you see Officer Avery, ma'am? I don't think he ever came back."

Andrea felt light-headed as the boy's words sank in.

"Came back?" she asked, forcing herself to remain calm. The children were watching her.

"Yes, ma'am. Kyle freaked. He ran off. Officer Avery went after him."

"I'll find him, Jimmy. You kids stay put." Andrea's words were said on the run. If anything had happened to Doug, or to Kyle, either, for that matter...

She rounded the corner into what used to be a main thoroughfare of the school and stopped dead in her tracks. The entire hallway was a mass of plaster and dust. The ceiling was nonexistent. Only the brick walls and roof were still intact.

Her throat was dry, her heart pounding so heavily it was practically choking her. She didn't see how anyone could be alive in that mess. She hoped Doug had made it far enough to get past it. There were no north walls here, so hopefully there hadn't been anyone in the area when it had been hit.

She was debating the advisability of picking her way through the rubbish when she heard a moan. It was very faint at first, but as she moved toward the biggest pile of drywall scraps, it grew stronger.

"Help!" She heard the word again, coming from the middle of the thoroughfare. She continued to pick her way toward the pile.

"Please, someone, help me!" The words were growing stronger by the second as Andrea neared the pile of plaster. She fought down panic. It was Kyle's voice. But where was Doug?

"Kyle?" she called.

"Over here!" The boy didn't sound as if he were too badly hurt.

"Keep talking, Kyle, until I find you. Have you seen Officer Avery?"

"He's here, ma'am, but I think he's hurt bad. I can't get him to move. He's crushing my right leg."

Andrea had pinpointed Kyle's position in the pile, and as she drew closer, she saw a patch of dark blue—the exact color of the standard-issue police uniform she was wearing.

"Are you hurt at all, Kyle?" she asked, the officer in her taking over as she realized the woman in her could no longer face what she might find.

"I don't think so. Except I can't feel my right leg anymore. I think it went to sleep."

Andrea kept Kyle talking while she pulled pieces of drywall from the pile covering them. She wanted so badly to ask if Kyle could tell whether or not Doug was breathing, if he could feel his heartbeat, but she didn't want to alarm the boy.

Andrea couldn't even contemplate the possibility that Doug might be dead. As she pulled and lifted, slowly uncovering his limp body, she could no longer deny that she cared for him—deeply, personally, as a woman cares for a man. At that moment, with Doug's life resting in the balance, the fact that she couldn't get involved didn't occur to her at all.

Sweat was trickling down her back and between her breasts. Her arms ached from lugging the heavy plaster, her throat was clogged with dust and unshed tears, but still she kept plowing through the rubbish.

After she'd lifted a particularly large piece of ceiling panel, Doug's back came into full view. He was frighteningly still. Not moving herself, she stared at him, waiting for any sign of life, willing it to be there. After what seemed an eternity, she was rewarded. There was an ever-so-slight movement. Doug was breathing.

"Officer Parker? Could you hurry? It's getting really stuffy down here."

"I'm almost there, Kyle. Just hold on a couple of seconds longer. Try to put your nose in Officer Avery's shirt. That should help block some of the dust."

She pulled away part of a two-by-four, and then a piece of what looked to be a heating duct. The duct had been resting against Doug's upper body, and by the looks of it, might have protected his head from being crushed by the board.

Andrea found herself noting every little detail with a detachment she would never have believed. She wondered if she was in shock, but kept on working as if she were someone else looking down on the scene, registering every sensation.

"Is everyone else okay?" Kyle's voice was starting to wobble.

"We're all fine, Kyle. The hallway's still completely intact. I can't tell about the rest of the school. We seem to be cut off from everyone else by this cave-in. Hopefully it's the only one."

Gathering her strength, Andrea removed the last piece of constricting rubbish. Doug still didn't move. He didn't even groan. She reached for his pulse, and was reassured to feel it beating strongly against her fingers.

"I have to check him over a little bit before I move him, Kyle. If he's broken anything we could make it much worse if we don't move him properly." She was running her hands up and down Doug's body as she spoke, neglecting to tell the boy that she was looking for signs of a broken neck or back. To move Doug under those conditions could be fatal.

"Please hurry."

"His legs seem to be all right," she said, trying to keep Kyle's mind off his own discomfort. She'd seen something she didn't want the boy to know.

And as soon as Doug was moved, Kyle wouldn't be able to miss the fact that his own leg was twisted grotesquely beneath him. His right leg had not gone to sleep. It was severely broken. She thanked God that Kyle was too numb to feel the pain.

"Officer Parker? Are you there?" The voice came from along the corridor, where she'd left the rest of the class.

"I'm here, Jimmy. I think the danger's over, but we need a paramedic here. Do you think you can get out that side entrance and try to go around the front to get help?"

"Sure thing, ma'am."

"Jimmy?"

"Yeah?" His voice already sounded farther away.

"Take someone with you and *be careful*," she yelled.

"Is . . . is something wrong?" Kyle was starting to cry. Andrea wondered if he was feeling more of his leg than he'd led her to believe.

"Nothing that can't be fixed," she said, hoping she was right. She didn't think Doug's back or neck were broken, but his stillness was frightening. She didn't even want to consider the internal injuries he might have suffered. She just knew that with Kyle's leg the way it was, she couldn't do anything more on her own.

It was only a matter of minutes before she heard someone coming in the side entrance of the building, but they were the longest minutes Andrea had ever lived through. Kyle was sobbing, and Doug remained as still as ever.

"Okay, what've we got here?"

Tears flooded Andrea's eyes when she turned and saw a paramedic crawling across the rubbish toward her.

"Officer Avery's unconscious. The boy beneath him is not."

She saw the paramedic take a quick scan of Kyle's leg. He lifted a handset from his belt and called for a splint.

"Has he moved? Moaned? Anything?" he asked, motioning to Doug.

"No."

"How long has he been here?"

"I don't know for sure. Twenty minutes, maybe."

The paramedic had taken Doug's pulse and blood pressure within seconds. And then his hands flew over his body, probably to determine whether it was advisable to move him.

"I don't think anything's broken, and his blood pressure's good." He reached for his handset again and called for another stretcher and someone to take care of the rest of Doug's students.

Ten minutes later Doug was on his way to the hospital. Andrea rode in the ambulance beside him. She wasn't about to be separated from him until she knew he was going to be all right.

She watched nervously as the driver turned off the highway. The hospital was just around the corner.

"So you finally decided to take me to bed, huh?"

Andrea's head jerked toward the stretcher beside her. Doug's eyes were wide open, gazing up at her with just a touch of the sardonic humor she'd missed these past weeks. *Thank God.*

"H-how do you feel?" she asked. She felt for his pulse, encouraged by its steady strength.

"Like my head got hit by a steamroller."

"Do you hurt anywhere else?" She continued to hold his wrist.

"Everywhere else, I think. But most especially here." He lifted his other hand slowly and dropped it against the fly of his trousers.

She smiled down at him through a haze of relieved tears as she read the message in his eyes. He was going to be all right.

"You can talk to the doctor about that in just a minute."

"I don't think he can help me with this."

The look in his eyes made the past weeks of missing him melt away. She was only sorry it had taken a tornado to bring that look back.

"SO HOW'S KYLE?" Doug asked early that evening. He was half lying across the passenger seat in Andrea's cruiser. He felt like hell, but other than a few stitches, many bruises and a concussion, he was fine. He'd refused to stay in the hospital, and Andrea had refused to take him home to stay by himself. They'd compromised by his agreeing to stay at her place for the night.

"He's going to be all right. They had to do surgery on his leg, but they think it'll heal fine. He'll be playing baseball again by spring."

"Poor little tyke."

"Yeah. He's feeling pretty bad about running off. He says he'll never forgive himself if you don't get better."

"I'll try to call him tomorrow."

"I'm glad. He made a mistake, but don't we all."

Her statement reminded Doug of a thought he'd had right before the world had come crashing down on him. He'd been a fool to think that Andrea wouldn't be able to see him for the man he was rather than the boy he'd been. A woman with as much capacity for caring as she had would surely be able to forgive him for his past mistakes.

"So how'd everybody else do? The doctor said that hallway was the only one with any damage."

"Pretty much so. There were a few broken bones, a few kids needing stitches, but other than Kyle, everyone was treated and released."

"Will they be closing school for a while?" Doug was getting sleepier by the second, but he loved the sound of Andrea's voice. He'd keep her talking as long as he could.

"It's too early to tell, but they think they can use mobile units until the hallway's rebuilt."

"We were lucky," Doug said, hoping his words didn't sound as slurred to her as they did to him.

"Yeah. We were lucky..." He didn't think he'd ever heard that particular tone in her voice before. She sounded so...so personal.

"I'M NOT GOING to throw you out of your bed." Doug insisted. He was swaying on his feet.

"You're not sleeping on the couch. The doctor said you needed to rest."

"He said I have a concussion. He said you have to wake me up every hour all night. What kind of rest is that going to be?"

"You're not sleeping on the couch."

"I'm not taking your bed."

"Doug, please lie down before you fall down."

"Only if you lie down with me."

"I'm not sleeping with you!"

"That's a relief. I'm not sure how good I'd be with a freight train running through my head."

"You know what I meant."

"I know that I'm not getting in that bed until I have your word that you aren't going to go sleep on the couch."

Andrea eyed the armchair in her room. "Okay, I promise. Now will you please lie down?"

"Do you mind if I shuck these first? They're a little dusty." He tugged on the waistband of his uniform trousers.

Andrea blushed, feeling foolish all of a sudden. "Of course."

She turned quickly toward her closet, telling herself to get a grip. She'd been married, for heaven's sake. This wasn't the first time she'd had a man in her bedroom. She thought of the look he'd shot her in the ambulance. Of the fact that he still wanted her.

She heard the rustle of his clothes, the rasp of his zipper, and almost dropped the sweat suit she was reaching for. She remembered that night in the spa, how he'd looked with the water splashing around his thighs. She remembered how affected she'd been by his heavy strength, and thought of that strength touching her, surrounding her, entering—

"You can turn around now. I'm safely tucked in."

She swung around, the sweat suit clutched against her breast. He was tucked in, but not safely. Her bright yellow comforter was pushed down to the end of the double bed. The matching sheet was barely covering his hips. His stomach was naked and darkly sensual, tempting her to forget why she couldn't want a man—any man—like she wanted Doug Avery.

Her gaze traveled slowly upward, until it met the heavy bandage taped to his chest just beneath his collarbone. And the sight of that stark white bandage against his dark chest hair made her remember the reason he was lying in her bed. The man had been battered by half of a school building. She had no business lusting after him. She looked at the scar on his shoulder, the one she'd noticed all those weeks ago in his hotel room. Had that been a result of heroism, too?

THE NIGHT WAS TOO LONG, and yet in some ways not long enough. Andrea hated having to wake Doug every hour just so he could be reminded of how badly his head hurt. She hated to interrupt the sleep he so desperately needed. But she loved having him in her home, in her room, in her bed. *Just for this one night,* she told herself, though without much conviction.

Gloria called after the ten-o'clock news. She'd heard about Andrea's part in the rescue mission and took turns praising her daughter's courage and asking for reassurances that she was indeed uninjured. Andrea did her best to answer her mother's thousands of questions, watching the clock all the while. She finally had to resort to a white lie about needing to use the rest room so she could get off the phone in time to wake Doug again.

She spent the first half of the night in the armchair, like she'd promised herself she would, but by the early hours of the morning, she was just too exhausted to make herself move from Doug's side. With a weary shrug she put her alarm back on her nightstand and crawled in beside him.

SHE WAS UP by the time Doug awoke the next morning, but he knew she'd been there. The last few times she'd had to wake him she'd fallen back to sleep before he had, and he didn't think he'd ever forget the feel of her womanly thighs nudging against him, or her soft breath on the back of his neck. For the first time in his life, the thought of sharing his bed with a woman all night long enticed him.

He looked around her room, seeing in the eclectic decor both sides of the woman he was coming to know. Everything was in place, neat and controlled, but her passion was obvious, too. The room was done completely in yellows—bright, bold, vibrant yellows—from the curtains at the window to the cover on the big, overstuffed armchair. He wondered if there was any possibility of him ever finding out if that armchair was big enough for making love....

But enough was enough. It was time for him to go home. He wanted to make love to Andrea, but there was a lot more between them, and inside him, that was going to have to be settled first. Because he knew that, for the first time since he'd lost his virginity to Cindy Lou, he wasn't going to be able to settle for an hour or two of great sex. If he was going to make love with Andrea, he wanted more than just physical satisfaction. He just didn't know what that "more" was, or whether or not he could ever have it. And he didn't know what the cost would be to him if he couldn't.

ANDREA BATTLED with herself all day Thursday after she dropped Doug off in the sterile studio apartment he called home. There he was, all alone with only a generic tweed couch and a portable TV for company. The doctor had ordered another two days of rest. So who was going to take care of him? Who was going to feed him? Should she take him dinner? Did she dare? Shouldn't she walk away now while she knew she still could? Was she so weak that she couldn't take an injured man a plate of food?

She showed up at his door at four forty-five, carrying two bags of groceries with her including the makings of Gloria's manicotti.

Doug was watching TV when he heard the knock at his door. He jumped up, eager to have someone to talk to even if it was the paperboy, and then had to stop a minute to let the stars clear from before his eyes.

"I thought you might like some dinner," Andrea said, as soon as she opened the door.

Doug smiled at her. He couldn't help it. She looked so damned cute standing there like she'd been caught looting the principal's office. She was still wearing the uniform she'd had on when she'd dropped him off that morning, he realized as he led her to his small kitchen.

"I'd planned on eating," he told her.

"Then maybe you can show me where your pans are."

That stopped him. "You're cooking?"

"Unless you want to eat raw pasta."

He didn't know which was better, the novelty of having someone cooking for him or the aromas that were soon drifting around his one-room apartment. He turned off the television and sat at his old formica table while she worked, content just to watch her.

"Where'd you learn to do that?" he asked as she whipped up a batch of sausage meatballs.

Andrea grinned at him over her shoulder. "My mom. I learned how to be a wife before I learned how to read."

Her words slammed into him. Had she been anyone else but Andrea, Doug would have read her comment as a hint, and she'd have been out of there so quickly her head would have been spinning. But with Andrea he knew better. With her, he almost *wished* it had been a hint. *The concussion must still be screwing up my head,* he thought wryly.

"You didn't have to do this. But thanks," he said as she sat down across from him, passing him a plate of pasta. No one had ever eaten with him in his apartment before.

She looked up from the salad she'd been dressing, meeting his gaze, smiling that smile that lodged someplace deep inside of him. "I wanted to."

Dropping his eyes from hers, he picked up his fork. "So how was school today?"

"Fine. The kids were full of questions. They'd heard about the tornado on the news."

"You didn't tell them I passed out on one of my students, did you?"

"No. And you didn't pass out. You were knocked out."

"Yeah, well. Same thing." Doug applied himself to his pasta.

"We did your role-playing exercise," she said a couple of minutes later.

"Yeah?" He was kind of surprised that she'd followed his lesson plan. After all, he was just a rookie—she was the pro. "How'd it go?"

"Did you know that drinking alcohol could make you pregnant?"

Doug choked on his ice water. "What?"

Andrea laughed. "Just think how I felt when I heard that one, sitting there with twenty-six intent faces gazing up at me."

"Did you, uh, correct the assumption?" he asked.

"I started to."

"You *started* to?" Doug was smiling now, too. He could just picture it, Andrea all prim and in control in front of a classroom full of blooming adolescents. He sure as hell was glad it hadn't been him.

"Well, it seems that if you drink, you're more apt to let a boy, *you* know, and you're also less likely to be thinking about what time of the month it might be, or whether or not there would be any consequences...."

Doug laughed outright. "So, would you like some wine?" he asked, sending her a suggestive smile.

"I'm not allowed to drink on school nights...."

Andrea stayed until almost nine o'clock. They had the dessert she'd brought, and then did the dishes together. Doug was almost falling asleep on his feet by the time she said good-night, but he felt better than he could ever remember feeling.

He'd been tempted to kiss her good-night, to see if he could convince her to stay. But he still wasn't feeling so hot, and he didn't want to start something he couldn't finish. At least, that's what he told himself as he locked his door behind her. It was easier to believe that than to wonder if he might have just been too chicken to risk rejection.

ANDREA WAS TEMPTED to use the tornado as an excuse to miss the mystery-weekend adventure with Mark, but it was precisely because she was so tempted that she didn't. She was afraid that if she wasn't safely tucked away with Mark in Cincinnati, she might be tempted to take dinner to Doug on Friday night, and that he'd be feeling good enough to...

She arranged to meet Mark at her mother's house. He'd be bringing the boys over anyway, so it seemed like a logical choice. It had nothing to do with the fact that she didn't want another man in her apartment so soon after Doug had been there.

"Did you pack a nice dress?" Gloria asked as soon as Andrea walked in the door Friday afternoon.

"The black one I wore to the Christmas party. Will that do?"

"Yeah. You looked good in it," Gloria said, leading the way back to the kitchen. She was baking chocolate-chip cookies for her little houseguests-to-be.

"How's Scotty doing?" Andrea asked. She leaned over to snitch a fingerful of cookie dough.

"He got an *A* on his science project."

"Yeah? What'd he make?"

"I'm not sure what it was, but the teacher was impressed. It had lights and wires and did things."

Andrea laughed. "Not like the moldy bread I used for my project, huh?"

"Thank God," Gloria said with a chuckle.

The backdoor rattled, and footsteps sounded from the laundry room. Andrea looked up, expecting to finally get a glimpse of the man she was going away with for the weekend.

But the body that filled the kitchen doorway was not that of a man.

"Oh. Sorry. I'll be out in the garage."

Andrea told herself she wouldn't cry. She swallowed. She blinked. She took a deep breath. A tear fell anyway, trickling slowly down her cheek.

Gloria watched as her teenaged son turned abruptly and left, then she hurried around the counter to take her daughter in her arms.

"He doesn't mean to hurt you, Andi. He's just so ashamed."

"He hates me, Ma. But it's okay. I don't blame him. Sometimes I hate me too." She gave her mother a squeeze and then pulled away, reaching for a tissue from the box on the counter.

His sandy blond hair was longer, he'd gotten new glasses and he'd grown a couple of inches—he looked great. Until he'd seen Andrea, that was. Until the sullen look she'd become accustomed to over the past four years had tightened his features again.

Still, she was glad she'd been there. She hadn't seen her baby brother in almost a year. She was desperate enough to take what she could get.

CHAPTER ELEVEN

MARK WAS GORGEOUS. He was tall and tanned, with light brown hair that was thick and full. He had stunning blue eyes. He wasn't embarrassed about kissing his kids goodbye, yet he walked with enough of a swagger to proclaim his healthy male ego. He was charming and witty, he listened, he had interesting things to say. He was intelligent. He was successful.

He wasn't Doug.

Andrea knew five minutes after she'd gotten into Mark's Explorer that he was everything she could have hoped for. More than that, she liked him. But it still wasn't going to work. He didn't take her mind off Doug.

And she needed that more than ever now. Seeing Scotty had been as painful as it had been wonderful. It had been a powerful reminder to her of why she was alone, why she had to stay alone. She tended to lose perspective when she loved. And she'd caused enough pain, been hurt enough, for one lifetime.

"THE ONLY TWO ROOMS they had left were adjoining, but I want it understood right from the beginning that I don't expect you to unlock the connecting door—not unless you want to, that is," Mark said as they arrived at the hostel. They had an hour to unpack before all the weekend's participants had to meet in the lounge for the revealing of the crime.

"I'll keep that in mind," Andrea said, taking her key from her handsome companion. She would, too. Maybe she wasn't giving Mark enough of a chance. Maybe if she allowed him to kiss her, to touch her, the memory of Doug's heat might be obliterated from her heart.

And maybe pigs can fly, Andrea thought late that night. She'd held Mark's hand. She'd cuddled up to him a little bit in the elevator. She'd flirted with him. She'd even welcomed his good-night kiss. And she felt like trash. She felt like she was being unfaithful, like she was tarnishing something valuable. She'd never felt so alone in her life. She lay in bed, curled into a ball, and wondered what Doug had had for dinner.

ANDREA WAS UP EARLY Saturday morning, and rather than disturb Mark, who rarely had a chance to lie in bed in the morning, she dressed and went sleuthing. By midmorning she was pretty sure who'd "dun it," but after sharing breakfast with the woman she'd been interrogating, she decided to keep her suspicions to herself.

Amy was a charming young woman, an interior decorator who'd lost her husband in a boating accident the year before. But she'd reached the point where she had to live again, and the mystery weekend was her first attempt to meet new people.

"How'd you like to meet a wonderful man?" Andrea asked Amy as the two women walked down to the lake behind the hostel after breakfast.

Amy laughed. "Who wouldn't?"

"No, really. I mean it. I can introduce you to him if you'd like."

"You don't mean that gorgeous hunk I saw you get in the elevator with last night, do you?"

"He is hunk-of-the-month material, isn't he?" Andrea mused. What was wrong with her? She was throwing away a perfect date.

"I only saw him from behind, but what I saw was pretty spectacular. How come you're not—I mean, didn't you two come together?"

"He's my mother's next-door neighbor. He's a great guy, but really, we're just friends. You wanna meet him?" Andrea hoped her mother's telepathy was on the blink. Otherwise she could expect a lightning bolt from heaven to strike her at any moment.

"If you're sure you don't mind." The petite brunette smiled, losing some of the shadows that were haunting her lovely eyes.

GLORIA DROPPED Scotty off at Lizzie's house with an impatient wave and a promise to return in time to take the two of them to play miniature golf that evening.

She pulled her car out into the street, turning in the direction of home, just in case he was watching, and then did an illegal U-turn in the next block. She knew her family was not going to approve of where she was going. But there were some things a mother just had to do. And one of them was to listen to her instincts. Gloria's were screaming loud and clear.

She pulled the newspaper article out of the pocket of her shapeless shift, looked at the picture again and returned it to its place for safekeeping. The photographer had captured a miracle. Andrea's face was filled with longing, with love, with worry, as she gazed at the man being pulled from the rubbish and placed on a stretcher. It was the same man she'd been looking at during the DARE culmination breakfast. His name was Doug Avery.

Gloria found his apartment with only one wrong turn, pulled into the visitors' parking area and picked up the homemade brownies from the seat beside her. She'd never met a man yet who didn't like her brownies.

He answered on her first knock. "Can I help you?"

He was wearing black sweats that had been cut off at midthigh and a black T-shirt. His feet were bare, his hair rumpled and his face looked like it hadn't seen a razor since the tornado. Gloria eyed the silver-studded, black leather wristband for a moment and then met the man's eyes. That's when she fell in love.

"I think so. May I come in?"

ANDREA HAD BUTTERFLIES as she entered the hostel dining room with Mark at her side. What if he and Amy hated each other on sight? Maybe she should have left well enough alone. Just then Amy spotted her—it was too late to change her mind.

"Mark, this is Amy. Amy, Mark," she said, stopping beside Amy's table.

"Mark Bishop?"

"Amy Jordon?"

"You two know each other?"

"I can't believe it's you. You look great!"

"So do you!"

"How long have you two known each other?"

"What happened to Sharry? I thought you two'd be married long ago by now."

"We were. We're divorced."

"I can't believe you two know each other."

"I heard about Danny. I'm sorry, Amy. Really sorry."

"Me too. He was the greatest. But I gotta go on, you know?"

Andrea looked from Amy to Mark and back again. They were looking at each other like they'd each won the lottery. They'd forgotten she was even there.

She backed away from the table, excused herself to their waitress and headed for the coffee shop across the street. Matchmaking was a funny business. She was happy for her two friends, and lonelier than she could ever remember being.

"I'M WORRIED ABOUT my daughter."

Doug didn't know what to make of the large woman sitting on the other end of his couch, claiming she was Andrea's mother.

"From what I've seen, she's perfectly capable of taking care of herself," he said.

The big woman harrumphed. "I know my daughter, young man. I know when to worry."

Doug shook his head, wondering if he was going to wake up soon. Maybe he was having another concussion.

"So why are you telling me about it?" he asked.

"Because I think you care."

"What ever gave you that idea?" he asked angrily. This woman hadn't even met him until today. How could she possibly know something about him that he didn't even know himself? What right did she have to barge into his house and accuse him of things?

"You telling me you don't?" She glared at him with eyes that were exact replicas of Andrea's.

Doug opened his mouth to tell her just how wrong she was, but he couldn't lie to those eyes.

"That's what I thought," she said when he remained silent.

"Why do I get the feeling Andrea wouldn't approve of you being here?" he queried, trying to make sense of it himself. He wasn't sure why he didn't just ask the woman to leave and be done with it.

"Because you're smarter than you look. Now listen. My daughter's been through hell and back, except she can't quite seem to make it back. She used to argue with me all the time, quite well, I might add. Now all I ever get is 'Yes, Ma,' 'No, Ma'."

Doug's head was spinning, and he was pretty sure it wasn't from the bump he'd received. "You're worried because your daughter won't argue with you?"

"I'm worried because she's not happy. That jerk she married walked out on her at a time when she really needed him. Now even her tears are without passion.

She just lets them fall, doesn't sob like she used to. She doesn't feel things like she used to. There's no fire.''

Was he getting this right? The problem was that Andrea didn't cry properly?

"Uh, where do I fit into all this?" he asked, not sure he wanted to know.

"She's all shut away. I think you might be able to get her out."

Doug wasn't sure the woman wasn't just plain crazy. "Why me?"

"Because Andrea's never mentioned you...."

ANDREA SPOTTED DOUG as she hurried across the parking lot after school on Tuesday. He was heading her way. She walked faster. He walked faster.

"Have dinner with me tonight."

"I'm sorry, Doug, I can't," she said, trying to get to her car before she gave in. She'd only been back in town two days and already she was losing focus.

"Why not? I owe you one. You gotta let a guy pay his debts." He followed her to her cruiser, holding on to the door as she got inside and tried to shut it.

"You said that last night."

"Yeah, and you said you had plans."

"I did have plans."

"But you don't tonight, do you?" His arms were draped over the top of the door and the roof of her car as he leaned in toward her.

Doug Avery in small doses she could resist. Having him filling the interior of her car was another matter.

"If I have dinner this once, will you consider the debt paid and quit bugging me?"

He smiled that wicked smile that went straight to her belly. "Am I bugging you?" he asked.

"Doug." She drew out his name in warning.

"Okay. You have my word. I'll stop harassing you about who owes who what."

Andrea knew that his concession was a far cry from what she'd asked. But he looked so vulnerable suddenly as he stood there waiting for her answer.

"Okay, I'll have dinner with you. Where do you want to meet?"

"I'll pick you up at seven," he said, swinging her door shut and striding away before she could suggest an alternative.

For a man whose posture was lazy at best, he sure could move quickly when he wanted to. Andrea smiled, and knew she was in deep trouble.

DOUG WAS ALMOST HOME when he saw the grubby blond boy coming out of a 7-Eleven. Jeremy Schwartz. Slowing his car, he watched as the boy walked away alone, huddled in against himself, his hands shoved deeply into the pockets of his oversize pants. He'd bet there was contraband in those pockets. He'd bet his life on it.

And he'd bet it wasn't chewing gum or candy, either. It was probably peanuts. They were small, easy to conceal and full of protein. They didn't cause aches on an empty stomach.

Or it could have been cigarettes. They were necessary for other reasons.

Doug followed the boy at a discreet distance until Jeremy cut through a couple of yards and hopped a fence. He still wouldn't have lost him if he'd been willing to risk exposure. But he didn't want the boy to know he'd seen him. He didn't want to make him any more defensive than he already was. He wanted Jeremy to trust him.

DOUG TOOK ANDREA to One Nation for dinner. Set on the top floor of the tallest building in Columbus, the revolving restaurant afforded an incredible view. The atmosphere and the food came in a close second. Doug wasn't sure how many chances he was going to get with her, so he wasn't taking any chances. He'd even put on a tie with his white oxford shirt and Dockers.

"Tell me about your ex," he said as he poured them each a glass of wine from the bottle of chardonnay he'd ordered.

She shrugged and looked out the window beside their table. "There's not much to tell. We wanted different things."

A week ago Doug might have believed her.

"What things?"

"I wanted to be a cop. He didn't want it." She was wearing a teal blue cotton top and miniskirt. The rich color was reflected in her eyes.

"So why'd you marry him?" That was one of the questions Gloria hadn't answered.

Andrea took a sip of her wine, studying the golden liquid as if life's answers floated there. "We were high-school sweethearts. I couldn't imagine not marrying him. We were married for almost a year before I knew I wanted to enter the academy."

"Was he against it from the beginning, or just after he got a taste of the life?"

"From the beginning." She smiled sadly. "I loved him enough to give him the world. I thought he loved me enough to come around once he saw how much police work meant to me."

"When did you know it wasn't going to happen?"

Doug would never have asked if he didn't sense that her answer was a critical one. He'd done a lot of thinking after Gloria had left the other day, and he figured that if he was ever going to have a chance with Andrea, she was going to have to deal with whatever had happened in her past.

Being a cop himself, Doug was pretty certain that she must have had a case go bad, that she must have been questioning her ability, as any good cop does at such a time. And that her husband, instead of standing beside her, had deserted her.

Andrea didn't answer his question. She swirled the wine in her glass. She took a sip.

"What happened?" Doug asked softly. He slouched down in his seat, resting his forearms on the edge of the table.

He still wasn't sure he was what Andrea needed. He still wasn't sure she'd be able to forgive him his past. But for some reason it was important to him that she live again, that she be happy.

"I made a mistake," she finally said softly. "A big one. He blamed me. He told me either I give up being a cop or he'd leave."

"The bastard," Doug said. He didn't realize how forcefully he'd said the word until she glanced up and smiled at him.

How could any man who'd had this woman have left her? he wondered. How could he have left that damn smile?

Andrea watched the expressions chase themselves across Doug's face. Just knowing he was on her side made her feel better.

"How come you've never married?" she asked. It was something that she'd been wondering about a lot lately.

Doug shrugged, running his index finger up and down the stem of his wineglass. "It never seemed like the thing to do."

His vague answer frustrated her.

"Haven't you ever been in love?"

He grinned at her over his glass. "What is this, twenty questions?"

Andrea gave up. He wasn't going to answer her. She'd had enough experience as his mentor to know that Doug Avery was a master at prevarication.

Doug knew he'd disappointed her. He set out to be his most charming as they ordered lobster for dinner and laughed over his bungled attempts to eat it. He never should have asked those questions about her personal life. He had no business courting confidences he wasn't going to return. He was just going to have to find some other way to reach her.

"You going to invite me in for coffee?" he asked as he walked her to the door of her apartment later that evening.

"You don't drink coffee."

He'd forgotten that he'd told her that the morning after the tornado.

"I know."

He trailed his fingers up her forearm as she reached to unlock her door.

"No, Doug."

She opened her door just enough for her to slip inside. Doug stopped her as soon as he realized that that was just what she intended to do. He pulled her against him, fitting her thighs in between his, molding her breasts to his chest. He lowered his mouth to hers before she could work up another protest.

Her response was instantaneous and hot, just like the last time he'd held her. She met him thrust for thrust, as if she'd been waiting all night for him to touch her, as if she hadn't just rejected him seconds before. She gave him a taste of the passion he suspected she was keeping bottled up tightly inside herself, and Doug knew that he was in danger of becoming an addict again. But this time he wasn't so sure about his chances of drying out.

And then, just as he was about to take her in to her bed, to finish what they had started two months ago, he found himself standing alone at her door. She'd pushed away from him so fast he'd hardly known what was happening. She was inside before he could figure out a way to get her back in his arms. He heard her dead bolt click and knew that he'd had all of her he was going to get that night. *Damn!*

DOUG SOUGHT JEREMY OUT on the playground that next Monday. DARE officers were encouraged to mingle with the kids during their lunch and recess times, and Jeremy was one kid Doug was becoming more and more eager to mingle with.

"How about a little one-on-one?" Doug asked, bouncing a basketball toward the kid.

Jeremy looked at him out of eyes that were cynical enough to belong to a fifty-year-old man. He didn't even bother to comment. He just turned and walked away.

Doug followed him.

"Hey. I asked you a question. You didn't answer," he said, falling in step with the boy. The basketball was lodged between his forearm and his side.

"*I* didn't ask for no do-goodin', man. Lay off."

"Yeah. I guess you didn't."

Doug continued to walk beside the boy, hoping the kid would say something. Anything. Even cussing him out would be better than this wall of silence.

"You haven't done any of your reports," Doug finally said. If the kid wasn't going to talk, he would do what he could to get a rise out of him. He saw too much of himself in Jeremy to just let the kid slip away.

"Get real, man. Like some damn report's gonna make any difference."

"It could." Doug cursed himself for sounding like a cop.

"Yeah, and I could join the Boy Scouts if I wanted to, right?"

The bell rang, signaling the end of recess, and Jeremy took off like a shot, heading toward the school.

But even then, Doug noticed that he was the last one
to go inside. The kid always kept his back covered. If
he was last in line, there was no one behind him, no
one who could be stabbing him. Doug nodded his
head. He understood. He was always last in a line
himself.

Andrea watched Doug from across the playground. She saw him approach Jeremy, saw Jeremy
turn away and saw Doug go after him. She held her
breath, hardly daring to believe what she was seeing.
Doug was reaching out, on his own, without being re-
quired to do so.

She watched as the man and the boy walked together across the field, their hands in their pockets.
And her heart split in two when Jeremy turned and ran
away from Doug.

And that's when Andrea knew for certain that she
was irrevocably in love with Doug Avery. It tore her up
to think of him risking his heart and being rejected.
She wanted to wring that boy's neck. For the first time
in four years, Andrea's kids weren't coming first.

But, somehow, they were going to have to be
enough. Because just as Andrea knew she loved Doug,
she knew she couldn't handle the responsibility of that
love.

ANDREA'S PHONE RANG late the following Friday
night. She wasn't in the mood to talk to anyone, especially not her mother. She reached for the receiver
after the eighth ring.

"Hello?"

"Hi."

She sat up. Doug? Why was he calling her? "Is something wrong?"

"I need your help."

"Sure. What can I do for you?"

"I'm going to Stan's house tomorrow night for dinner. I need you to come with me."

Andrea wanted to say yes, and the word almost slipped out.

"Why?"

"Because if you don't, they're going to ask Myra's sister to make up a fourth."

Andrea told herself she couldn't go. There just wasn't any point.

"Who's Myra?"

"Stan's wife. Ever met her?"

She smiled at his aggrieved tone, curling her toes underneath the covers. "Nope. I've only met Stan once."

"Myra's a real sweet woman, she's a good wife, but she's about as meek as they come. Except for her sister, of course. She's even worse."

"You've met Myra's sister?"

"Twice. And I scared her to death both times."

Andrea grinned again. "I can see your dilemma. Why not just make up some excuse not to go?"

Doug grunted, sounding frustrated. "I can't do that to Stan."

His response surprised her. It sounded like he had some kind of commitment to Stan Ingersoll other than just a former working relationship. She hadn't thought Doug had ties with anyone.

"Why not?"

"Because he asked me to come, that's why. Please say you'll come, Andrea. It's only dinner."

"Okay. I'll come."

Maybe, as Doug's training officer, she should observe his relationship with the man who inspired such fierce loyalty in him. And maybe she was just too weak to say no.

"STAN COMES ON a little gruff at times, but he's really a good guy," Doug said the next evening as they approached the door of Stan's Tudor-style, two-story house.

"Like someone else I know?"

Doug looked down at her, taking in the grin that was spreading across her face, appreciating the figure-molding bodysuit she had on underneath her thigh-length jacket. She was dressed in his favorite color, all black, and it looked great against her soft white skin and perky blond hair. He figured he was feeling good enough to let her comment pass.

Andrea liked Stan and Myra. They welcomed her into their home as if she was a visiting dignitary. And Doug they treated like a son.

"You gonna help me with all the ladies again this year, Doug?" Stan asked, spooning himself a second serving of potatoes.

"I'm always eager to take ladies off your hands, Stan, you know that," Doug said with a cocky grin.

"You boys stop right now," Myra piped up from her side of the table. "They helped several of the ladies at church unload their cars last year at the bazaar," she explained to Andrea.

Andrea watched enviously as Myra attempted to send her husband a chastising look across the table. Somehow, by the time it reached Stan, it had changed into a smile that promised private retribution at a more appropriate time. They both looked like they were looking forward to it.

Doug leaned over the corner of the table. "You look gorgeous tonight," he whispered in Andrea's ear.

Andrea blushed, thankful that her host and hostess were otherwise engaged. "Behave," she said as sternly as she could manage under her breath.

"Doug tells me you gave him a hard time down at the Hetherington Hotel," Stan said later that evening while they all nursed after-dinner coffee.

"Did he also tell you he fell asleep during my first session?" she asked, taking a sip of her coffee. She'd teach Doug Avery to mess with her.

"Yep. He did at that. He also told me you did one hell of a good job getting him in shape to hit the schools. He was really sweating that one."

Andrea sent Doug a surprised glance. He'd *talked* to Stan? She'd thought details about Doug Avery's life, his inner musings, were strictly off-limits.

"And if you say any more, Stan, my man, you'd best be taking your gun to bed with you tonight."

Now that sounded more like the Doug she knew.

"So you guys've known each other a long time?" she asked Stan. She wasn't giving up yet.

"Ever since I stumbled on this punk in—"

"Long enough." Doug cut him off, pushing away from the table. "It's getting late and I promised Andrea I'd have her home early," he said stiffly.

Andrea thanked the Ingersolls for a wonderful evening and followed Doug out to his car. She was silent as he drove her home and left her with just a brief kiss. She couldn't help wondering what it was that Stan had been about to say—what it was Doug didn't want her to know. She wondered if she'd ever find out.

THE NEXT WEEKEND Doug managed to talk Andrea into a drive-in movie. He congratulated himself on a near-victory. She was becoming easy. He'd be making love to her before the month was out.

The movie was billed as a drama and rated for teenage viewing, but the heat emanating from the screen had Doug squirming in his seat long before the film was over. Tom Cruise was gazing at the woman lying in his arms as if he could barely restrain himself from devouring her. Her look was innocent and hungry at the same time.

Andrea sat next to Doug, with a full two feet separating them, chewing on popcorn. Her eyes were riveted to the screen. She seemed indifferent to his presence in the car. So much for his near-victory.

Or so Doug thought. The first time she glanced his way, he figured she was just checking to see if he was enjoying the movie. The second time she could have been looking to see if he needed more popcorn. By the third time, it dawned on him that she wasn't as immune to him as she appeared.

"Come here," he said, pulling her across the seat. He put his arm around her shoulders and moved his leg until it was flush with hers. His denim rasped against hers.

"Aren't we a little old for this?" she asked half-heartedly. Her eyes were still trained on the screen, but she didn't make any effort to move away from him.

Doug decided not to push his luck with an answer.

He turned his eyes back to the screen in front of him, but try as he might, he couldn't concentrate on the movie they'd come to see. He was too aware of the woman sitting next to him. She was wearing white jeans and a purple pullover sweater that outlined her full breasts to perfection. He ached to touch them.

She moved. Just a fraction of an inch. Just enough to rest the side of her hand against his thigh.

He tried to adjust his swelling penis into a less uncomfortable position.

She ran the tips of her fingers along the side of his thigh, so lightly he could barely feel the movement, and it was as if he'd had the breath knocked out of him. In answer, he trailed his fingers from her shoulder to her neck and up into her hair. He loved the way the strands of her hair slid through his fingers, almost like a caress.

Andrea's gaze was still glued to the screen, but she tilted her head, moving into his touch like a cat looking for a reason to purr.

Doug lowered his head to her neck, running his tongue along the side she'd exposed, nipping her gently just above her collarbone. She smelled like roses and woman. He reached down to unbutton the fastener at the top of his jeans, giving himself just a little more room.

Andrea still held the carton of popcorn on her lap, but she'd stopped eating. She was clutching it against

her like it was all that held her together, all that held
her apart from Doug.

He touched her breast, palming it gently, stroking
it with the pad of his thumb. Her nipple hardened almost instantly. Andrea moaned, sliding down until her
head rested against the back of the seat. Her eyes were
still on the movie.

He turned in the seat, cupping her other breast. A
torrent of liquid heat built up inside of him, uncon-
trollably, as his fantasies finally took form and shape.
He'd waited too long for her. His body was done
waiting.

Her lips parted as her breathing quickened and he
leaned over, opening his mouth over hers, sliding his
tongue inside of her. He'd lost all track of time, of
space, of where they were. All that mattered now was
his pulsing body and the release it craved. All he asked
for was that Andrea need him as badly as he needed
her.

Her popcorn spilled all over the floor of his car as
she reached up and wrapped both of her arms around
his neck. She gave him kiss for kiss, wantonly mating
her tongue with his, pressing her breasts more firmly
into his grasp.

Doug slid his hand beneath her sweater, shaking
with his eagerness to know her more completely. He'd
been dreaming of her for so long he could hardly believe he was finally touching her—that she was welcoming his touch. That she was touching...

"Oh baby," he groaned against her lips, lifting his
hips up as Andrea's hand pressed against the fly of his
jeans. He was so full he ached, but her gentle touch

brought such sweet pain he knew he'd rather die than stop her. She molded her hand to the length of him, squeezing him as he thrust against her. He felt his passion building, nearing its peak.

"Stop," he said, holding her hand still against him. "Not here. Not like this. Let's go home. I don't want to take this trip alone."

Andrea pulled her hand back, clenching it together with the free hand in her lap. She scooted over on the seat—not very far, but much too far.

"What? What's wrong?" Doug asked. He was going to lose his mind if she turned away from him now.

"I can't, Doug."

"What do you mean, you can't?"

"I just can't. It wouldn't be fair. To either of us."

"Fair? It wouldn't be fair? My cock's so hard I'm about to lose my mind, and you call that fair?"

"Look, I'm sorry. I know I was wrong to let things get so out of hand. I just wanted to make you feel good. I guess I got carried away."

"You got carried away? You haven't even begun to get carried away, baby. That I can promise you."

"I can't start anything with you, Doug."

"You gonna tell me why not?"

"I tried this before, and I screwed up badly. I can't go through it again. I can't be responsible for putting you through it. I've already hurt two people I've loved."

"You can't just turn your back and walk away, Andrea."

"Please don't ask me to do this, Doug. You could talk me into it with very little effort, but I know I'd regret it."

Doug sat in his seat, his arms folded across his chest, focusing on the screen in front of him. He had to get home, to take a cold shower, before his frustration made him say something he'd regret. This was not just about sex. Somewhere along the way Andrea had become his friend. And he had precious few of those, too few to want to lose one over a little pain in his groin.

"Then what was this?" he asked, wishing he didn't need so badly to know.

"It was—it was...you turn me on, Doug. More than anyone ever has in my life...." He started to reach for her again, but she slid over to the other side of the seat. "But I also care about you, too much to make either of us into a one-night stand."

Her words made no sense. "And you think that's what we'd be?"

"It's what we'd have to be. I'm not open to any other possibilities."

"So what now? We just stop wanting each other? We just ignore what being together does to us?"

"I don't think we have any other choice."

Doug looked over at her, at the determination in her eyes, at the fear she probably didn't even know was there. He was afraid to push her. He was afraid she'd never want to see him again.

He reached for his keys, started the car and drove her home, leaving her with a tender but chaste goodnight kiss. He thought of the way Gloria had de-

scribed her daughter before her divorce, how lively
Andrea must have been then, how full of brimstone.
And he vowed that someday, somehow, he would have
that woman in his bed.

CHAPTER TWELVE

DOUG SAT IN HIS CAR thinking about Andrea as he waited for Jeremy Schwartz after school one Monday, about ten weeks into his first semester as a DARE officer. He wondered what he could do to get Andrea to take a chance on life again. If there was anything he *could* do.

The school buses had long since left, and the after-school crowd of kids dispersed by the time Jeremy sauntered outside. His ratty jean-jacket was slung over one shoulder, and he wasn't carrying any books. He glanced around and then crossed the playground, heading out behind the school.

Doug got out of his car, shutting the door quietly behind him, and carefully followed the skinny blond boy. Jeremy cut through a couple of yards and turned into an alley a few blocks from the school. Doug kept a discreet distance as he headed down the alley after Jeremy, ducking behind dumpsters anytime the boy turned around. He didn't blame Jeremy for keeping his back covered. The neighborhood on the other side of the alley wasn't anything like the one they'd just left behind.

It still amazed Doug how quickly the scenery could change. How strange it was that the children of successful businessmen played with relative safety on their fresh green lawns just one block away from some of the city's worst squalor.

Jeremy reached the end of the alley and headed up a street that hadn't seen grass in at least a decade. Doug followed him.

"Jer'my, how ya doin', boy?" a drunk called out from the doorway of a vacant building.

"Just cheesy, Butch, just cheesy." Doug heard the sarcasm in the boy's voice even if the drunk didn't.

Jeremy walked on, nodding to some of the people he passed, avoiding others, until he came to another alley. It was deserted except for the overflowing trash bin that sat there. The boy dropped his jacket, approached the trash bin and weeded through it, coming up with an open coffee can. He set the can high on top of the pile of trash and backed up about eight feet. He bent down, picked up a rock, adopted a perfect basketball stance and shot the rock straight into the coffee can. Doug listened as four more rocks, one after the other, clinked into the can.

Jeremy continued shooting rock after rock, changing his stance, his angle, his distance from the can. And stone after stone met its mark with uncanny precision. Doug was impressed as much by his determination as by his talent.

He finally had a way to reach the boy, maybe even to help him. Doug walked out into the alley, picked up a rock of his own and lobbed it toward the can.

As the rock flew by him, Jeremy jerked, swung around and reached for the knife that was hidden at his waist.

Doug held both hands up and away from his body. "Hold on there, guy. I was just about to suggest a game of one-on-one at the Y, nothing else."

Jeremy lowered the knife, but his defensive, belligerent expression didn't change. He spat at Doug's feet.

"Get lost, cop."

Doug studied the boy for another couple of seconds, then turned around and left.

ANDREA PEDALED FURIOUSLY, barely listening to the news blaring from her television set as she tried to work off images of Doug in her apartment, looking so out of place at her glass-and-brass kitchen table, filling her living room with energy even when he was suffering from a concussion, lying in her bed, his bare chest—

Her doorbell rang, saving Andrea from following where her thoughts were trying to lead her. She slid off her exercise bike, panting heavily, pretending that her lack of air was due entirely to exertion from her physical workout.

She looked through her peephole, and was actually glad to see her mother standing on her doorstep with a package under her arm.

"Hi, Ma!" she said, flinging open the door. "Come on in."

Gloria frowned, peering closely at Andrea. "You okay?" she asked.

Andrea took her mother's free arm, dragging her into the living room. "I'm fine, Ma. Really. I was just riding my bike."

Gloria frowned again as she glanced over at the exercise bike in Andrea's living room.

"It's not right, making your living room look like a gym. How's a man supposed to relax after a hard day's work with that thing staring him in the face?"

"So what man's gonna be relaxing in my living room?"

Gloria harrumphed. "My point exactly."

Andrea refused to rise to the bait. She didn't have the energy to fight both the world and her mother.

"I bought these for you today. They were on sale," Gloria said, handing Andrea the package she'd brought.

Andrea opened the bag hesitantly, knowing better than to get too excited. The last time Gloria had found a sale, it had been on the laciest, skimpiest teddies Andrea had ever seen. Her mother had bought seven of them. They were in one of Andrea's dresser drawers with the tags still on.

"Ma! They're beautiful!"

Andrea held up the oversize cotton shirt and leggings her mother had brought. They were black, with tiny silver studs outlining a striking leafy design from the right shoulder to the left ankle. It was an outfit Andrea would have bought for herself in an instant if she'd been able to afford it.

It reminded her of Doug, of the silver-studded wristband he never took off.

Gloria was running her finger along Andrea's coffee table, checking for dust.

"I did it yesterday," Andrea said. "Ma, they weren't on sale, were they?"

"It's not polite to ask the price of a gift, Andrea."

Andrea walked over to her mother, wrapping her arms around Gloria's ample girth. "Thanks, Ma."

"Mark and Amy are getting married."

Andrea pulled back from her mother, too excited for her new friends to care about the accusation in Gloria's words. "They are? That's wonderful! When?"

"They haven't set a date yet, but it'll be soon, I'm sure. Someday you're going to have to try it again, Andrea. I'd hoped it was going to be Mark, but just because it isn't doesn't mean the show's over you know."

"There's no law that says a woman has to be married, Ma."

"You're not happy alone."

"I'm happier alone than when I was married."

"But that's because you married the wrong guy."

"I don't want to discuss this anymore, Ma."

"Isn't there anyone, Andrea? Anyone who makes your knees just the least bit wobbly when you think about him?"

Andrea had passed the stage of wobbly knees weeks ago. She was into hot flashes and heart palpitations these days. "Nope."

"No one, Andrea? Are you sure? You always went for dark hair. Don't you know anyone with dark hair? Or what about eyes? All the guys you ever dated had brown eyes. Surely you can think of someone who attracts you?"

The image of Doug in her bed came back to haunt Andrea. If only Gloria knew how close she was....

"No, Ma. I don't. Now just leave it alone."

Gloria studied her, seeming to come to some decision.

"I'll leave it alone if you'll agree to meet Mabel Stewart's brother. He's moving to Columbus and he's staying with her while he looks for a place to live."

"Mabel Stewart from the supermarket? She's your age, Ma! You want me to go out with someone your age?"

"He's her step-brother from her mother's second marriage. He's younger than she is. He works at the supermarket, too."

"How much younger is he?"

Gloria looked away, straightening a pillow on Andrea's couch. "Years younger. Believe me, Andrea, Blake isn't too old for you. He's a really nice young man, takes the time to help all the old ladies at the market. And he's gorgeous, too. He's got this thick head of brown hair and a body that all the ladies talk about."

Andrea was tempted. Here was an opportunity to prove to herself that Doug didn't have any hold on her. "No, Ma. You know I don't go in for blind dates."

"But I already told him you would, Andrea. I'll never be able to show my face at the market again if you don't at least see him once. Come on, Andrea. What's one dinner?"

Doug's image popped up in front of Andrea's eyes again. His big brown eyes were half-closed, hazy with desire, and the sheet had slipped so low on his hips it might as well not even have been there at all....

"Okay, Ma. I'll go." *I'll prove once and for all that Doug's kisses aren't the only ones that make me so desperately hungry....*

DOUG WENT to school early the following Monday. He entered the gym, calling out for Rich Peterson, the junior-high basketball coach. Rich doubled as the elementary gym teacher on Mondays. Doug had met him in the lunchroom several weeks before.

"Back here." The words came from a little office at the side of the gym. Doug headed in that direction.

"Officer Avery," Peterson said when he spotted Doug, and he got up from behind his desk to shake his hand.

"Call me Doug." Even after all these weeks he wasn't used to the respect he got from the staff at the schools. He was more comfortable with people calling him "pig" and spitting at him.

"What can I do for you, Doug?" Rich asked.

"I got a favor to ask you," he said, shoving his hands into the pockets of his uniform trousers. He felt like a fraud cashing in on the reputation of his badge.

"Sure, Doug, whatcha need?"

"I'd like you to take a look at one of my students. The kid can shoot."

"Sure. I'll look. Who is he?"

"Jeremy Schwartz."

"Schwartz? Are you kidding, Doug? That kid's nothing but trouble."

Doug's jaw clenched as he bit back the response on the tip of his tongue. "He's not the nicest kid I've ever met," he said instead, "but he can shoot a basketball like I shoot a gun. He's right on every time. Maybe if we give him something to do with himself, he'll straighten out."

The coach studied Doug. "You're trying to find him one of those alternatives you're always talking about, right?"

"Could be. But what could it hurt to take a look at him? If he's not as good as I say he is, you've wasted five minutes of your day."

"Have him here at lunch. I'll take a look." Rich walked back around his desk and sat down. "But he'd better be good...."

Doug decided to wait until lunchtime before approaching Jeremy. He didn't want to give the boy any time to back out on him. But when they were seated at the lunch table and Doug broached the subject, Jeremy stood up, picked up his lunch tray and walked away.

Doug followed him to the trash can and then over to the window where Jeremy dropped off his tray. "What can it hurt, Jeremy? All you have to do is shoot a couple of baskets."

Hope flashed briefly on the boy's face, but it was gone so quickly Doug wasn't sure he hadn't just imagined it. "No way, cop. When you gonna get the picture? I ain't no charity case."

Doug followed Jeremy to the door of the lunchroom. "No, you're not. But you're one helluva good shot, Jeremy. What's wrong with giving yourself a chance?"

"A chance at what?" Jeremy asked bitterly, stopping in the entrance to the lunchroom. "Look at me, and look at them." He nodded toward the clean-cut young boys at the table nearest the door. "I ain't gonna get a place on that team, and you and I both know it."

"You're never going to get any chances if you don't try."

"Go away, man."

When Doug didn't move, Jeremy pushed open the door and left the room.

He couldn't force Jeremy to meet with Coach Peterson. He couldn't force Jeremy to do anything—but he couldn't give up, either. Lord knows, he'd tried. But Jeremy just kept coming back to haunt him. Here was a chance for him to do things over, to save a young man from the hell that had been his own life for too many years.

DOUG TOOK ANDREA out for an ice-cream cone after school that afternoon. It was November, and too cold for ice cream, but he knew she had a soft spot for the creamy confection. And he needed to talk to her.

"I'd like your opinion on something," he said as soon as they were back in his cruiser licking their cones.

"Shoot." She looked at him over the top her cone, and Doug felt his groin clench. Even in her uniform she took his breath away.

"What?" she asked when Doug continued to watch her without saying anything.

He told her briefly about his attempts to get through to Jeremy Schwartz. "I've tried everything I can think of and so far nothing's working. Got any suggestions?'' He took a bite of his cone.

Andrea stopped licking. "You can't do it, Doug."

He stopped crunching. "What?"

"You can't abandon an entire classroom full of students to concentrate on one boy."

Doug rolled down the window and tossed the rest of his cone to the birds.

"I'm not abandoning the class," he said carefully. What the hell was she talking about?

Andrea bit into her cone. "You're running that risk if you pick out one child to befriend over the others. You've already done more than you should have, approaching Coach Peterson like that. What if any of the other boys found out?"

Doug was getting angrier by the minute. "I don't get it. I show them I care about them. I give to them all day, everyday. I get them to trust me—but I can't help the one little boy who probably needs me the most?"

"That's just it, Doug. If you lose even five of the twenty-five kids who are learning what you're trying to teach them, would helping Jeremy be worth it? Five kids who have a great chance, for one who probably won't make it anyway?"

He pounded his hand on the steering wheel. "How can you say that? How can you sit there and decide a boy's fate, like it's nothing more than old cat litter?"

Andrea threw out the rest of her own cone. She pulled a tissue out of his glove compartment and wiped her hands.

"Do you remember that last session I did in training?" she finally asked.

"Yeah. I remember," he said. He remembered that he'd hated every word she'd had to say. He remembered her condemnation of people like him—druggies who walked the streets, too hardened to care about the people they were hurting. And he remembered again feeling that he'd never have the right to share the life of someone as soft, as lovely as Andrea Parker.

"It's not right or good or easy. But it's a fact. There are some kids we're just not qualified to help. As wrong as it might be, there are some eyes that have seen too much, some emotions that have been too trampled, some bodies that have been stripped of their hearts."

Doug heard her. He supposed she was right, to a point. But he knew he couldn't give up on Jeremy Schwartz. He just kept wondering where he'd have ended up if Stan Ingersoll hadn't broken some rules to help him. He owed it to Jeremy to give the boy the same chance Stan had given him.

He'd pursue Jeremy on his own time from now on. He'd make sure none of the other kids were slighted. But one way or another, he was going to help Jeremy Schwartz.

ANDREA AGREED TO MEET Mabel's brother, Blake, at a restaurant in Gahanna, one of Columbus's northern suburbs. She took a lot of time with her appearance, wearing the new outfit from her mother and fluffing her short hair until it bounced. But when she approached the table where she'd been told her date was waiting, she could hardly believe her eyes.

She supposed Blake was the heartthrob her mother had claimed he was, but he would need to add at least ten years to his age before he could even begin to get her attention. The boy still had peach fuzz! And not enough savvy to know that he should have shaved it before going on a date. The whole thing was ludicrous. If this kid actually had a paying job at the supermarket, he surely wasn't more than the bag boy. Her mother had really gone too far this time.

Andrea saw Blake turning around, slowly scanning the restaurant. She ducked behind a potted plant. As soon as he turned back to the table she hurried back the way she'd come, out into the parking lot to her car. There was no way she was going on a date with a boy barely out of his teens.

She drove until she found a pay phone. Looking up the restaurant's number, she had Blake paged.

"Hello?" A hesitant, wobbly voice came on the line. It sounded like it belonged to a sixteen-year-old. *Give me a break,* she thought with a weary shake of her head. She'd never be this desperate.

"Hello, Blake. This is Andrea," she said, impulsively disguising her voice to sound like an old woman. Gloria was going to pay for this one. It wasn't the kid's fault he'd been born ten years too late.

"Andrea? Where are you?" he asked.

"Well, that's just it, Blake. I'm not going to be able to make it tonight." Andrea's throat hurt with the effort it was taking her to keep her voice so unnaturally shaky. "My arthritis is acting up something fierce and I don't want to be too far away from my pills. But I could make it up to you some other time. We could go to that nice cafeteria down by the medical center for lunch...." She laughed gleefully to herself.

"No! I mean, that's all right, Andrea, really. I'm probably going to be moving back with my mother soon, anyway. But it was real nice talking to you."

Andrea drove home slowly, a satisfied grin on her face. She wished she could be there the next time Gloria showed her face at the supermarket.

She knew she was breaking her own rules, but she called Doug when she got home, thinking that maybe they could meet for pizza and beer. For once in her life she needed to feel like a desirable woman.

His phone rang and continued to ring. Andrea listened to the lonely peal for a full minute before she finally had to accept that he wasn't home. She shouldn't have expected that he would be. After all, it was Saturday night. He probably had a date.

CHAPTER THIRTEEN

JEREMY'S NEIGHBORHOOD smelled like unshowered bodies and hot cooking grease. Doug leaned against the wall of an out-of-business gas station, watching the Saturday-night action. There wasn't much to see. Most of the things that happened in that neighborhood weren't things people did for show.

Which was fine with Doug. The less he saw that reminded him of his adolescence, the better. He wasn't there for a trip down memory lane. He'd just as soon never take that trip again as long as he lived. He was there to find Jeremy.

And this time Jeremy would see the man, not the cop. Doug was wearing his favorite black jeans—the faded ones with the hole just below the hip pocket—a black leather jacket with the sleeves pushed halfway up his forearms and a rolled bandanna around his head. He wasn't wearing his wristband.

He scoured the neighborhood for a couple of hours, trying to ignore the sights, the sounds, the smells. He passed a group of rough-looking teenagers who were huddled around a fire in the middle of the sidewalk. They were all gazing silently into the flames, as if fascinated by them. Doug wondered what the current code name was for LSD, and then decided it hardly mattered. No matter what they called it, the trip was the same.

He crossed the street when he saw a McDonald's up ahead, figuring he'd get himself some dinner before continuing his inspection. It might be a long night.

He was still half a block from McDonald's when he spotted Jeremy. The boy was crouched on the side of the building, a white garbage bag in one hand.

Doug stopped, watching Jeremy from a distance, waiting to see what the boy was doing. It didn't take him long to figure it out. He'd known a lot of kids who'd cleaned up trash for a meal. He'd done it himself. It was part of the initiation into hell.

Jeremy filled his bag and then headed to the back door of the restaurant. He pounded on the door once, probably harder than necessary, handed in the bag of trash and then went around to the front of the building to collect his "pay." Doug hoped the boy was wise enough to wash his hands first.

Giving him time to get his food and sit down, Doug approached the restaurant. He spotted Jeremy immediately, sitting at a table back by the rest room, stuffing his face so fast Doug had to wonder how long it had been since he had had a decent meal. Except for the days when kids on assistance ate free, Jeremy hardly ever ate at school. He always said that he didn't like the school's food, or that he'd forgotten his lunch. Doug should have known better than to believe that old line.

He wondered why Jeremy even attended the school he did. Ghetto kids went to ghetto schools, that was the unwritten rule that everyone around there just sort of understood. Ghetto kids knew they had to get tough early on. Jeremy must have slipped through the system—the one exception that proved the rule.

Doug ordered his dinner, adding an extra order of french fries, carried his brown plastic tray back to the table where he'd seen Jeremy and sat down. He unwrapped his burger, took the lid off his cola, salted his fries and took a bite, never once looking at the boy across from him.

"Don't bother, cop. It ain't gonna work." Jeremy's words weren't quite as sullen as usual. Doug figured his fancy duds must be doing their job.

Minding his own business, Doug ate his burger, drank his cola and finished half of his fries. He wiped his hands on a napkin, and pushed his tray away. It was no accident that the tray moved in Jeremy's direction.

"The first time my father sucker-punched me across the jaw I couldn't open it for three days. I lived on french fries the whole time. They were skinny enough to fit between my lips and didn't need much chewing." Doug said, looking at Jeremy for the first time.

The boy didn't look at him. He didn't respond to his comment, either, but Doug could tell by his unnatural stillness that the boy was listening to him. It was all the encouragement he needed.

"I didn't get it much at first, when my old lady was around. She took most of his abuse back then, and I just had to stay out of his way when he was drinking. 'Course, listening to her take his punches was almost as bad as taking them myself."

Jeremy looked up, fire in his eyes. *Bingo.* The boy was feeling.

"So you got whacked now and then, cop. Lotsa kids do. There're worse things," he said bitterly.

Doug didn't look away from Jeremy. He didn't let the boy's words push him away. He was finally making headway. "Yeah? Like what?"

"You'd probably barf up that burger if I told you. What kinda house did you grow up in, cop? One of them fancy little numbers across from the school, all painted up nice with a yard full of green grass? I bet your ma made roast beef for dinner every Sunday and baked cookies while you were at school, too. Go back where you came from, cop—you ain't needed here." Jeremy slid from his seat, picking up his trash from the table.

"Sit down," Doug said. His voice was no longer kind or the least bit gentle. He grabbed a fistful of Jeremy's old flannel shirt and shoved the boy back into his seat.

"Let me tell you a thing or two about life, *boy*," he said. He leaned forward, pinning him with the same hard glare that had cowered drug dealers in his earlier life.

"This place is paradise compared to where I grew up." Doug pointed to the littered street outside McDonald's. "We didn't have a house. We had two rooms in a building that should have been condemned. My old lady didn't cook or bake. She didn't even bother to hang around. More often than not my Sunday dinner was the day-olds out of somebody's trash.

"And before you start on him, my old man wasn't much to speak of, either. The only time he knew I was alive was when he was trying to kill me. The rest of the time he was too drunk to know his own name, let alone mine.

"You want to talk about losing your dinner, I could tell you stories that would make you never want to eat again. I got memories in my head that would've sent some guys to the nut farm. I was seven years old when I learned about the facts of life. My old man was doing some girl on the living-room floor when I came home from school. He saw me, but he didn't stop. He told me I could watch. Now you still think you got something to tell me I don't already know?" He practically spit the last words at the boy. He hadn't expected helping Jeremy to hurt so much. He'd thought it was a deed he would do, like arresting a thief or busting a prostitution ring. He hadn't expected to *feel* anything.

"How old were you when she split?" Jeremy asked. His voice was low, hesitant. He stared across at Doug with a look too knowing for his years.

"Five or thereabouts."

"I was six when my old man left us."

In the space of nine words, Doug Avery opened his heart completely for the first time in more than twenty years. He opened his heart and let a troubled little boy inside.

"How many of you did he leave?"

"There's four more, younger 'n me."

Doug remembered one of his pals from the old days, before he'd started trading in friendship for fixes.

"With you being the oldest, I bet your old lady leans pretty heavy on you, huh?"

"When there ain't some guy there humping her."

"I can't make it go away, Jeremy. But I can help. I can understand. I can listen. I can feed you now and then. I can help you find a way out, eventually. But you're going to have to trust me—to let me be your friend."

Doug picked up one of his leftover french fries and lifted it to his lips.

"Oh my God, man! You're a Rattler. Nobody messes with a Rattler. I can't believe you're a Rattler. I thought you were just a cop! I can't believe it. A cop Rattler."

Doug lowered his arm, shocked that he'd lowered his guard so completely that he'd forgotten not to expose his wrist. He'd left the wristband off as a precaution, in case he needed it in his search for Jeremy. He'd forgotten it wasn't there.

"I've been a lot of things that might surprise you, son. But the point is, I got out. I can help you get out, too. It's up to you."

Jeremy deliberated for another minute or two. He ate a couple of Doug's fries, as if testing the waters. And then he reached across the table, holding out one very clean, young hand.

"Friends?" he asked solemnly.

Doug took the skinny fingers into his, forcing himself to shake the boy's hand and let it go. He was filled with an unfamiliar urge to pull the boy into his arms and hug him. Jeremy smiled, and Doug finally had a glimpse of what caring was all about.

DOUG WANTED TO TELL Andrea about his weekend, about Jeremy, but it was precisely because he'd spent the weekend with Jeremy that he kept silent. He knew she wouldn't approve. He knew, too, that nothing was going to stop him from keeping his promises to the boy.

He had a few rough minutes at school, afraid that Andrea would see the miraculous change in Jeremy, afraid that he'd somehow favor him over the other kids. But other than a couple of covert, private glances, Jeremy behaved pretty much the same as always. The only difference was that, though Jeremy never participated in DARE lessons, Doug now suspected that the boy had been paying attention all along.

He took Jeremy to K-Mart for some new clothes on Wednesday. They weren't designer duds, but they were new and they fit. Jeremy not only thanked Doug, which was a shock in itself, but he offered to wash Doug's car for the rest of his life. Doug wished again that he could share these victories with Andrea. Though he wasn't sorry to be spending time with the boy, he wished the three of them could do things together, even though he knew that wasn't possible.

"You got a girlfriend?" Jeremy asked the following Saturday afternoon as he and Doug waited in line at the movies. Jeremy was looking at a young couple about his own age who were chewing gum and holding hands.

"Sorta." Doug answered as honestly as he answered all of Jeremy's questions. His idea of a girlfriend was a woman in his bed, which he definitely hadn't had in a while. But he did have kind of a relationship with Andrea—surely they were friends, at least—and she was a girl.

"Is it Officer Parker?" Jeremy asked in a teasing voice.

"Why do you ask?"

"You guys look at each other kinda funny sometimes."

"I didn't think you ever looked at us."

"I look. I listen sometimes, too. But some of that stuff ain't for real. I mean, look at that stupid teddy bear. Like he could really make me feel warm all over when the heat's been turned off again."

Doug was relieved they weren't talking about Andrea anymore, but he didn't like the turn of the conversation.

"You got something that does keep you warm?" he asked.

Jeremy shut down.

Doug took a deep breath, wishing they weren't in the middle of a movie line. "It's okay, kid. I could name a thing or two that kept me warm nights. But the problem with my solution was that it gave me more problems. Bigger ones."

"You know? You know I'm a user and you're still here with me?"

"I suspected, Jeremy. It's kinda hard to live where you live for eleven years and not get sucked in."

"I don't use nothin' hard, Doug. I swear it. I just smoke a little pot now and then. It's easier to go home when I'm high."

Doug forced himself not to react. He leaned one shoulder against a cement column outside the theater, sliding his hands into his pockets.

"It was easier for me, too. Until the pot wasn't enough."

"You tried harder stuff?"

Doug was stuck. If he said yes, would Jeremy run out and try it, too? But what kind of chance would he be taking if he lied to the boy?

"It's not the answer, Jeremy. You said you'd trust me, and you gotta trust me on this. It's not the answer. Listen to what we're telling you in school. Arm yourself with alternate choices, with ways to reduce stress, with answers to gang pressure. Those are the tools that are going to get you out of there. You're already well on your way. We're going to be learning about the importance of support systems next week and you've already gotten yourself one of those."

Doug punched Jeremy lightly on the shoulder, letting his arm fall around the boy's shoulders for a minute to propel him forward as the line began to move.

"You aren't going to turn me in, are you?" Jeremy asked just before the lights went down and the movie started.

"Stay off the stuff and I won't have any reason to make that decision, will I?"

ANDREA MISSED DOUG. He hadn't made some excuse to see her outside of school for over two weeks. She knew she'd have to live without him very soon anyway, since his first semester was over in just a matter of weeks and she'd have no more reason to see him every day. But she wasn't ready to give him up yet.

She became so obsessed with the idea that he'd found a girlfriend that she finally had to ask him. His denial was curt, to the point and not very friendly.

Something was up with him. She was sure of it. But if it wasn't a girlfriend, what else could it be? Was he turning back into to the solitary man he'd been when she'd first met him? Had he ever really stopped being one? Had she just thought he was changing—losing her perspective in her desire for his kisses?

She'd almost convinced herself he was purposely avoiding her when he showed up on her doorstep one Sunday afternoon.

"Hi," she said, wondering if he could tell how glad she was to see him.

"I missed you," he said, leaning one shoulder against her door frame. Those didn't sound like the words of a man who preferred to live in a vacuum.

"I missed you too."

"You wanna drive out to Alum Creek?"

"Yeah."

"You wanna take a blanket and make love out there?"

"Yeah."

He shot away from the door frame, penetrating her with his intense brown gaze. "You do?"

"Yeah. But I can't."

He leaned back against the door. "You wanna tell me why not?"

"You know why. I drove my last lover away. I can't go through that again."

"Can't or won't?"

Andrea shrugged. "It amounts to the same thing, doesn't it?"

"Nope. If you can't, you can't. If you won't, you can. I just have to convince you to."

Andrea laughed. It was so good to be with him. "I'll let you know which it is when I figure it out."

"So we going to the creek?"

"You still want to?"

"I always want to," he said with a suggestive grin.

He was back. And though she knew it was wrong, Andrea wanted him to stay.

ANDREA WAITED for Doug after school on Monday. Thanksgiving was just over a week away and she had gone around and around with herself deciding whether or not she should ask Doug to spend the day with her. She wouldn't be going to her parents' house. She wasn't going to force her little brother out of his own home on a holiday.

And as far as she knew, Doug would be alone, too. She was afraid to spend the day with him, afraid of her traitorous heart, but she hated even more the thought of Doug all alone at a time when everybody had someone.

She looked around the deserted school-yard, wondering where he was. She'd thought he was right behind her. She was about to go back inside, to see what was keeping him, when she saw him out on the playground. He was watching Jeremy Schwartz shoot baskets. And right beside him stood Coach Peterson.

Andrea was a mass of conflicting emotions as she watched the scene unfolding before her. There was a thrill of elation so acute it almost hurt as she realized that Doug had opened his heart enough to continue trying to help the skinny blond boy. But there was also fear.

Andrea had seen Jeremy's kind before. The boy was as hard as they came. He was sullen and disrespectful. Andrea would bet her life that he was already a regular user. She knew the signs, and Jeremy had all of them. He lied, his grades had dropped, he had no straight friends, he took no part in school activities, his attention span was sporadic, he had fits of anger and his eyes alternated between being glassy and bloodshot.

Andrea was frightened beyond belief that Doug had set himself up for disillusionment the very first time he opened his heart. But she was also filled with anger. She'd told him about the other kids that could suffer if he did this very thing. Any of the other boys could have come outside and seen Doug standing out there with Jeremy. Why hadn't he listened to her? Why was he jeopardizing everything?

She drove home, changed out of her uniform, left it lying across her bed and pulled on a pair of blue jeans and a black thermal sweatshirt. She slipped into a pair of tennis shoes and headed back out, not bothering even to run a comb through her hair.

She met Doug just as he was pulling into his apartment complex. She had to take several deep breaths before she got out of her car, reminding herself that he was only going to get defensive if she blasted him.

"This is a nice surprise," Doug said as she caught up with him at his parking slot. He ran his liquid gaze from her head to her toes, saying more with his eyes than he did with his words. His scar was barely visible.

Andrea fought against the heat that flowed through her, the weakness just being near him caused in her. She had to concentrate on the job at hand. She had to keep things in perspective. She fell into step beside him as he headed toward his apartment.

"I needed to talk to you for a sec."

"Shoot."

"It can wait until we get inside. How come you're so late getting home?"

"I had to stop by the cleaner's."

Andrea knew he was lying. She knew it not just because she'd seen what he'd been doing, but because he looked away from her when he spoke.

"So where are your clothes?" she asked, glancing down at his briefcase, the only thing he was carrying.

"I was dropping them off, not picking them up."

He was so smooth it scared her. This was a side of Doug she'd never met before—a man who could lie through his teeth without missing a beat. How much more was there that she didn't know about? How much more had he concealed with all his vague answers and closemouthed conversations?

He went into the bathroom to change. Andrea looked around the room, noticing once again that it was the most impersonal apartment she'd ever been in. There wasn't even a pair of shoes by the door or a book on the coffee table.

She sat down on the brown tweed couch that pulled out into his bed at night, wondering again where Doug had come from. There were no pictures hanging on his walls, no snapshots sitting on his tables. She didn't even know if the furniture belonged to him.

The bathroom door opened. Andrea's breath caught in her throat when she looked over and saw him standing in the doorway.

He was wearing a pair of faded black jeans—and that was all, except for the wristband that he never seemed to take off. His hair was mussed and his chin was dark with the day's worth of stubble. He looked more like one of the rough characters she would expect to meet in a redneck bar than the respected policeman she knew him to be. And still she wanted him.

"What's up?" he asked, lowering himself to the couch beside her.

She tore her hungry gaze away from the dark hairs curling over his chest, from the firmly defined muscles his uniform usually hid, from the scar on his shoulder, and met his hooded eyes. He knew something was up. He was retreating from her.

"I saw you," she blurted out. It was nothing like the calm words she'd rehearsed.

He raised one eyebrow in question, saying nothing.

"With Jeremy. And Peterson."

She waited for him to defend himself, to tell her to mind her own business, to go to hell. But he continued to watch her with his piercing brown eyes until she felt like she was the one who was in trouble.

"I warned you to stay away from him, Doug."

"I remember."

"But you didn't."

"Nope."

"He's a user, Doug. All the signs are there." She forced herself to speak evenly when she badly needed to yell, to force some sense into him.

"Isn't that why we're there—to steer kids straight?"

"It's more like to keep them straight. And yes, maybe, to steer the occasional user toward other choices. But Jeremy's not an occasional user. I've seen his kind before. You're setting yourself up for a fall and risking the faith of the rest of the class in the process."

Doug stayed calm as long as he could. He listened to Andrea. He tried to hear fairly. He already knew he'd made a mistake that afternoon by sticking around with Jeremy and Peterson. Andrea had been right there. He'd risked hurting the other boys, making them jealous, losing their trust. But when Jeremy had agreed to shoot for Peterson only if Doug came along, he hadn't been able to refuse. Jeremy's best hope was basketball. It could set him up for life. It offered not only a time-consuming outlet for his energy, but the potential for scholarships, and a future.

"We have only so much time in each class, Doug," Andrea continued. "Sometimes it's just too late."

He couldn't take any more.

Doug shot up off the couch, walked angrily toward the door and then wheeled around. He stopped in front of Andrea, leaning over with one hand on the back of the couch behind her shoulder, the other on the arm of the couch beside her, trapping her.

"It's—never—too—late." He said each word separately, leaving her no doubt that he meant each one.

He pushed away from the couch with such force that it scooted backward a couple of inches. He walked over to the window, forcing himself to calm down.

He was so filled with frustration he was ready to explode, but he knew it wasn't all her fault. Part of it was from wanting her for so long, being around her every day, having nothing but cold showers for company. But another part was a frustration that was all his own making. It was born of his past, and it lived with him each moment that he dared consider a life with Andrea.

He turned around, finding her in the same position he'd left her in. She wasn't crying, but she looked as if it wouldn't take much to make her start. His time was up.

"If there were a 'too late,' I wouldn't be here right now," he said, knowing that he was killing any chance he'd ever had to be this woman's lover.

"What do you mean?" Her lips barely moved as she spoke. She sat stiffly on the couch, as if trying to ward off any blows, physical or emotional, that he might throw at her. But she didn't look frightened. Doug was thankful for that, at least.

"I took my first hit of acid when I was seven. I'd been alone with my dad for a couple of years by then. I didn't think I'd make it for another two. I was addicted by the time I was eight.

"And you know that skit Steve and I did? Most of it wasn't fiction. Only his name wasn't Steve, it was

Chuck, and there were no little kids or an older brother. And it wasn't my first time with drugs, only with the magic white stuff. I was eleven. Jeremy's age. By the time I was twelve I'd done it all. Needles, pills, pipes—you name it, I knew it. And I didn't care who I had to hurt to get it. And you know why?"

Andrea looked up at him, her eyes filled with pain. She shook her head.

"Because it hurt me more not to have it."

Doug slumped down on the couch, as far from Andrea as the old piece of furniture would allow. He wasn't going to give her the chance to scoot away from him.

"How badly did you hurt them?"

Doug knew what she was really asking. He supposed he couldn't blame her. "No one ever spent the night in the hospital as a result of my handiwork, or the morgue, either."

He saw the relief in her eyes, and for once was thankful for the truth. But there was more. He had to tell her or she'd never understand.

"For my twentieth birthday I threw a party. It was on the roof of an old warehouse, and the invitations were few, but mandatory. After fifteen years on ghetto streets, I'd earned myself a reputation. I had power. Everybody brought presents, just like I'd told them to—blue ones and yellow ones, capsules, pills and vials. I provided the syringe."

Andrea cringed, but she didn't look away from him. She held his gaze as boldly as everything else she did. Doug had never wanted her more than he did while he sat there watching his chances slip away.

"The party turned out to be even more than I had envisioned. Sometime after midnight, I hallucinated that I was on a flying trapeze. I'd had dreams of running away with a circus when I was a kid. I suddenly thought I could fly across the street to a telephone pole. It was breathing, you see, and I wanted to check it out. I flew, all right—right off the rooftop. It was four floors up."

Tears were sliding down Andrea's cheeks. Doug didn't even know when she'd started to cry. He'd been lost in memories, reliving that night, wondering at just what point it had been too late for him.

He crossed his arms across his chest, staring at the blank TV set. Andrea watched him, her tears falling down her face unchecked.

"What happened?" Her gentle words were almost his undoing.

"I landed in a dumpster, but I still broke more bones than I knew I had. The only good thing was I was so high I didn't feel any pain. Not until the next day, when I came to in the hospital. I hallucinated for six more days after that."

"How did you get into the academy with a record like that?" Andrea asked. He'd wondered when she'd get around to the question.

"No charges were ever filed."

"Didn't they notify the police when you were brought it?"

"They notified Stan Ingersoll."

"Sergeant Ingersoll?" Andrea asked.

Doug nodded. "He was on call that night. And I'll never know what he saw in a punk like me, but he gave me a chance, Andrea. Me. A loser. A druggie. He visited me in detox, got me a room in a boardinghouse across town from where I'd grown up and enrolled me in high school. You have no idea how difficult that was, being twenty years old and a junior in high school. Studying didn't come too easy, either, after the way I'd been frying my brain for years, but eventually my thinking got clearer. I graduated when I was twenty-three."

"And entered the academy?" Her voice sounded small.

"I'm going back out there, Andrea. I'm going to get on the Drug Task Force and get every dealer, every pusher, every gang member who preys on kids like I was, like Jeremy is—kids who think they have no other choices in life, who need the escape to get through the hell of living."

"Is that what happened to you? Did the gangs pressure you into using?"

Doug shook his head. If only it were that simple. His heart was numb as he removed his wristband. He turned his arm over, holding it out toward Andrea, exposing the lethal-looking little snake burned into the skin of his wrist.

"Oh my God," Andrea said, sucking in her breath. She stared at his wrist, horrified, and then looked back at him.

"You're a Rattler?" she whispered, as if she couldn't believe the evidence in front of her eyes.

"Was." Doug knew the distinction didn't really matter. It didn't change what he'd been. Nothing could, which was why he'd never had the tattoo removed. "I founded the Rattlers when I was fourteen. My personal membership was current until my twentieth birthday."

Andrea fell back against the couch, staring blankly at the opposite wall. Doug knew he'd shocked her. He'd probably killed any affection she might have had for him. But it really hadn't been for him, anyway. It had been for the man she'd thought he was.

He waited for her to say something. But when several minutes had passed without a word from her, he got up from the couch and went into the bathroom, shutting the door behind him. He'd give her a couple of minutes to clear out, without having to put them both through any awkward platitudes, without forcing her to lie. And then, somehow, he'd get on with the rest of his life....

Andrea heard the door click as Doug shut the bathroom door. She pulled her knees up to her chest, resting her chin on them, hugging them so tightly it hurt. She welcomed the physical pain, using it to ward off the ripping of her heart.

She hurt for herself, for the fact that she loved Doug so completely and was so frightened to admit it. But mostly she hurt for him, for the life he'd been handed, for the memories that would always haunt him. She felt completely helpless as she sat there, unable to make any of it better for him, unable to change anything, to promise anything, to love him as he deserved to be loved.

"You're still here."

Andrea jumped up off the couch. She hadn't heard the bathroom door open. "Did you want me to go?" she asked. The thought hadn't even occurred to her.

He shrugged. "Only if you wanted to." He stood in the middle of the room, his hands in his pockets, as if unsure what to do next.

Andrea understood then. He'd expected her to be gone. He'd expected her to be so shocked, so repulsed, that she'd want nothing more to do with him.

He couldn't have been further from the truth. She walked up to him, slid her arms up his naked chest and locked them around his neck.

"Nothing you've said here today changes the way I feel about you, friend. Except to give me a new respect for the depth of your courage."

He encircled her with his arms, pulling her against him so tightly she could feel his heartbeat against her chest. He stood there holding her, nuzzling his face in her neck, more vulnerable than she'd ever seen him.

Andrea let her hands run slowly along his back, caressing the broadness of his shoulders, reassuring him in the only way she knew. "How'd you get this?" she asked softly, fingering the scar on his shoulder.

"My old man came home late one night shortly after my fourteenth birthday. He apparently decided I was sleeping too peacefully, because he landed on me with a knee in my back and his hand in my hair. He only got me twice that time before I got loose. I took off, looking for someplace to spend the rest of the night. I fell asleep leaning up against the dumpster behind our building."

Andrea laid her head on his chest while she listened to him, marveling that he was such a good man in spite of the memories he carried around in his head.

"The next thing I knew I had a knife in my shoulder. When I opened my eyes, I was surrounded by a group of Scorpions. I was trespassing on their space. It was the only home I'd ever known, but it was their space. The next day I scoured the streets with a pocketful of pills. I bribed every guy I could find to join my gang. That night, the Rattlers fought their first brawl. And we won back my dumpster."

She looked up when he finished, smoothing the hair back away from his face, wishing she knew how to soothe his soul as well. Her fingers brushed against the scar at his temple.

"Was this from that brawl?" she asked.

Doug caught her hand, bringing it to his lips as he shook his head.

"That's the result of a piece of flying glass from a holdup at Tremont's Jewelers a couple of years ago. Our suspect tried to escape the hard way."

He pulled her against him again, just holding her.

"Did you get him?" she asked, her voice muffled against the warmth of his chest.

"What do you think?"

He loosened his hold just enough to look into her eyes, telling her things he'd never said in words, things he might never be able to say but that she desperately needed to know. All the love she felt for him was in her eyes as she tried to answer him.

"Will you make love with me?" he asked. He'd asked the words before, but never like this, never like her answer mattered to him.

Andrea fought with herself. She loved Doug. Making love with him would only be an extension of what she was already feeling. But would it be fair to him? Would it be fair to start something she wasn't sure she could carry through for the long run? Because while she wasn't afraid to make love with him tonight, she was terrified to consider committing herself to a lifetime with him. Not because of him—she had complete faith in Doug. It was herself she couldn't trust.

Doug must have read her silence for an answer. He pushed her away before she could reach any kind of decision. If he'd only kissed her, there wouldn't have been any decision to make. She wouldn't have been strong enough to deny herself, or him, anymore. But he didn't kiss her. He walked back over to the window, looking out into the falling darkness.

"I really don't know where you get off, lecturing me about my feelings for Jeremy. You're hardly an authority on the subject, Andrea."

She heard the disappointment in his words, but she heard honesty as well. "What do you mean?"

He turned around to face her, and the look on his face shocked her. She saw pity there. Pity from the man she'd once thought so cold he'd forgotten how to feel.

"You care for the kids at school. You give your all to them. As a group. But did you ever stop to think that you never—*ever*—care for anyone one-on-one?"

"You don't know what you're talking about. I love my parents very much."

"Sure you do. Because they're safe. Their role in your life is predetermined. They're the providers, not the providee. You don't have to worry about shaping their lives, or even sharing them."

Andrea felt the blood drain from her face. She wrapped her arms around her chest, holding on.

"You ask others to care—hell, you even *teach* them how. But you don't practice what you preach."

"That's not true." Her words sounded weak even to her own ears.

"You're the most giving, unselfish person I've ever met, Andrea. You really make a difference in this world—you save the lives of children who might not have made it without your compassion. But you're afraid to take on anything personal, aren't you? That's why you feel so threatened by my involvement with Jeremy, isn't it? That's why you won't let me make love to you."

He walked up to her until their bodies were so close she could feel his heat, but he didn't touch her.

"Well, I got news for you, lady," he said, sounding angry now. "I *am* personal. And I'm not going away."

Andrea looked up at him, wanting so badly for him to hold her, knowing that all she had to do was ask him. She thought of Scotty, of her ex-husband. She thought of disappointing Doug like she'd disappointed them. She thought of losing Doug like she'd lost them. And then she ran.

She didn't stop until she was locked in her own apartment. She fell down onto her bed, shaking, out of control, knowing her life was nothing the way it should be.

CHAPTER FOURTEEN

"I'M SORRY."

"Where are you?" Doug's voice came over the telephone line, deep, forceful, so totally Doug.

"At home. I came straight home." She couldn't believe it was only three hours since she'd left him. It felt more like three years.

"Are you all right?"

"Yeah."

"Good. Good. Well, thanks for calling."

"Doug?" She couldn't let him hang up. She might never work up the courage to do this again.

"Yeah?"

"I want to make love with you." She said the words so quickly her tongue tripped over her teeth.

"Are you sure this time?"

"As sure as I'll ever be."

"I'm on my way." The line crackled.

"Wait! I mean, that's not all."

"What's not all? Oh. You need me to stop by the drugstore on my way?"

"No! I'm on the pill, but..."

"If you're worried about my health, I was tested just a couple of months ago."

"I'm not worried. And you don't have to worry about mine, either." She'd never thought this would be so difficult.

"Then what is it?"

"I want to make love with you, but only if it's one time at a time."

"What the hell's that supposed to mean?"

Andrea stood at her living-room window, gazing out into the darkness. If he couldn't give her this, she couldn't give him anything. "No commitments, no future, no promises."

The line hung with dead silence. "Is there any other way?" he finally asked.

"Don't make it sound like that, Doug. What I feel for you, the way I want you, is like nothing I've ever felt before. But I'm no good at commitments. I don't want to ruin things."

"You can't break promises that aren't made, is that it?" His disappointment was barely concealed.

Andrea could feel tears burning the back of her eyes again. "I'm sorry," she said. "I shouldn't have called."

He sighed. "Yeah, you should have. It's okay, Andrea. The only promises I'm making are for today. I'm on my way, baby, and it's going to be perfect—I give you my word on it."

Andrea smiled, leaving her living room behind as she carried her cordless phone toward her bedroom. "How soon can you be here?"

DOUG KNOCKED ON HER DOOR, his hair still damp from the shower he'd taken, his face freshly shaved.

His legs looked strong and firm in their form-fitting black jeans. His zipper was already bulging.

Andrea was glad she'd changed into the black silk teddy, even though she'd had to send up a quick prayer when she'd cut off the tags that Gloria's radar was turned off for the night.

She fell against Doug, throwing her arms around his neck, sure that she was doing the right thing. There was no more denying the frightening hunger he'd woken within her.

"Let's go to bed," he growled against her ear. He kicked the door shut behind him and half led, half pulled her across the living room and down the hall.

He pulled off his black leather boots as soon as he reached her bedroom doorway, letting them fall behind him as he followed her to the bed. His jacket and T-shirt dropped to the floor halfway across the room. His impatient fingers went to the button on his jeans.

Andrea sat on the edge of the bed, her legs crossed demurely, watching him unzip his pants. She'd never felt such desire just from looking at a man, from thinking about what lay ahead. She'd never known anticipation could be so powerful. He kicked off his jeans, taking his briefs with them.

Liquid warmth flooded Andrea's crotch as he stood, proudly jutting, in front of her. There was nothing shy or hesitant about Doug Avery. There never had been.

Doug had to force himself not to manhandle Andrea as she sat so temptingly on the bed, her beautiful body mostly revealed by the thin layer of black lace she was wearing. Her breasts were full and creamy, and falling out of their brief covering. Her nipples were already hard, puckering against their satiny confines.

Her waist was slim, the perfect complement to her rounded, womanly hips. And her thighs... Doug leaned forward, sliding his arms beneath hers, propelling her backward. He couldn't even look at the sweet black curls peeking out from the juncture of her thighs. He knew the limits to his self-control. He knew he was already dangerously close to reaching them.

She fell back on her bed, reaching up to run her fingers through the hair on his chest. Her touch was electric. Doug felt a satisfaction broader, bigger, better than anything he'd ever known before because her passion was for *all* of him, scarred as he was.

He looked down at her, sprawled beneath him on her satiny white comforter. Her eyes were wide open. She was with him all the way.

"You're not going to be sorry for this. I'll make sure of it," he said, his voice husky with need.

"I'm not sorry, Doug. It hurts too much to want you. I can't stand it anymore."

"That makes two of us, lady," he said. He reached his hand down between their bodies, unsnapped her teddy and slid his fingers boldly between her legs.

"You're ready already," he said with satisfaction. He'd never had such an eager woman in his arms before. He gave up trying to fight what she did to him.

Andrea smiled, spreading her legs a little wider beneath his as she too reached down between them. "It seems I'm not the only one in that condition."

Doug leaned on his elbows, taking a breast in each of his hands.

"Oh God, Andrea. This isn't how I planned it," he groaned, just before he plunged into her.

Andrea clutched Doug's buttocks, riding the tense muscles while he rode her. She met him thrust for thrust, so filled with love, with need, with him, that she was losing all traces of coherent thought.

Her mouth was consumed by him, his tongue sending spirals of desire down her back and between her legs. Her breasts were possessed by him, tingling and heavy beneath his touch. Her body was one with him, giving a whole new meaning to the physical union between a man and a woman.

Their need was too great, their desire too long denied for them to have time for foreplay. Andrea's hips accommodated Doug's body, driving with him, pushing him harder and harder until she thought she'd go mad. She felt him stiffen, heard his gasp as his body exploded within hers, and then suddenly she was spiraling alone, up and away to a realm where only sensation existed. Everything she was, everything she had ever been, became centered in that space, pulsing around Doug's body until she was weak and spent, and lay beneath him resplendent with peace.

Doug rolled off of her, lying flat on his back with his arm flung over his face. "God, lady, what'd you do to me? I've never embarrassed myself like that before. I swear it."

Andrea laughed. She couldn't help it. She couldn't ever remember feeling so good.

"Don't laugh. My ego's already small enough as it is."

Andrea reached her hand down. "But you're still plenty big where it counts...."

She leaned over and licked his nipple, needing to taste him, to feel him, to become as familiar with his body as she was her own, now that she could be patient enough to enjoy the journey.

"Andrea." His voice held a note of warning.

"You wouldn't want me to think it's always 'wham bam, thank you, ma'am' with you, would you?"

Doug pulled her over on top of him, lifting his hips against her as he ran his fingers down her back and across her bottom. Andrea shivered.

"Let's see how much you can take, shall we?" he said, catching her nipple between his teeth.

Andrea couldn't believe herself. A wild woman had taken over her tense, controlled existence, lighting a fire within her that she wasn't sure would ever be extinguished. She touched Doug, giving in to her heated flesh, hoping that neither one of them would get burned by her actions.

THE DAYS THAT FOLLOWED were out of space, out of time. Andrea didn't think about the past. She didn't look to the future. She didn't let herself make love to Doug nearly as often as she wanted to. And she never let him spend the night. She kept hoping that her desire for him would lessen, that her love would wane. It never did.

She knew Doug was still spending time with Jeremy. She'd stopped by Doug's apartment Tuesday evening and found the boy there with him, making a pizza. They'd invited her to stay, but she'd refused.

She was still convinced that Jeremy was only paying lip service to Doug. She was still scared silly that Doug was setting himself up for a major fall. She still thought Doug was wrong to have singled out the boy. She decided to spend Thanksgiving alone.

DOUG'S PHONE RANG early on Thanksgiving morning. He rolled over in his sofa bed, fighting the bitter taste of disappointment as reality intruded on his dreams and he realized that he was in bed alone. He reached for the receiver.

"Avery." He sat up, leaning against the back of the couch. There was no evidence anywhere in the room that Andrea had been there the night before, loving him like he'd never been loved. The woman could pick up and leave more quickly than he'd ever done.

"Doug? It's Gloria Parker."

"Gloria? Has something happened to Andrea?"

"She's the same as always, Doug, same as always. Which is why I was wondering if you wouldn't mind doing me a favor—that is, if you're still feeling about my daughter the way you felt last time we talked."

"Depends on the favor."

"Andrea's planning to spend the day alone."

"Some people like it that way."

"Not Andrea. She hates it. She's just too damn stubborn to admit it."

That sounded a lot like Andrea. "And you think I can do something about it?"

"She wouldn't turn you away if you showed up on her doorstep."

He'd planned to spend the day on his couch, watching football and feeling sorry for himself. "Maybe I'll give her a call."

"No!" Doug pulled the phone away from his ear as Gloria's panic resounded in his eardrum. "If you call her, she'll say no. I know she will. But my daughter's got a big heart. She won't be able to turn you away if you show up on her doorstep all alone, looking for someplace to spend the day, especially if you have a turkey in your arms."

The woman was something else. He pictured Andrea growing up with her mother, getting the best of her now and then. The vision made him smile.

"Cooked or uncooked?"

"Oh, uncooked, definitely."

Doug swung his legs to the side of the bed, keeping the sheet across his naked hips. "I'll think about it," he said, unwilling to let the woman know how completely he could be manipulated.

And he did think about it. For the five seconds it took him to get from his bed to his bathroom. The thought of spending the whole day with Andrea, alone in her apartment, was too good to pass up. But he drew the line at the turkey.

"I'M GLAD YOU CAME," Andrea said late that evening. She and Doug were curled up in her bed, sated and replete. It wasn't the first time they'd been there that day.

"Mmm. Me too," he mumbled against her breast. And he was. But he wasn't satisfied. For the first time in his life he wanted more, dared to allow himself to hope for more, wasn't satisfied to take what he could get.

"I don't know what possessed me to buy such a big turkey," she said dreamily. "I'd have been eating leftovers till Christmas."

"Mmm..."

"You hungry? We still have lots left."

"We can have it for breakfast in the morning." His words hung in the air between them.

"I, uh, don't eat breakfast."

"You could watch me eat it."

"Doug. Don't do this."

Doug pushed away from her, getting up to slip into his jeans. He zipped them, but left them unbuttoned. He stalked back to the bed, leaning down to place one hand on either side of her, his face only inches from hers.

"What am I? Some kind of damn gigolo? Good enough to romp with, but nothing else? What? I might soil your sheets if I stay in them too long?"

Tears welled up in Andrea's eyes. Doug tried not to see them. He couldn't stay angry with her if she was going to cry.

"Don't say that." Her words were barely above a whisper. "You promised. No commitments."

"As I recall, it was no promises, either. But that was then. Andrea, for the first time in my life I want more than good sex. I want what other guys have, what Stan Ingersoll has—a woman in his bed at night, the same woman every night. I want to hold you in my arms when I go to sleep, and find you there when I wake up. Why is that so much to ask?"

"Because you're asking the wrong woman."

"Why? You let me enter your body, but cringe at the thought of me holding you while you sleep?"

She met his gaze steadily, her eyes filled with resolution—and a hint of something more, something painful. "I cringe at the thought of you leaving my bed when it goes sour."

"And how do you know it will?"

"I don't know. I just can't take that chance. I'm no good at loving, Doug. I lose perspective. I let people down."

Doug swore, pushing away from the bed to stalk across the room. "That's bullshit. Who have you let down? A man who didn't love you enough to stand by you when you needed him? Who else?"

"It wasn't like that, Doug. I let him down first. And it wasn't just him." She got out of bed, shrugging into the terry-cloth robe she'd worn earlier when they'd gone to the kitchen for dinner. "Look, what you're asking for isn't unreasonable. It isn't even unfair. But I'm just not the one to give it to you. I told you that two weeks ago."

"So this is where you kick me out of your life, is that it? All clean and neat. I've served my purpose and now I'm supposed to walk, like a good little boy?"

She leaned against the wall, tears pooling in her eyes again, this time falling slowly down her face. But she didn't back down.

"I'm not ready to lose you. I don't know if I'll ever be ready. But I can't make promises I might not be able to keep. I tried that once and it didn't work."

Doug studied her, seeing her pain, her unhappiness, but her resolution as well. A part of him acknowledged the irony of the situation. Here he was, a man who usually could barely wait for his heartbeat to return to normal before he jumped out of a woman's bed, finally ready to stay put—and the woman wasn't offering.

"So where does that leave us?"

Andrea walked over to him, smoothing her slim hands up his chest. "We're here together now. Can't we just have this? Please, Doug. It's been such a perfect day. Just hold me."

She laid her head on his chest, cuddling up to him, and Doug felt his arms going around her, doing her bidding, even while he knew that he was heading for disaster. He was getting in too deep, and he feared that the lady wasn't getting in at all.

THE DAYS SEEMED to fly by after that. Each one was precious to Andrea, because she feared her time with Doug was going to end. He wanted more from her than she was giving him. He deserved more from her. But she was just too damn scared to give it. She'd rather die than live through more broken promises, more expectations she couldn't live up to. She'd rather die than believe in a future with Doug Avery, only to have it swept away by her own incompetence.

She was dusting her apartment the Saturday after Thanksgiving, wondering if Doug would be stopping by sometime that evening, when she heard his familiar knock at her door.

Andrea stopped for a quick glance in the mirror to be certain she didn't have dirt smudged across her nose. She would have preferred to have changed out of her jeans and sweatshirt into something a little more provocative, and to have run a comb through her hair so it didn't look as if she'd been running her fingers through it all afternoon. But knowing Doug, she figured she'd be out of her clothes soon enough anyway, and she hurried toward the door with the fierce heat of anticipation spreading throughout her body.

Doug looked awful. He stood in her doorway looking at her as if he were drowning and she were a piece of driftwood. His face was ashen, his lips tight, his eyes glassy with shock.

Andrea took hold of his arm, her heart pounding in her chest. She pulled him forward, trying to draw him into her arms, to hold him, to make whatever it was go away.

He brushed past her into her living room, standing by the couch, looking around as if he didn't know how he'd gotten there. His nostrils were flaring with the obvious effort it took him to keep a hold on his emotions. Andrea's heart filled with fear.

"It's Jeremy."

The two words were all he said, but they were all Andrea needed. She knew. In the space of two words she knew exactly what Doug was facing. She knew the disbelief, the recriminations he was putting himself through. And she knew about the guilt that lay ahead. She knew it, not because she could guess, but because she *knew*. She'd been there before, once. She'd never made it back.

"Where is he?"

Doug looked over at her, his eyes hard with self-loathing, his breathing heavy with guilt. "Children's Hospital."

So Jeremy was alive. She'd been afraid to ask.

"Let's go."

Andrea never hesitated as she picked up her purse, locked her apartment and followed Doug to his car. She knew she was walking into something she wasn't ready to handle, something that could very well strip her of the little control she had left, but she went anyway. Doug needed her.

The hours in the empty waiting room were endless. Doug paced. He sipped the coffee Andrea brought him, and nagged the nursing staff until Andrea finally had to intercede on his behalf. Jeremy was still alive. That's all anybody would tell them.

"Is there anybody we should contact?" Andrea asked when it seemed like their vigil was sure to continue on into the night. She needed something to do. She'd been on this floor before, waited in this very room for the same interminable hours. The memories were suffocating her.

Doug shook his head. He slouched back on the vinyl seat beside her, staring at the floor between his outstretched feet.

"Won't his parents wonder where he is?"

He turned his head to look at her, his eyes bitter. "His old man quit wondering years ago, when he took off. And if his old lady ever bothered to wonder now and then, Jeremy wouldn't be in there fighting for his life."

Andrea swallowed hard, forcing her own demons aside. She couldn't let herself think about another fight like this one, another young life hovering on the brink of death. She was too worried about the boy whose life hung by a thread right now, about the frightening coldness that was consuming Doug.

"Who found him?" She'd been afraid to ask, afraid to make him relive any part of the tragic day, but now she was afraid not to. She couldn't just let Doug slip back to the lonely hell he'd inhabited before DARE had come into his life.

He didn't answer her.

"Doug? Who found him?"

He didn't look up. He didn't even move, but finally he murmured, "A Rattler." The next words came as an afterthought. "The kid had seen me around. He'd ragged on Jeremy once for hanging out with an old guy. Jeremy told him who I was. The guy's been looking after Jeremy ever since."

"Where'd he find him?"

"Relieving himself in a mailbox slot a couple of blocks from home. Apparently Jeremy'd been partying since six o'clock last night. God only knows what all he's on. Someone said he fell off a wall while watching the sun rise six times. Both of his wrists were broken. Jeremy didn't even know it." Doug's voice was a monotone.

"He's hung on this long, so his chances are getting better every minute," Andrea said, repeating words she'd been told four years ago, even though she had a feeling they were going to help Doug as little as they'd helped her.

"Yeah. He may pull through and have a wonderful life sitting in a chair, being fed from a spoon like a baby. Who the hell do you think's going to take care of him? His old lady? Or maybe one of the strangers she brings home at night?"

Andrea reached over to run her hand along Doug's forearm. His skin was icy.

"Don't, Doug. Don't do this to yourself. If it's bad, there'll be plenty enough time to deal with it when we know. He may pull through just fine."

"He may." Doug's jaw clenched. Andrea could tell he wasn't buying it. If Jeremy didn't make it, she was afraid that Doug wasn't going to make it, either. She knew exactly how he felt.

It was another two hours before the doctor finally appeared. He was an older man, tall, with gray hair and stooped shoulders. Or maybe his slumping shoulders were just a result of the day he'd had. Either way, Andrea's stomach knotted with dread when she saw him heading toward them.

"Doug Avery?" he asked, looking at Doug's bent head.

Doug shot out of his seat, grabbing Andrea's hand on the way, pulling her up beside him. "That's me," he said.

Andrea wrapped her arms around his waist, hoping he could find some strength from her presence. There were no thoughts of tomorrow or yesterday, no worries about promises made or broken. There was only Doug's need, and her compulsion to love him.

"I'm Dr. Sandborne. You know the boy's parents?"

"Yes."

"We've been unable to reach them as yet. Perhaps you know where we might find them?"

"No. How is he?"

"I'm afraid I'm not at liberty to say until I've met with the family. If we can't locate them, we'll need to call in the police."

Andrea felt Doug's muscles clench. Her nerves were shaking.

"We're police officers, Dr. Sandborne. Officer Avery is responsible for the boy's welfare. His father's gone and his mother is most likely too drunk to be much good to him. We'd be most grateful if you'd let us see him." Andrea spoke quickly, but as calmly as she could manage, inserting all the authority at her command. Her stomach was quaking.

The doctor looked both of them over, Andrea in her blue jeans and sweatshirt and Doug in his skintight jeans and leather jacket. She reached into her purse and pulled out her badge. Doug saw what she was doing and reached into his pocket for his wallet.

Dr. Sandborne looked at the photos briefly, and then at Doug. "Right this way," he said, leading them back the way he'd come. Andrea took a quick glance at Doug, uneasy about the tightness of his jaw, his pursed lips, uneasy about the too-familiar smells and sounds that were assailing her.

"How is he, Doctor?" she asked, as much for her benefit as Doug's.

"He's a lucky young man. We pumped his stomach and his vital signs have stabilized, though he'll probably suffer from flashback hallucinations for a while. As far as we can tell, his brain waves are normal. His right wrist is badly broken. It's going to require surgery within the next day or so, so we'll need his mother's signature on the release form. I've already set the left wrist.''

The doctor paused outside a door that stood slightly ajar, his craggy eyebrows knit into a frown. Andrea wondered how many of his days were like the one he'd just had.

"It looks worse than it is," he said. "We're flushing his system and monitoring his oxygen intake, but the biggest danger has passed."

With that, he pushed open the door and stood aside for Andrea and Doug to enter the private room. A nurse was busy beside Jeremy's bed. She glanced over as they came in, but didn't stop attending to her patient.

Andrea stood back by the door. Jeremy was going to be all right. She kept concentrating on that thought. The helpless, shockingly pale boy surrounded by beeping machines was Jeremy. And he was going to be all right. The tubes that were coming from all parts of his body were helping him. He was Jeremy. And he was going to be just fine.

The blackness came upon her so quickly she didn't know what was happening. She only knew that the cool relief it offered was too strong for her to resist.

DOUG FORCED his concentration onto the road in front of him. Only a couple more blocks and he'd have Andrea home. She sat silently beside him. Doug wasn't even sure she was aware of the tears that were falling slowly but steadily down her cheeks.

She let him help her from her car and into her apartment, as listless as a stunned animal. Dr. Sandborne had told him that she was suffering from emotional overload. He'd recommended that Andrea take the tranquilizers he'd prescribed. Doug wasn't so sure that was such a good idea.

He didn't think Andrea was simply reacting to the trauma of Jeremy's overdose, as the doctor had assumed. Doug was pretty certain that she had been harboring whatever was bothering her for a long time. And he didn't think she needed to hide from it with prescribed numbness. His instincts told him that if she was ever going to live again, to live wholly, she was going to have to face her pain and put it to rest. He wasn't going to let her run away again.

He led her to her bed and took off her tennis shoes and socks. She flopped back against the pillows he stacked up for her, looking like she didn't have the desire to ever move again. Doug settled beside her, taking her in his arms. She started to cry harder, until her sobs were shaking the bed. He handed her some tissues from the nightstand and held on. The pills Dr. Sandborne had prescribed were still in his pocket. He only hoped he was doing the right thing.

Doug lost track of time as he held her and listened to the pain racking her. He felt so lost, so damned helpless as he tried to absorb her pain without knowing what was causing it. He felt like his heart was breaking into as many fragments as hers.

He held her, he stroked her, he murmured to her. And finally her trembling quieted, her tears slowed to trickles, her sobs to an occasional hiccup. Doug had no idea what to do next, what was best for her, what she needed from him. Should he let her sleep? Suggest she take a shower? Fix her something to eat? He felt almost panicky as he realized he had no idea how to take care of another person.

"Scotty's lips were bluer."

Her soft words ripped into the night, searing Doug's soul. Who the hell was Scotty? Was he supposed to ask? Or would his question silence her?

"He looked so little, so helpless lying in that bed. And all those tubes..."

Her voice trailed off as she gazed sightlessly across the room. Doug was frustrated by his inability to share whatever pictures were playing themselves out in her head. He didn't even know who she was seeing. She could have been describing Jeremy. Maybe she had been.

But another possibility suddenly occurred to him. Had Andrea been through this before? Had there been another young child, another overdose? Had Andrea, as a young cop, been the one to find him, to bring him in? Had that been the time of need Gloria had referred to? The time when Andrea's husband had walked out on her? Suddenly it all made horrifying sense.

Doug had a hard time sitting still on the bed. He needed to do something. To hit something. To kill the bastard who had locked Andrea up in this emotional hell.

"Jeremy's going to be okay, Doug. The doctor said he was a lucky boy."

"I know, sweetie. By tomorrow the tubes should be gone."

"Scotty had the tubes for almost a week. He was so tiny, so innocent. He just lay there with the shadows getting darker and darker beneath his eyes." Her voice was distant.

Doug's dread increased. Had the boy lived? He was afraid to ask.

"No matter how long I sat there, how much I talked to him, how many times I prayed, he just wouldn't wake up. I thought we were going to lose him for sure. And it was all my fault."

"Wait a minute there, lady. You're a cop, not God. You told me yourself you can't help them all. Sometimes it's just too late before you get to them."

Doug hoped she bought the words better than he had. He was still reeling from his own self-disgust, tasting the bitterness of his own guilt. He understood only too well how she could have shouldered the blame for the little boy's condition, and how her husband's desertion would only have deepened the quagmire of destructive emotions.

"I was there before it was too late, Doug. I missed the signs. All of them. The new set of friends, lower grades, unusual requests for money, disappearing allowance, lost interest in basketball, truancy. I thought they were all a phase—you know, like the terrible twos. Even the nosebleeds didn't clue me in."

She laughed a humorless, shallow laugh. "He was nine years old and addicted to cocaine, and I thought it was the terrible twos."

Doug was alarmed by the self-loathing he heard in Andrea's usually sweet voice.

"You can't expect yourself to see the symptoms in every child when you deal with hundreds every week," he said, rubbing her arm gently, trying to work the circulation back into it.

"I wasn't a DARE officer then, Doug."

"Then you have even less reason to blame yourself. How many cops do you know who can keep track of the everyday lives of the people on their beat? What were you, a truant officer?"

Andrea took a deep, shuddering breath and shook her head, and then shook it again.

"I was a sister." Her words, when they finally came, were barely audible, thick with tears, but they hit Doug with the impact of a bullet. Dear God, he'd never imagined anything like this. He hadn't even known she had a brother.

And now he had to ask that question. He had to know.

"Did he make it, baby? Did Scotty get lucky, too?"

Andrea nodded, but her tears continued to fall relentlessly. Doug pulled her onto his lap, cradling her against his chest. He was prepared to shoulder as much as she would let him. She was his woman.

"Talk to me, Andrea. Tell me what happened."

"It started as a dare out on the playground." Her voice faltered. "Some bigger boys, sixth-graders, offered to let him lick some 'sugar' off a mirror. He was always such a shy little boy, small for his age and smart as a whip. Most of the kids teased him, called him 'teacher's pet,' made fun of his thick glasses. But that day, the most popular boys in school were being nice to him. Scotty licked. And when he got into gym class that afternoon he was a star.'' Andrea was calmer now, reciting facts. "He was making baskets he'd never made before. The teacher told him that if he kept shooting like that, he'd let him work out with the sixth-grade team. Scotty had always dreamed of making the team, but he'd never thought he had a chance because he was so short. But that afternoon he felt like he could do anything. The girls that had always made fun of him were fighting over who would walk with him back to class, and Scotty was able to talk to them without tripping over his tongue.

"The next day, when those same boys were out on the playground, he worked up the courage to ask them if they had any more of that sugar. They laughed and talked him into some 'better' stuff. They kept him supplied long enough to get him hooked."

Doug felt Andrea shudder against his chest. He tightened his hold on her.

"Then they put it to him. Before anyone knew what was happening, he was addicted to crack."

"How long before you knew?"

"He'd been using regularly for over a month. He was getting low on funds and I refused to give him any more. I thought he was blowing it on video games at the arcade." Her words were bitter again, condemning. Doug had a terrible premonition that there was more to come.

"When it got to the point that he could no longer afford his usual stash, he settled for some cheaper stuff. It was bad. He had an allergic reaction to the stuff that afternoon at school. They had to rush him to Children's Hospital by helicopter. They almost didn't get him there in time."

"What about your parents? I can just imagine how they felt, having missed all the symptoms when he was living in their home...."

Andrea slid off Doug's lap and got up from the bed. She wrapped her arms around herself as she headed for the bathroom across the room. She turned to face Doug just before she shut herself inside.

"They were out of town, Doug. They'd been saving all their lives for a European cruise. That year was their thirtieth wedding anniversary and they celebrated with a month on the Atlantic. Scotty had been staying with me...."

CHAPTER FIFTEEN

ANDREA FELT a little better after her shower. In four years' time she'd never once talked about Scotty, never once shared her anguish with anyone. But while it had helped to talk about it, to be wrapped within the secure cocoon of Doug's arms, the guilt was still just as bitter, as unrelenting as ever. How could she ever promise to love and to cherish again? What did those empty promises mean? She'd promised to look after Scotty. Her parents had left an innocent little boy in her hands and had come home to a nightmare.

"Mmm. That smells good," she said, finding Doug in her kitchen ladling tomato soup into two bowls.

He sat down across from her, passing her a package of saltines. "I called the hospital. Jeremy's sleeping peacefully."

"Thank God." Andrea had never meant two words more in her life. Maybe they could just put the past twelve hours behind them.

"So where does your divorce fit into all this?"

She looked at Doug over the spoon suspended halfway between her bowl and her mouth. He was watching her intently. It wasn't over yet.

Andrea's first instinct was to throw him out, to plead fatigue, to lie to him, but she couldn't. She loved

Doug. She couldn't give him promises, she couldn't give him commitments or a future. But she could give him the truth. He deserved that, at least.

She put her spoon back in her bowl, leaving it there.

"As soon as we knew that Scotty was going to make it, John jumped on the incident as proof of my inappropriateness for police work."

Doug dropped his own spoon, disgust flaring across his stubbled face.

"Wait." Andrea held up a hand, forestalling what he might say. "In a way he was right. As a cop, I should've seen the signs long before Scotty snorted that bad batch. But that wasn't what broke up our marriage. It was the way I had failed at home. I was trained to see the signs, to protect the public from people like those who'd started in on Scotty to begin with, and I'd been so complacent in my knowledge that I lost perspective. I never put two and two together where my brother was concerned. John was worried that I'd fail my own kids like I failed Scotty, that I couldn't do my job and take care of a family, too. He wanted children. He just didn't want me to be their mother. Not unless I gave up my career."

"And you couldn't do that."

Andrea felt so incompetent. "Nope. At the expense of my marriage, in spite of the vows I'd taken till death do us part, I chose my career over my husband. I was served with divorce papers exactly one month after Scotty's overdose."

Doug swore, getting up from the table to pour his soup down the sink. He didn't say anything else, but the rigid set of his shoulders told her what he thought of John's sense of timing. It felt good to have someone champion her, even though she'd been in the wrong.

She helped Doug with the dishes and then followed him back down the hall to her bedroom. She pulled on her sleep shirt while Doug showered, listening to him set the soap in the dish, wondering if she'd ever share a house with him. She doubted it. After all he'd heard, she doubted that Doug would ever ask her to.

"I'd like to meet Scotty." His words were easy enough as he came through the door into her bedroom, but they sent Andrea into a panic.

"You can't." She sat frozen at the foot of the bed, staring at him.

Doug stood rooted to the spot, his towel slung loosely around his hips, beaded drops of moisture clinging to the hair on his chest. "Why not?"

The words were more challenging than curious.

Andrea felt trapped. She'd never intended to confess the rest. It was her biggest humiliation.

"He hasn't spoken to me in almost three years."

"What?" Doug was staring at her as if he'd never seen her before.

"He hates me," she said flatly.

"That's ridiculous. He was the one who made the mistakes. How could he hate you?"

Andrea rose to her little brother's defense. "He was a child, Doug. A little boy just waiting for someone to catch him, to help him out of a situation that was too big for him to handle. He'd trusted me to watch out for his welfare, to guard and protect him. I failed to do that."

"You're not God, Andrea. He can't hold you responsible for thugs on the playground."

"He can do whatever he chooses to do, Doug, and I, for one, can't say I blame him. Things haven't been easy for him. After his overdose became public knowledge he was forced out of his Cub Scout troop, and that summer, scared parents didn't want him in T-ball. The couple of boys that used to be Scotty's friends weren't allowed to play with him anymore. He'd always been a shy boy, slow to make friends. How could he have been expected to deal with total rejection? He felt like I let him down. And he's right, I did."

"Didn't your parents fight it? Didn't they try to reason with the parents who were blackballing him?"

"*I* tried. Mom and Dad were too busy dealing with Scotty. But people are a funny lot when they're scared. Scotty's mishap, as the other parents termed it, hit a little too close to home. They were horrified by the danger that had entered their upper-middle-class elementary-school hallways through my baby brother. They were running scared. They didn't bother to be tactful when they let me know that I'd blown it. After all, I'm a cop. Why hadn't I prevented things from getting so out of hand?"

Doug threw down his towel. "I don't believe this. What about Scotty? Didn't you try to reason with him? He's your brother, for Pete's sake. You can't go through life ignoring each other."

Andrea felt tears choking her throat again. When would she ever have cried enough?

"I tried to talk to Scotty," she said, meeting Doug's gaze squarely. "Even after I visited his hospital room and he demanded that I leave, even after he'd told me repeatedly that he hated me, I still tried. I wanted to apologize, to do whatever I could do to help him through the mess he was so ill-equipped to handle. But my attempts only seemed to upset him more. At first he screamed at me every time he saw me, and then later, the few times he'd talk to me at all, he was formal and awkward, as though I were some great-aunt of his. It was his counselor who finally suggested that Scotty might need some time, and mine who reminded me that I could only bang my head against a wall so many times before I broke. So I've been giving him the time he needs, for more months than I care to count."

Doug grabbed up Andrea from the foot of the bed, crushing her in his arms, doing his gut-level best to erase her loneliness, to fuse it with his own. But even as he held her, he doubted that he'd ever really have her. They weren't just dealing with a failed marriage, with scarred emotions. Her ex-husband's words were too deeply embedded in her heart, her own crucifixion of herself too complete, her brother's condemnation ringing too loudly in her ears for her to ease up on herself. Doug wasn't sure she'd ever recover. He had no idea how to make things better for her.

He led her to the bed, tucking her under the covers, wondering if Andrea's self-loathing might just be bigger than both of them. He wanted so badly to lie with her, to hold her through the night, but he knew better than to try. Now he understood why Andrea insisted on being alone.

He was zipping up his jeans before Andrea realized that he was going to leave her. The walls of her apartment closed in on her, reverberating with all the words they'd absorbed that night, replaying memories that were demons just waiting to destroy her.

"Don't go. Please don't go." She heard her voice begging Doug to stay, and didn't even care. She couldn't bear to be alone. Just for one night, she couldn't bear to be alone.

Without a word Doug slipped out of his jeans again and crawled in beside her, pulling her back into the safe haven of his arms. His leather wristband pressed comfortingly between her shoulder blades.

"It's okay, baby. I'm right here," he said in the most tender voice she'd ever heard him use. It slid over her skin, touching her in all the right places, offering her forgetfulness within the magic of his desire.

She snuggled against him, desperately eager for him to take her away from herself, from her thoughts and fears, from her belief that she was a lesser being, and transport her to a place where she was desirable, beautiful, courageous.

She waited for Doug's fingers to trail across her skin, to take possession of her breast, to tease her to the point of insanity. She expected the hair-roughed heaviness of his thigh to slip between her legs, to spread them apart and ready her to take his most intimate offering. But he didn't. He simply lay with her.

Andrea lay awake long into the night, refusing to cry. She didn't blame Doug for not wanting to love her. It had been a long time since she'd loved herself.

LITTLE SPIRALS OF HEAVEN spun down Andrea's body, settling in her womanhood, nudging her awake. She didn't move. She didn't even want to breathe, for fear that she'd make the magical dream go away.

Calloused fingers captured her breast beneath her nightshirt, teasing the tip of her nipple. Every ounce of Andrea's concentration settled in that spot, glorying in the miracle of her awakening.

She shivered as the covers rolled away, but she welcomed the bite of cool air on her skin. Her nightshirt slid up her body, exposing her belly and then her breasts to the early-morning light. And then she felt one of her nipples being grazed by bearded stubble, by the hot velvety sleekness of a tongue, by lips that suckled her with fierce longing.

Andrea abandoned herself to the magic that only Doug could give her, refusing to allow thought to interfere with the perfection he was creating. She opened her eyes, relinquishing sleep so she could join Doug in the world he'd made for them.

He lay on his stomach beside her, his naked buttocks tight and firm to her hungry gaze. His dark head nestled against her chest as if he had come home, as if he was where he'd always belonged, as if her body was his haven.

"It's about time you joined me, woman." He lifted his head from her breast, fondling her moistened flesh with his thumb as his gaze bore into hers.

She slid her fingers boldly over his behind and then back up to fan out over his shoulders. "All you have to do is ask," she said, meeting his gaze.

"Oh, I'm askin', lady. I'm askin' real hard."

He pushed his thigh between her legs, spreading her open, and climbed on top of her.

"See how hard I'm askin'?" He nudged her womanhood with his bulging penis.

Andrea nuzzled her face into his neck, inhaling the musky male scent of him, tasting the saltiness of his flesh, flooding her senses with all that was Doug. She spread her legs wider, accommodating his swollen flesh, and rocked her hips upward, taking all of him in one brazen thrust.

"God, woman. How do you do this to me?" He ground her hips into the bed, taking over from her, filling her body so completely that she couldn't possibly feel empty again. He pulled out slowly and plunged again, and again, and again, giving Andrea the most exquisite pleasure she had ever known.

And by the time his body was pulsing with release, flooding her with his seed, Andrea had never felt so cherished in her life. She clutched him to her even after he was spent, marveling at his ability to take a mass of knotted string and make it feel like spun gold.

GLORIA WAS REALLY getting mad. She'd done everything a mother could do, even a couple of things that most mothers probably couldn't, and still Andrea was alone. Gloria didn't get it. She'd thought for sure when she managed to pull off Thanksgiving that Andrea would finally at least announce that she had a boyfriend, maybe even bring him around for dinner. But nothing of the sort had happened.

She was beginning to worry that there was something fundamentally wrong with her daughter. Maybe that jerk ex-husband of hers had done more than desert her. Maybe he'd turned her off from men in the biblical sense. Of course, even fundamental wrongs could be fixed. And it was Gloria's job, as Andrea's mother, to do the fixing. After all, if a girl couldn't talk to her mother about sex, who could she talk to?

Gloria chose her time carefully. She wanted to have an entire afternoon free of the guys so she wouldn't have to embarrass Andrea by announcing that they were having 'woman talk.' On the first Sunday in December, she sent her husband and son to a Cincinnati Bengals game and then called Andrea over to help wrap Christmas presents.

"That pile over there on that chair are Scotty's gifts and these on the table are your father's. No, Andrea, don't use that paper yet—those rolls of paper are for Scotty's gifts, and for the ones we're taking to the orphanage. Use the green foil on Pop's, and save the red foil so I can do yours."

Gloria surveyed her dining room, taking a last look at the order with which she'd arranged everything. It was likely to be chaos by the time they were finished.

"How're Mark and Amy, Ma? Have you seen them lately?" Andrea reached over her mother to rip a piece of tape from the dispenser on the table.

"I think they're flying to Vegas to get married over Christmas."

"They're eloping? Did they tell you that?"

"Of course not, Andrea. You don't tell someone you're eloping, or else it wouldn't be eloping. You just run off and get married, all by yourselves, just like it was any other normal day. And then afterward—after you've done it and you're really married—then you tell everybody." Gloria figured it couldn't hurt to make sure Andrea had a thorough understanding of these things.

Andrea smiled. "Then how do you know they're going to do it, Ma?"

Gloria's heart turned over. Her daughter really did have a beautiful smile. She carefully folded in the corners of the paper she was wrapping around a shirt box.

"Just wait, Andrea, you'll see. They'll be married by the New Year."

They wrapped in silence, while Gloria tried to work up the guts to talk to Andrea about sex. Should she just come right out and talk about climaxes—female ones? Or should she approach Andrea more subtly, maybe ask a couple of leading questions first?

And then she remembered there was something else she needed to ask.

"How's that boy you were with at the hospital last weekend?"

"Jeremy? He's really doing okay, Ma. He has some tough times ahead of him, but so far he's pulling through. They have him in detox and he's still having hallucinations, but he seems to be ready to go straight. That's most of the battle won right there."

Gloria nodded. Her whole family was pulling for the boy. They all knew, firsthand, what the young man was going through. They knew all about the hell of rehab.

"You'll let me know if there's anything I can do, won't you?"

"Yeah, Ma. I'll let you know."

The packages were almost all wrapped. Gloria watched Andrea reach for the last box in Scotty's pile. She watched her daughter measure and cut a piece of paper to fit the package, and took a deep breath.

"Do you like sex?"

"What?" Andrea dropped the scissors, putting a nick in the dining-room table.

"You know—sex. Do you like it?"

"No offense, Ma, but that's really none of your concern."

"Just answer me, Andrea. Do you like it?"

"Sure, I like it. Who doesn't, if it's with the right person?" Andrea paused in her wrapping to study her mother. "Wait a minute, Ma. Are you having troubles? Is there something wrong between you and Pop?"

Gloria snorted. Leave it to Andrea to try and turn the tables.

"No. There is nothing wrong between your father and me. He's as randy as ever, and I still tingle every time he touches me. But what about you? Do you ever, you know, tingle?"

Andrea's face filled with color. She resumed her wrapping. "That's none of your business, Ma. Now how about we change the subject?"

Gloria was encouraged by the blush on her daughter's cheeks. Maybe that Doug Avery was as good as he looked, after all. Maybe they'd have a very merry Christmas yet.

"I'm only trying to help, Andrea. You're a grown woman. It's not natural for you to go so long without sex. Your body needs the, uh, release."

"Stay out of it, Ma."

"Andrea, sex is natural, it's necessary—"

"Ma! Shut up!"

Gloria smiled. *Yep. It just might turn out to be a glorious Christmas, after all.*

"OKAY, GANG, we've got time for one more before we wrap it up for the week. Someone throw out a pressure situation."

"This really rad girl invites you over for a party. You get to her house and find out it's just you and her. Her folks are gone for the weekend. You're sitting next to her on the couch, getting up the guts to make a move on her, and she pulls out this joint and wants you to try just a toke or two."

Doug listened to Jay Wilson describe every boy's dream. "Okay, Jay's got a good one. Shane? What would you do?"

"Take a stand?"

"How?"

"Tell her she's so cool she doesn't need that stuff?"

"She doesn't buy it," Jay called out.

"But she's so beautiful and smart. She could have any guy she wanted. Why would she want to mess herself up like that?"

"She's bored. Nothing's exciting anymore."

"I guess that means I'm not exciting, and if that's the case, I don't feel so good about being there anyway."

"Catch." Doug tossed Shane a miniature DARE Bear. He'd earned it. Doug was glad. Shane had been the only student in the class who had yet to earn a bear.

Doug looked over at Andrea as the kids packed up for the day. She was leaning against a desk, talking to a pretty red-headed girl. The girl had been crying during recess. Now she was smiling. Andrea was great with the kids. He didn't know what he would have done without her in the classroom with him these past months.

Which raised a question that had been nagging at him more and more. Next week was graduation. What was going to happen to him and Andrea after that?

"You got plans for the weekend?" he asked her as they walked together out to the school parking lot.

"I've got to get to the mall. I've barely started my Christmas shopping."

"You could pick up some great things at Winterfest."

"What Winterfest?"

"Down at King's Island. Stan was telling me they've turned the whole amusement park into a winter wonderland. Some of the rides are open, and all of the shops, of course."

"But King's Island is two hours away. That's kind of far to go just to shop, don't you think?"

"I wasn't just thinking about shopping. I was thinking about having you all to myself, taking you on an old-fashioned sleigh ride, having to cuddle you to keep warm.'' Doug paused and then jumped in feet first. ''I was thinking about staying in the hotel there and having our own private Christmas.''

''Oh, Doug. Don't do this. I want so badly to make you happy. God knows you deserve it. But I just can't do something that's going to make things even harder.''

''But why does it have to? Did something terrible happen last Saturday night when I slept with you all night long?''

She sighed, stopping beside her car to look up at him. The sadness in her eyes pierced Doug.

''More than you know. I haven't been able to sleep all week for missing you beside me. And that was after only one night. You're like an addiction. It scares me.''

Doug got the feeling that a lot more than a weekend was at stake here.

''Just what are you saying?'' he asked carefully. He slid his hands into his trouser pockets.

''I don't know,'' she said, sounding as confused as a child. ''I'm trying so hard to find a way out, to forgive myself, but it's just not working. I'm beginning to think it never will. And I just can't risk losing it all again.''

''So what are you saying?''

She looked up at him, her eyes pleading for understanding. ''I guess I'm saying it would be best if we don't see each other anymore—in a personal sense, I mean.''

Doug digested her words in silence. He felt there was something he should do or say, something he could give her that would help her find the courage to try again. But as he stood there in the semideserted parking lot, he couldn't find that elusive something.

"I guess if that's the way you want it..." He took a long last look at her, then walked away.

CHAPTER SIXTEEN

DOUG LOOKED AT the address in his hand. It was written with faded ink on a yellowed scrap of precinct notepaper. He remembered the day he'd written it there. Someone had come up to him just as he was finishing, and he'd ripped it off the pad so quickly that he'd torn the edge. But he'd kept the information.

He ran his calloused finger over the jagged edge of the paper, thinking back to the man he'd been seven years before, the man who'd told himself he was relieved—glad even—to see that the address was in such a nice part of town. And suddenly he was consumed with rage. He crushed the scrap of paper, wadding it up in his fist, and threw it across his living room.

He thought of the mass of grief and guilt Andrea had subjected herself to on behalf of her baby brother and her ex-husband, the penance she was paying still. And he thought of the sacrifices his mother had never made. He thought of the tears Andrea had shed for those she loved, for him, and the tears his mother had never shed.

Still seething with anger, Doug grabbed his keys off his coffee table, stuffed his arms into his leather jacket and strode out of his apartment as if the devil were at his heels.

Andrea needed something from him. He knew that. He knew he hadn't pushed her hard enough to not give up on them. And he had a pretty good idea why not. In his own way, he was as frightened as she was.

Doug got into his car and sped across town to the elite neighborhood where politicians and doctors lived. He slowed as he turned onto the street he was looking for, and came to a complete stop before he was in front of the right house.

He gazed at the huge white building, noting the freshly painted black trim, the perfectly manicured lawns, the mass of brightly colored flower beds. Anger was replaced by a childish fear, resentment by a lost piece of innocent hope. Maybe there was some explanation, something that would make the betrayal less damning, something that could explain the years of abandonment, of pain, of lovelessness.

Doug zipped up his jacket, slid his keys into one of its pockets and adjusted his wristband. He strode up to the front door of the imposing mansion as if he had every right to be there.

"Yes? May I help you?"

Lord. They even had a maid in a uniform.

"Yes. I'm looking for Dora. Dora Littleton."

The hired help looked him over, from the scuffed toes of his boots, along his tight, faded jeans, to the hair he probably should have had cut weeks ago.

"Who may I say is calling?"

"D-Deputy Douglas."

"Just one minute, sir."

The door swung toward him, and Doug had the sudden notion that the woman meant to shut it in his face and lock it. He grabbed the edge of the door with one hand, pushing it inward as he stepped up onto the marble floor of an incredibly luxurious foyer.

"I'll just wait in here, if you don't mind. It's unbelievably cold out today."

The maid looked like she was going to protest, but with one glance at Doug's face, she apparently thought better of it.

"Yes, sir. I'll get Mrs. Littleton."

So much for loyalty, Doug thought, scuffing the toe of his boot along the grouting that held two slabs of decorator marble together.

Now that he was there, he wasn't even sure why he'd come. He wondered how she'd look, if her hair was still the soft brown he remembered or if she'd turned graciously gray. He wondered if Mr. Littleton might be home.

"What's the meaning of this? Who are you and what do you want?"

He recognized her voice. He couldn't believe it. He actually recognized her voice.

But that was all he remembered about the woman standing before him. Gone were the stooped shoulders, the weary eyes, the gentle lips. The woman was regal, tall, erect and as cold as a headstone. Her lips were taut with displeasure.

Doug pulled out his wallet, flashing his ID, seeing the whole bizarre scene as if from a distance. A safe, unemotional distance.

"The name's Avery. Doug Avery. Mean anything to you?"

He felt a queer sense of satisfaction as he watched the color drain from her perfectly made-up face. It was good to know, after twenty-five years, that she still remembered him.

"Doug? Oh my God. Doug? What do you want? Why are you here? You want money, don't you? How much?"

Doug felt his heart sink like a stone. "Hi, Mom. I'm glad to see you, too."

"Doug? Why are you doing this to me?" Her silk pantsuit trembled around her.

"I wasn't aware that *I* had done anything to *you*," Doug said, trying to find some spark that would prove the woman's humanity.

Doesn't she feel anything? Isn't there any kind of maternal instinct inside her? Isn't there something that binds us together?

"You've got to go. Chad's due home any minute. He can't find you here."

"I meant to ask you about that. I know I was young, but I remember the guy's name as Philpot, Larry Philpot." His words were bitter, but they only portrayed the tip of what he was feeling.

She looked distracted for a minute, and Doug had the funny feeling that she was trying to remember if she'd ever known a Larry Philpot.

"He, uh, turned out to be something of a bum. Never could keep a job."

"Guess you were a little too hasty there, huh? At least Dad worked." As soon as the words had escaped his lips, Doug remembered the sound of his father's hand smacking his mother's face, and felt ashamed for having said them.

But then he remembered the feel of that hand against his own head, the anger that had been turned on him because of this woman's desertion, and he didn't feel sorry for hurting her.

"What do you want from me?" Her words were pleading. Suddenly she looked her age, even older. Her years of hard living seemed to have caught up with her in the space of two minutes.

"Why? Why did you do it?"

She looked impatient. "How can you ask that? You know what he did to me—"

"I don't mean that." Doug cut her off. "No one could blame you for leaving him. But what about me? Why did you leave me there with him? I was just a little kid, for heaven's sake, barely out of diapers."

She started to cry then, small tears that were wiped away before they could smudge her eye makeup. She looked around, as if fearing the servants' sharp ears, and then led Doug into a private sitting room to the right of the hall.

Doug refused the seat she offered him. He refused the drink, too, surprised that she didn't immediately help herself to a stiff glassful from the fully stocked sideboard.

"You've certainly done well for yourself. How long have you been living in the lap of luxury?"

"I met Chad twenty years ago, when I was waitressing at the Morse Road Golf Club. He didn't care

that I didn't have a good family name. He only cared
that I was pretty and innocent."

Doug cringed. "How'd you pull that one off?"

"I'd learned how to pretend almost anything, by
then. And Chad saw what he wanted to see."

"So the poor fellow married you, not knowing that
you'd ever lived with another man, let alone borne his
son?"

"I did what I had to do, Doug. And I've been a
good wife to Chad all these years. I learned what I had
to learn to fit in with his family and friends, and I've
been faithful to him since the moment we met. I'd
even have given him children if he'd wanted any."

Doug stood in the middle of her elegant little room
and wanted to throttle her. Like, he was supposed to
be impressed by her fidelity? "Where was all that loyalty when I needed you?"

Dora sank down onto a velvet-covered sofa, running her fingers through her meticulously styled and
frosted hair.

"You're all grown up now, Doug. I can see how
tough you are. You were tough then, too, tougher than
I ever was. Sometimes your courage frightened me,
because I couldn't find any myself, but mostly it made
me ashamed. I wasn't fit to be a mother—especially
not yours. I couldn't take care of myself. How was I
supposed to take care of a kid who had more of the
answers at five than I did at twenty-five?"

"You thought I'd be better off with *him?*"

"No! But Larry wouldn't take you with us. And I just couldn't stay anymore. Your father found out about Larry. If I'd stayed, he'd have killed me."

At least something finally made sense, Doug thought, strangely relieved to know that there'd been some logic to his mother's desertion.

"And Littleton still doesn't know any of it, does he? He doesn't know about my father, or Philpot, or even about me, *does he?*"

Dora shrank back at the anger in Doug's voice. She looked toward the door of the sitting room and shook her head.

"And you aren't going to tell him, are you?"

She looked up at him, her eyes pleading with him not to make waves. "I'll give you money, as much as you want. You can set yourself up anywhere you'd like, take a cruise, go to the Bahamas. I'll buy you a yacht."

Doug smiled derisively. "Yeah? And how would you explain that to Chad?"

"I give to charities all the time."

She gave to charities, but she'd never bothered to look up the son she'd left behind in the slums.

Doug shoved his hands into the pockets of his jacket and headed toward the door. "Well, thanks, but no thanks. In case you didn't notice when you looked at my wallet, I'm a cop. Here. In Columbus. And I've got a job to do. A job I wish someone had done back when I was a kid."

He looked over his shoulder at the woman who'd given him birth, almost as if waiting for some kind of approval for the good he'd made of his life, some kind of maternal pride at what he'd accomplished. What he saw was the stricken look in her eyes. She didn't care what he was; she was only afraid of the threat his existence posed to her well-ordered life.

"Don't worry, *Mother*, I'll keep our little secret."

Her relief was so palpable it was almost sickening. And that's when Doug's anger turned to pity.

"I've got a question for you," he said, turning to face her when he reached the doorway.

"What?" She didn't sound too eager to hear it.

"Did you ever consider leaving with me, instead of Philpot?"

"Come on, Doug. You said you're a cop. You have to know that life isn't really sweet and pretty like they show you on TV. How far do you think I'd have gotten if I'd had a child hanging around my neck? It would have taken one hell of a man to have been willing to raise your father's son. I'd never have gotten farther than the next block."

Doug swallowed hard. He wished he'd never asked. "You could've tried." She could have gotten a job then, tried to support him herself.

"This is the real world, Doug. And the reality of it is each man for himself. When the chips are down, that's all you've got. There's nobody out there who'd have made the kind of sacrifice you're asking. Life doesn't work that way."

Doug thought of Andrea, of her warmth and generosity, of the kindness within her that wouldn't allow her to take a chance on failing him. And he realized then what he had that he could give her. His love.

He looked at his mother for the last time. "You're wrong. It can be that way."

He walked out of the house, away from the past, without looking back.

CHAPTER SEVENTEEN

"ALICIA EDWARDS, age ten." The voice of Mike Cooper, sixth-grade athlete of the year, was subdued as it broke the silence in the auditorium. Andrea watched the young man light a candle, leave the stage and take his seat in the darkened room.

"Molly Schumaker, age seventeen." The voice belonged to a young girl this time, but the lighting of a single candle, the solemnity of the scene, was the same. She crossed the stage, stepped down and took her seat.

"David Billings, age six."

"Brenda Williams, age twenty-seven."

"Brian Henly, age sixteen."

One by one Doug's students crossed the stage, lit a candle and walked back to their seats, until the auditorium was a mass of glowing, flickering shadows. Andrea had been to many DARE graduations, but she'd never seen a program like this one. She sat next to Doug at the side of the stage, missing him like she'd never missed anyone before, needing him like she'd never needed anyone before. The room was full of parents, students and school personnel, yet as she watched the stage, lonely and afraid, she felt as if she'd been cut adrift. She'd never felt less in control in her life.

"John Doe, age two."

Suddenly a song began softly in the back of the auditorium. Teenage voices sang about love that ran deep, time that was stolen, bodies that would never hold or be held again. And as the song faded away, a single gust of air extinguished all the brightly glowing candles, leaving the room in darkness—the darkness that comes when a life has been shamefully cut short as a result of alcohol and drug abuse.

Tears filled Andrea's eyes, brimming over to trail slowly down her cheeks. There was so much darkness. No matter how much she pressed forward, there never seemed to be enough light to show her the way. A tear dripped off her chin and landed on her wrist. And Doug's fingers wrapped around hers, bringing them to rest against the solid muscle of his thigh.

The lights came on and the school principal stood up to address the parents.

"We've been telling your young people that there are many alternatives to drug use. Today we're honored to present you with one of them. Ladies and gentlemen, I present you with the award-winning DARE dancers."

Andrea had seen the DARE dancers before, but she still felt the same thrill of excitement as they bounded out onto the stage. Her tears were forgotten as she watched the young girls, dressed dramatically in black-and-red bike clothes, performing an amazing jazz routine to the DARE theme song. Their attitudes said it all. Even the little five-year-old abounded with positive energy as she danced against drugs, her steps as well executed as those of the older girls around her. Andrea noticed Doug's hand tapping the beat of the music against his thigh.

The dancers finished their numbers and ran offstage, back to their seats. Andrea looked out at the mass of young faces and saw the empty seat that was supposed to have been Jeremy's. Doug's students were not all graduating. One had already made the wrong choice.

"And now I give you DARE Officer Doug Avery."

Andrea felt a very private pride as Doug stepped up to the microphone. He looked stunning in his full dress blues, every inch a man, but it was the person living inside his handsome body that Andrea had grown to love with all her heart.

"Okay, gang. This is it. We made it." Doug smiled at his Monday kids.

Andrea smiled, too. She alone knew the significance of that "we."

"And I want you to remember, every day of your lives, that we did it together. We all have value, and rights, and choices. And we all need each other. Don't ever think that what happened here these last couple of months was just a job for me, or another lesson for you. It was life, folks, and I signed on with you for the long haul. If any of you ever find yourself needing a friend, I'm available—always."

One by one Doug called the names of his graduates, and one by one they crossed the stage to receive their DARE T-shirt, their diploma and a hug from their DARE officer. Andrea felt a peculiar mixture of heady joy and great sadness. Doug had completed his journey. He didn't need her anymore. Her job was done.

As the last student left the stage, Doug looked out over the sea of smiling parents. "Ladies and gentlemen, may I present to you the graduating—"

A door at the side of the room creaked open, letting in the afternoon sunlight. Heads turned as a little blond boy entered the auditorium. All eyes watched as the boy, skinny but clean, approached the front of the room. He hesitated, looking at Doug, as if asking for permission to continue.

Doug motioned the boy toward the seat that had been empty for most of the ceremony. But Jeremy didn't join his classmates. Instead, he stepped up on stage, to the microphone.

He pulled a wrinkled piece of paper out of the pocket of his blue jeans.

"I, uh, I know you guys read your essays last week in class so you could graduate today. Since I wasn't here, I figured, maybe if I—well, anyway, here it is."

Jeremy looked down at his paper, his voice muffled as he started to read.

"DARE is good. It teaches kids that life isn't always all bad. It teaches them that they actually have choices, and even teaches them how to make some right ones. DARE gives courage, and maybe, if you don't waste it, it might give friends. DARE is about life. It pro'bly saved mine."

Jeremy's choppy words slid softly into Andrea's being, soothing her wounded soul. She might not ever be able to atone for the sins of her past, but at least she was contributing to the future. She was helping to make a difference. Peace settled over her, a kind of tentative truce that had eluded her for four long years.

Jeremy stepped back from the microphone with his head bowed, as if he was embarrassed to have exposed himself in front of the classmates he'd shunned all year, as if he expected rejection. He turned to head off the stage, but he didn't make it three steps.

Doug waylaid the boy with a hand on his shoulder, handed him a DARE T-shirt and hugged him like he'd never let him go. Jeremy wrapped his skinny arms around Doug's waist, holding on so tightly that his fingers turned white.

And suddenly someone in the audience was clapping, followed by another and another until the whole auditorium thundered with applause. Jeremy turned to face his classmates, looking incredulously out over the sea of smiling faces, and a grin split his own face— a grin so big, so happy, so innocent that it lit up the room. For the first time since she'd met him, Andrea thought, Jeremy Schwartz looked like a little boy.

"Ladies and gentlemen, I present to you the graduating DARE class of Filmore Elementary School," Doug hollered into the microphone, but even then his voice could barely be heard over the cheering.

The sixth-graders raised their arms, donned their DARE T-shirts and sat back down, several parallel rows of black and red.

Andrea watched the children, sharing in their joy, satisfied that another group of young people were well armed to face the world they were entering. She couldn't help sneaking a peek at Doug, too, wishing she had the right to share this moment with him, wishing she knew how to take what he was offering.

Doug was looking at her, too. His gaze was hungry, and strangely pleading as a sudden hush fell across the room. Confused, Andrea looked to the side of the stage, toward a commotion she'd been only vaguely aware of, and saw another young man stepping up to the microphone. But this boy wasn't alone. He was accompanied by her mother.

Doug saw the color drain from Andrea's face, and knew a moment of unadulterated fear as he considered the possibility that he might have made a terrible mistake, that he might have overstepped his bounds. He moved to sit beside her, sliding his arm around her waist, and prayed that the next several minutes would not be her undoing.

"I'm here today to tell you all about the reality of drug abuse," the young man said into the microphone, looking straight out at the sixth-graders in front of him.

"My name is Scotty. I was a cocaine addict." He paused, took a deep breath. "To most of you the lessons you've learned these past weeks didn't touch you personally. I'd bet that most of you think they never will. That's the mistake that'll get you. And before you know it, it's too late."

Doug listened to Scotty, pulling for the shy young man who'd been willing, at his bidding, to stand up in front a roomful of strangers and give his very private testimonial. He glanced at Andrea, worried by her pallor, by the tears streaming openly down her face. He pulled her more solidly against him, reaching for her hand with his free one. Her nails dug into his fingers.

"It happened to me at school, a school just like this one, where the kids were clean-cut and there weren't any gangs or anything. It started out as a dare, and I buckled. Cocaine made me feel invincible and I was stupid enough to believe I was. I lost my friends, Little League, my scout troop—everything. There was only one group of guys left who wanted me, but they didn't really care about me, only about the money they could make off me." Scotty reached to push his glasses up his nose. His hand was trembling.

Doug's muscles clenched as Andrea swayed, leaning her head against his shoulder. Her tears dribbled down to soak his shirt, her lips trembled, but she didn't make a sound. Her gaze was still glued to her little brother.

Scotty shifted his weight from one foot to the other, and back again. "See, the thing is, what happened was my fault. Just like you, I'd been taught never to accept things from strangers, but I did. I knew that drugs could hurt me, but I took them anyway. I wanted to fit in, to be cool." The children's gaze never left Scotty.

"And if you guys think it's never going to happen to you, if you think no one's ever going to offer you some dope, if you think you won't ever be at a party where you might look like a geek if you don't at least try it, then you're fooling yourselves. I thought that, too, and I paid for it big-time."

Scotty paused, looking like he was trying not to cry. Gloria stood in the shadows behind him. Her own cheeks were wet with tears, but she kept her distance.

"I got ahold of some bad crack because I couldn't afford the cocaine I needed. I almost died from it. Sometimes I wish I had, 'cause I lost something almost as precious as my life over it. I lost my big sister."

Andrea jerked upright, rigid as stone, her gaze fixed on Scotty as if bracing herself for what she might hear next. Doug let go of her. He figured this was something she had to get through on her own. But he stayed close beside her.

Scotty looked out at the audience in front of him. "See, my sister's a cop. How do you think it made her look, having a kid brother hooked on drugs? How do you think it made her feel? I let her down big-time. She used to think I was the greatest. But I made her the laughingstock of the whole police force. I hate to think what she went through because of me, what the guys at the station put her through. And I hate most to think of what she thinks of me now." The room fell silent. Scotty stood at the microphone, his mouth working as if trying to form words, but nothing came out. The children in front of him sat as still as statues, watching him, waiting for him to continue.

Andrea jumped up from her seat, moving toward the stairs that would take her up onto the stage.

"You can't sit around and wait for your parents to take care of you, to catch you doing something bad and make you change. 'Cause when someone loves you that much, they believe the best of you." Scotty was still looking at the children in front of him. Doug had a feeling that he was afraid to look toward Andrea's seat, afraid of what he might see in his sister's eyes.

"My sister loved me that much. While I was busy snorting coke, knowing I was getting in too deep, waiting for her to come down on me, she never even considered, for one second, that I might be on drugs." Scotty stopped, adjusted his glasses again and then rushed on. "That's what I lost—her unconditional love. Your parents probably love you that way now. Don't blow it like I did."

Scotty turned away from the microphone, looking for Gloria, his shoulders straight and stiff. Behind him, Andrea moved up onto the stage. Her short blond hair was standing on end where she'd run her fingers through it, her dress blues were creased, but she looked almost ethereal when the stage lights glinted off her badge.

She put her hand on Scotty's back. And as she took her baby brother into her arms, he buried his face against her and wept.

"YOU GET THAT Christmas shopping done?" Doug asked Andrea as they left the empty auditorium. Gloria had taken Scotty back to his own school to finish out the day, but he and Andrea had a date for later that evening. Brother and sister were going to shoot baskets at the high school.

Andrea looked at him, as if surprised by the innocuous question. "What?"

"That Christmas shopping you were supposed to get done last weekend. Did you do it?"

Andrea shrugged. "Not all of it. Doug, can we, uh, go someplace? You know, so we can talk?"

"I really need to get my Christmas shopping done."

Her step slowed, losing a little of its bounce. "Oh. Well, then, I guess I'll see you later." She started to veer off toward her car, but not before Doug saw the hurt cloud her eyes.

He snagged the sleeve of her police jacket. "You could come with me."

Her gaze locked with his. Doug tried his best to look reassuring, when he really felt like hightailing it to the next century. If she turned him down again...

"Okay. I've still got a few things to pick up. Where do you want to meet?"

"I'll pick you up at your place in half an hour. Will that give you time to change?"

DOUG TOOK HOLD of her arm as soon as she climbed out of his car in the mall parking lot. He propelled her forward to the door, into the mall and through the crowd.

"Hey, I thought we were going to shop," Andrea said, half laughing at his urgency.

Doug slowed. He was doing this all wrong. "Right. Sorry."

He forced himself to walk casually beside her, listening to her comment on the holiday sights, all the while looking for one particular store. He gritted his teeth through the first store she wandered through, and waited outside the door of the second. And then he saw the store he'd been watching for.

Andrea probably wasn't ready. She'd spent four years building up fear. He knew it didn't all just evaporate in the space of one morning. But he also knew that it never would if she didn't move forward.

"Let's go in here," he said, pulling her across the aisle to the other side of the mall.

She frowned at his gruffness.

Great, Avery. What charm.

He watched closely to see her reaction when she realized where they were going. It was frustratingly nonchalant.

"You got some lady you're sending jewelry to for Christmas?" She said it like a joke, but she wasn't laughing.

"Nope."

She didn't say another word. She just gave him a nervous look and followed him into the store.

"May I help you?" The saleslady was on them the minute they stepped onto the thickly padded carpet.

It didn't take Doug long to find what he was looking for. "That one. Can I see it please?"

He didn't look at Andrea as the woman pulled out a half-carat diamond solitaire with a unique oval cut. But he held tightly to her hand. She might not go along with him, but she was going to have to refuse him to his face. He wasn't going to have another woman walk away from him without saying goodbye.

The saleslady handed him the ring, an eager smile on her face.

"You've made a good choice, sir. That's one of our best diamonds. The clarity and cut . . ."

Doug took the ring gently, uncomfortable at handling anything so delicate and beautiful. He didn't even hear the saleslady as he took Andrea's left hand and slid the ring onto her finger. He didn't hear anything except the roaring in his own ears.

He stared at the beautiful ring on Andrea's slim hand and felt like a hero for the first time in his life. He couldn't look up at her, needing to savor the moment, afraid that this would be the only one like it he'd ever have. If he looked at her, if she shook her head, his moment of glory would be gone forever.

"It looks gorgeous, sir. A fine choice. Yes, a fine..."

A tear dropped onto their clasped hands, forcing Doug to face whatever was to come. He raised his eyes slowly, taking in trembling lips that were so sweet to taste, a small, pert nose and finally, eyes that were glowing behind their pools of tears.

"You like it?" It was as close as he could get to asking.

Andrea nodded, a tremulous smile breaking out on her face. "It's a perfect fit."

Doug nodded too, his relief so palpable he thought his legs were going to give out on him. And then he turned back to the saleslady, reaching into his jacket pocket for his checkbook.

"We'll take it."

"I MAY LET YOU DOWN."

"I can pretty well guarantee I'm gonna fail you sometimes, too. God knows, I'm far from perfect."

"I mean it, Doug. No matter what Scotty says, I'm still partially to blame. I should have been watching out for him more closely." Andrea lay in bed with her head on Doug's chest, afraid to believe, even now, in the happiness he'd brought her. After the basketball game, they'd spent the rest of the evening at her parents' house and Andrea had never seen her mother so quiet, or so content. Gloria had just sat and watched her children all evening, nodding and smiling, her glance lingering on the diamond on Andrea's finger now and then.

"You're human, Andrea."

"I let John down, too."

"He let you down, baby. He wouldn't let you be who you had to be. He wanted you to be who *he* needed you to be."

That might have been the case, but Andrea was still afraid. "I just need you to be prepared for the fact that it's probably going to happen. I'll probably lose perspective again. You just wait and see."

"If you're trying to get out of this, Andrea, forget it." He trailed his fingers down her naked back.

Andrea shivered, nestling closer to him. She could hardly believe this man was hers, that he'd chosen her to share his life. She was afraid she was going to make him regret that choice.

"I just need to know that you'll still love me when it happens."

"You can make mistakes all your life, baby. Just don't ever leave me. That's the only thing I'll ever ask of you. Just don't ever leave me."

The final knot in Andrea's stomach faded away. "You have my word on it," she whispered against his chest.

Finally, a promise she knew she could keep.

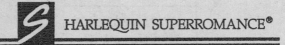

HARLEQUIN SUPERROMANCE®

The O'Connor Trilogy
by award-winning author KAREN YOUNG

Meet the hard-living, hard-loving O'Connors
in this unforgettable saga

Roses and Rain is the story of journalist Shannon O'Connor.
She has many astonishing gifts, but it takes a near-death
experience and the love of hard-bitten cop Nick Dalton to show
her all she can be. July 1994

Shadows in the Mist is Ryan's story. Wounded in his very soul,
he retreats to a secluded island to heal, only to be followed by
two women. One wants his death, the other his love.
August 1994

The Promise is the story that started it all, a story so powerful
and dramatic that it is our first featured Superromance
Showcase. Laugh and cry with Patrick and Kathleen as they
overcome seemingly insurmountable obstacles and forge their
own destiny in a new land. September 1994

**Harlequin Superromance,
wherever Harlequin books are sold.**

Harlequin® Historical

LOOK TO THE PAST FOR FUTURE FUN AND EXCITEMENT!

The past the Harlequin Historical way, that is. 1994 is going to be a banner year for us, so here's a preview of what to expect:

* The continuation of our bigger book program, with titles such as *Across Time* by Nina Beaumont, *Defy the Eagle* by Lynn Bartlett and *Unicorn Bride* by Claire Delacroix.

* A 1994 March Madness promotion featuring four titles by promising new authors Gayle Wilson, Cheryl St. John, Madris Dupree and Emily French.

* Brand-new in-line series: DESTINY'S WOMEN by Merline Lovelace and HIGHLANDER by Ruth Langan; and new chapters in old favorites, such as the SPARHAWK saga by Miranda Jarrett and the WARRIOR series by Margaret Moore.

* *Promised Brides,* an exciting brand-new anthology with stories by Mary Jo Putney, Kristin James and Julie Tetel.

* Our perennial favorite, the Christmas anthology, this year featuring Patricia Gardner Evans, Kathleen Eagle, Elaine Barbieri and Margaret Moore.

Watch for these programs and titles wherever Harlequin Historicals are sold.

HARLEQUIN HISTORICALS...
A TOUCH OF MAGIC!

HHPROMO94

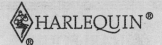

EXPECTATIONS
Shannon Waverly

Eternity, Massachusetts, is a town with something
special going for it. According to legend, those who
marry in Eternity's chapel are destined for a lifetime of
happiness. As long as the legend holds true, couples
will continue to flock here to marry and local
businesses will thrive.

Unfortunately for the town, Marion and Geoffrey Kent
are about to prove the legend wrong!

EXPECTATIONS, available in July from
Harlequin Romance®, is the second book in
Harlequin's new cross-line series, **WEDDINGS, INC.**
Be sure to look for the third book, **WEDDING
SONG,** by
Vicki Lewis Thompson (Harlequin Temptation® #502),
coming in August.

WED-2

MEN · MADE IN AMERICA

Fifty red-blooded, white-hot, true-blue hunks
from every State in the Union!

Look for MEN MADE IN AMERICA! Written by some of
our most popular authors, these stories feature fifty of
the strongest, sexiest men, each from a different state in
the union!

Two titles available every other month at your favorite
retail outlet.

In May, look for:

KISS YESTERDAY GOODBYE by Leigh Michaels (Iowa)
A TIME TO KEEP by Curtiss Ann Matlock (Kansas)

In June, look for:

ONE PALE, FAWN GLOVE by Linda Shaw (Kentucky)
BAYOU MIDNIGHT by Emilie Richards (Louisiana)

You won't be able to resist MEN MADE IN AMERICA!

This July,
Harlequin and Silhouette
are proud to bring you

by Request™

CONVENIENTLY
Yours

WANTED: Husband
POSITION: Temporary
TERMS: Negotiable—but must be willing to live in.

And falling in love is definitely not part of the contract!

Relive the romance....

Three complete novels by your favorite authors—in one special collection!

TO BUY A GROOM by Rita Clay Estrada
MEETING PLACE by Bobby Hutchinson
THE ARRANGEMENT by Sally Bradford

Available wherever
Harlequin and Silhouette books are sold.

HARLEQUIN® *Silhouette*®

HREQ6

HARLEQUIN®

Don't miss these Harlequin favorites by some of our most distinguished authors!
And now, you can receive a discount by ordering two or more titles!

HT #25551	THE OTHER WOMAN by Candace Schuler	$2.99	☐
HT #25539	FOOLS RUSH IN by Vicki Lewis Thompson	$2.99	☐
HP #11550	THE GOLDEN GREEK by Sally Wentworth	$2.89	☐
HP #11603	PAST ALL REASON by Kay Thorpe	$2.99	☐
HR #03228	MEANT FOR EACH OTHER by Rebecca Winters	$2.89	☐
HR #03268	THE BAD PENNY by Susan Fox	$2.99	☐
HS #70532	TOUCH THE DAWN by Karen Young	$3.39	☐
HS #70540	FOR THE LOVE OF IVY by Barbara Kaye	$3.39	☐
HI #22177	MINDGAME by Laura Pender	$2.79	☐
HI #22214	TO DIE FOR by M.J. Rodgers	$2.89	☐
HAR #16421	HAPPY NEW YEAR, DARLING by Margaret St. George	$3.29	☐
HAR #16507	THE UNEXPECTED GROOM by Muriel Jensen	$3.50	☐
HH #28774	SPINDRIFT by Miranda Jarrett	$3.99	☐
HH #28782	SWEET SENSATIONS by Julie Tetel	$3.99	☐

Harlequin Promotional Titles

#83259	UNTAMED MAVERICK HEARTS (Short-story collection featuring Heather Graham Pozzessere, Patricia Potter, Joan Johnston)	$4.99	☐

(limited quantities available on certain titles)

	AMOUNT	$
DEDUCT:	**10% DISCOUNT FOR 2+ BOOKS**	$
	POSTAGE & HANDLING	$
	($1.00 for one book, 50¢ for each additional)	
	APPLICABLE TAXES*	$ _____
	TOTAL PAYABLE	$ _____
	(check or money order—please do not send cash)	

To order, complete this form and send it, along with a check or money order for the total above, payable to Harlequin Books, to: **In the U.S.:** 3010 Walden Avenue, P.O. Box 9047, Buffalo, NY 14269-9047; **In Canada:** P.O. Box 613, Fort Erie, Ontario, L2A 5X3.

Name: _____

Address: _____ City: _____

State/Prov.: _____ Zip/Postal Code: _____

*New York residents remit applicable sales taxes.
 Canadian residents remit applicable GST and provincial taxes.

HBACK-AJ